{INSTA} BOYFRIEND

Book One

JEN ATKINSON

keeping it clean &
making you swoon
Jen Atkinson

For Gracie & Halle
Who once upon a time, had fake fiancés so they could try on wedding gowns.

{ I N S T A }

Boyfriend

Connection

Kiss

Family

Also by Jen Atkinson

{Insta} Boyfriend

BOOK ONE

ONE

Iris

The sun sits over the horizon, lowering down into the earth—and right in my eyes! Sure, it's pretty, but the glowing ball of fire right in front of my face is making it a real bugger to follow my GPS at the moment.

Driving into the sun and talking to my sister equals one too many jobs for my brain right now. Not to mention the bomb my cousin just dropped on me.

"Whoa. Slow down. Say that again, because there's no way I heard that right!" My sister's voice bellows through the cab of my vehicle.

"Ebony! I can't talk any slower, I'm driving to go see them right this second. I'm—" A clunking noise stops me short. "Crap."

"Crap? What?" she says through the speakers in my Volvo.

My heart jolts. "I think I just hit something." I hold back my wail and try not to picture anything dead left in my wake.

"Hold up, Snow White," Ebony says. "Don't panic on me now."

"I think I'm gonna be sick." My knuckles go white as I grip my steering wheel.

"What? Iris, what's going on over there? Do you need to call someone closer to you?"

My eyes prick with unshed tears and my throat swells to an ache. "There is no one closer to me than you, Ebony! We shared the same womb!" I dart a glance into my rearview mirror. A rabbit? Or... no! Bambi? I swear if I just killed Bambi I will never forgive myself.

"I mean like someone in the same state. Iris, I'm in Washington. You're in Colorado—what can I do from here?" She sounds almost panicked and my one minute older, hot shot, sports writing sister doesn't get panicked. She's cool, calm, and collected. Everything I am not.

"I don't know!" I squint into the sun, looking ahead and then behind in my rearview mirror—seeing if whatever I hit is limping away or in need of a funeral. "There's no one else on this stupid road." Besides me and Bambi.

Another clunk sounds, this time followed by smoke rising from my engine. "Crap!" I bellow again. I think I'm in trouble—which hopefully in the yin and yang world means that Bambi is okay. I sigh a little with the thought.

"That's it, Iris. Where are you? I'm calling Shelia."

"Don't you dare! Not after the bomb that traitor cousin just dropped on me. I'll be fine. I'll—" My car lurches and I realize probably five minutes too late that I really need to pull over and assess. "I'll call you back!" I tap the end call button on my steering wheel. But my car, my little Daredevil slows on its own, before I even hit the brake.

"This isn't good." I wish Hazel were here.

More smoke rises from my little red hood. "Nooo," I moan. "Poor little, Daredevil." I rub my hand over the dash of my Volvo and breathe out a tired sigh.

I am going to kill Shelia. "Maybe I'll get lucky and find out that instead of Bambi, I drove over my cousin a mile back." I like Bambi so much more than Shelia right now. "Bambi would never betray me." My voice sounds eerie in the quiet of the car. I clamp my mouth closed and look out into the twilight of the evening. The sun winks out, now instead of blinding me, or offering me a little light, it's hiding. *Jerk.*

Why did Shelia pick a late dinner for this meeting anyway? How in the world am I supposed to inspect the venue with the sun practically gone?

My pulse drums in my wrists and neck. My heart thumps— my entire body a live wire. I snatch my phone from its handy-dandy magnetic mount and type in Shelia's name.

`Running late. Car troubles.`

She doesn't text back. I don't know if she's gotten it. But then, she and *Travis* can sit and wait until they've expired for all I care.

I step out into the brisk forty-five degree weather, thankful to my trusty Converse for keeping my toes covered. Ebony may have talked me into a skirt for this sorry excuse of a business meeting, but I refused to wear pumps or even dressy flats.

No way.

Not now.

Not ever.

One day I will wed in a pair of white Converse tennis shoes. And if he's the right man, he'll be in black high tops.

If only I had been just as stubborn about this stupid skirt. But Ebony had insisted, "It's a business meeting. You need to look professional."

"It's Shelia and some guy who doesn't care about wedding photos," I'd told her.

But in the end she convinced me. As the wind swirls up my ankles to my thighs, I regret not buying those black slacks last month. Surely, Ebony would have thought black slacks dressy enough. However, my jeans and hello kitty leggings did not impress her.

At least my toes are warm inside my tennies.

I pop open the hood—to do what? I have no idea. A swirl of steam shoots up with the rise of Daredevil's top. "Cheese and crackers!" I squawk. I step backward and hold a hand over my mouth. And the smoke keeps rising, as if it's on a mission. There's a cylinder-ish metal piece that the smoke seems to stem from. I watch it for a second. I don't even know what the part is called, let alone what to do with it. I can't fix this.

So, I do what I do best. I grab my Cannon EOS, who I have lovingly named Snappy, from the passenger seat of my car and take a picture of the open hood and billowing smoke. I take another and peer back at the small digital image on my camera when a lone car passing by pulls over.

It's a white Jeep with a single person inside. He rolls down the passenger window and leans across the console to see me better. "Need a ride?"

He's cute. Mid twenties, with dark curly hair, short on the sides, and long enough on top that I can see the curls. Cuteness does not equal saneness though—I have Hulu. I've seen plenty of ads for horror films—so, I know. I mean, I don't actually watch any of those films, of course. I'm a pretty basic chick-flick and bachelorette kind of a girl. But I've seen the trailers—I know cuteness means nothing!

"Do you need some help?" the man inside the Jeep says, his voice low and smooth. The jury is still out on his axe murderer status.

"I've got it under control. Thanks."

His brows cinch together and he looks a little less daunting. "Really? Because it looks like your car decided to die."

"She isn't dead!" *Don't be dead Daredevil!* I peer back at the smoking parts inside her hood. *Crap.* She might be dead.

"What year is she?"

Again, his axe murderer status decreases—all for calling my car a "she". I've always thought of Daredevil that way.

"I don't know," I tell him. "I mean, I'm not really sure."

He keeps his deep blue eyes on mine—silently asking why I don't know.

"I bought her from my grandma last year." Bought is an over-statement. I took pictures of Gramgram's garden and canned two dozen jars of raspberry jam in exchange. But he doesn't need to know that.

"Oh. Okay. Well, I can take a look." He pulls his car in front of mine, but I don't want this strange man's help. I don't want anyone's help. I want to crawl into a cave with Bambi and die after the day I've had.

I walk around to the passenger side of my car and put Snappy back in her case on the seat. I see I have a text and though I'd rather never see my cousin again, I pick up the phone and read.

Well, hurry up.

Nice, Shelia. I tell you I have car trouble and all you can say is *hurry*. I ignore her message and write my sister. Ebony has sent four messages asking what's going on and threatening to call Shelia. I *cannot* let her do that. Besides, I've already texted Shelia. She's all sorts of torn up about my car troubles. Clearly.

I type, my thumbs on speed mode.

Don't call Shelia. There's someone here to help me.

Half a second later, a text from Ebony chimes in:

Someone? Who? You have mace right?

I write her back—just to ease her worries.

> I do. But no bad vibes. I'll be fine.
> DON'T CALL SHELIA!

If Travis and Shelia showed up to save me, I might fall down dead right here on this Colorado back road.

"Hey," the man says behind me—closer than I expected him to be.

I jump—my sister and her mace talk putting me more on edge. Still, I did see *The Strangers*. I didn't sleep for a week after Travis made me watch that stupid movie. Scenes are running through my head at the moment.

With half my body still inside the cab of my car, I flick open the glove box and toss all of its contents onto the floor of my car until I find what I'm looking for—pepper spray.

I hug it to my chest, holding it just so for my rescuer/murderer to see.

"Whoa. Hey," he says, backing up a step. "Sorry, I should have been smarter. I'm alone, you're alone. Maybe I shouldn't have stopped. But I saw the smoke and," he sighs, not finishing his sentence. "You don't live around here, do you?"

I shake my head. But then curse myself for giving that away. *No, stranger, I don't live around here and there's no one waiting for me at home either. Go ahead, make your move. Grab that axe!*

"This isn't a road many take. The sun is going down and I don't know who else will be coming through here." He runs a hand through the curls on top of his head. "I just want to help. You shouldn't be out here alone. It gets cold."

"I'll call an Uber."

His face scrunches. "I don't know many Uber's who make the trip out here this time of night."

"A tow truck."

He nods. "Sure. That'll work. I can wait with you." He points to his Jeep. "I can stay far away. No worries. I'll just be here in case you need anything."

I lick my lips and nod.

Facing me, he walks backward, moving toward his Jeep. He smiles at me, closed lip and child-like, almost *familiar*. "I'm Dean." The left corner of his lips turn up and he adds. "I like your shoes."

I look down at my favorite black Converse high tops, then back up to his face, still grinning at me. He might be the cutest possible axe murderer in the history of ever.

Dean trips on a rock the size of his head, but doesn't go down. He just stumbles and I find myself chuckling at him.

"What's your Instagram handle?"

`"What?" I clamp down on my bottom lip, thinking through his question. "Why?"

"You know, Instagram. What's your handle? I'm going to message you from my car."

The only reason I have an Instagram account is because Ebony made me make one. I have two posts and follow a whopping two people—Ebony and our friend Coco from college. In return, my private account has accepted two followers. Can you guess who?

"Umm…"

"I just want to send you a message."

I mean, it's not like he can see anything incriminating, my two posts are of my dog, Hazel. She's very photogenic. Still, I think it through and decide—there's not much for this stranger to learn about me through Instagram. Not to mention—he likes my shoes. I don't know why it makes him a little more trusting in my eyes, but it does. I grapple for my phone and open the app. If Instagram were an actual tangible *thing*, mine would be full of dust and moth balls. I don't even remember my handle without looking it up. "It's Iris underscore me."

He says the handle under his breath. "Got it." He gives me a thumbs up. "Now, go call that tow truck."

I sit in the passenger side of my car, make a quick call—only to learn it could take up to three hours for a tow to get out here at this time. Ugh. I sit back and wait for Dean's message. He doesn't need to wait three hours. I'm starting to think he is a decent human being who just wants to help. No axe murdering involved. Still, my pepper spray sits in my cupholder—just in case.

There's a message from Dean waiting for me when I hang up with the tow place. I didn't even have to accept him as a follower —so handy.

@deanlivingoutloud: Are you doing okay?

I'm not sure how I feel about this stranger looking after me.

@iris_me: I'm fine. Just late for a business meeting.
@deanlivingoutloud: I'd offer to get you there, but I'm afraid I'd get pepper sprayed.

I laugh—it is an absolute possibility.

@iris_me: Do you deserve it?
@deanlivingoutloud: Absolutely not. But I'm scared.
@iris_me: You should be.
@deanlivingoutloud: So, what's your business?
@iris_me: You really don't have to stay here.

I add,

@iris_me: The tow guy said it could be three hours.

I should text Shelia, but I'm going to make her stew for a bit.

She can wait. It's not like she'll hire another photographer. Before I knew what a traitor she was, I felt generous and offered her a family discount.

> @deanlivingoutloud: I'm not surprised. I guess we've got time then.
> @iris_me: Why would you stay?
> @deanlivingoutloud: I had a friend in high school named Iris. She was kind to me when others weren't.
> @iris_me: She sounds nice. But I still don't know why you'd hang out here, in the cold, for three hours.
> @deanlivingoutloud: She made me want to help others when life sucked.
> @iris_me: Does that mean your life sucked in high school?

This guy is sort of intriguing. I click on his face, and scroll through his public feed. His life does not suck... not now, not in the least. Dean's got pictures of himself skiing and snowboarding down hills, sitting in a hot springs pool surrounded by snow, snowshoeing over a mountain top. Geez, I wish I had taken some of these pics. After another thirty seconds of scrolling, another ping tells me Dean has sent more than one message.

> @deanlivingoutloud: Yes. 100 percent. High school hated me.
> @deanlivingoutloud: Iris?
> @iris_me: I'm here. Just thinking.

I lie. I'm not about to tell him I just scrolled through his last three dozen posts. Some of his reels have over fifty thousand views. People are watching him... ski down a mountain... *fifty thousand* people.

@iris_me: You stopped to help me long before you
    knew my name.
@iris_me: In fact… pretty sure I never told you my
    name. Stalker?

Probably not the best idea to ask your stalker if he is in fact a stalker, but I send the message before thinking it through.

@deanlivingoutloud: Not a stalker. I deduced. Your
    handle doesn't make it too complicated. Plus I
    don't mind helping people who aren't named
    Iris too.

I mean, he has a point. My name is in my Instagram handle. I told Ebony it was a bad idea. I should have named myself something like @snappyhappy… Or not.

@iris_me: Right. Gottcha.
@deanlivingoutloud: First name basis… So, are we
    friends now?
@iris_me: No.

I send the message too quick. I peer up from my phone to see Dean chuckling in his Jeep in front of me.

@deanlivingoutloud: Do you have trust issues?
@iris_me: No! I have single girl, deserted road
    issues.
@deanlivingoutloud: That's fair. Can I at least follow
    you on Instagram?
@iris_me: Nope.

Dean—living out loud—does not get to see my two posts about my beloved wirehaired pointing griffon. Hazel is the sweetest dog on the planet—except when she hops up on the kitchen counter and eats entire sticks of butter.

Who am I kidding?

Even then she's the sweetest. We just clean off her beard and sit on the back porch until the butter has seen the other side of Hazel.

Hazel will hate being alone so long. I better call Gramgram to go get her. Thankfully, my grandmother loves Hazel.

Before I can dial Gramgram, another message from Dean pops up.

> @deanlivingoutloud: You're a tough cookie.
> @iris_me: I'm a chewy chocolate chip cookie who
> doesn't make friends with strangers.

I dial Gramgram's number and wait, knee tapping. I got Hazel a year after Travis told me I wasn't "enough" for him. I love her more than anything—even my camera—and she loves me. She tells me every time she greets me at the front door that I am more than enough. Especially when I stop at Papa's Pets and pick up those bacon flavored chewies she likes so much.

"Gram!" I say, sounding more panicked than I intend to. I do not like worrying my eighty year old grammy. "Oh, hey Gram-gram," I try again, forcing coolness into my voice.

"Iris, is that you?"

"Yes, Gram. Remember my face pops up on the screen to tell you so."

"Well, I was just looking at a picture and then there you were. So, I thought that picture could have—"

"It's fine. Gram, can you go get Hazel? I'm going to be longer than I thought."

"Oh sure. Will she be staying the night?"

"Heavens, I hope not," I mutter. "Uh, maybe. Take her to go food bag, it's on the counter. Just in case."

"Sure thing, honey bunches."

"Thanks, Gramgram."

"All right, then. Hazel and I will just spend the night swooning over John." My grandmother has a not-so small obsession with Johnny Cash. And she's certain my griff is in love with him too. They watch Walk the Line together at least once a month.

"Perfect. Thank you, Gramgram."

"Hazel!" I hear her yell—she's forgotten to end the call. Again. "Grammy's coming for ya!"

With the pipes on that woman Hazel can probably hear her —we do live right next door.

I end the call to see there's a text from Shelia. I'm sure she's stewing—impatiently waiting without bothering to ask how I am.

Travis said you'd do this. Make some excuse not to come when you found out he'd be here. Come on, Iris. Can't you let your prejudice go? For me? We're family, for pete's sake. This is my wedding we're talking about. Can't you let Travis go? It's been years.

I swallow and the spittle is hard to get past the lump forming in my throat. *Let Travis go*—no problem. Why would she even say that? And *Travis said you'd do this...* Travis should never ever speak —ever—because all that will come out is stupidity!

My eyes are filling—with angry tears, not sad ones. Never sad ones! Not for Travis Cheesebro. I finished crying all of my sad tears over that man my senior year of college.

A banner with another message from Dean appears at the top of my screen.

@deanlivingoutloud: Too bad for me. Chewy chocolate chip are my favorite.

I don't know what that means. I have forgotten what we were talking about. But I like cookies. And I strongly dislike Travis Cheesebro. I step out into the cool evening and stomp over to where Dean sits in his Jeep. Hoping I don't regret every second of this whim of a decision.

His head tilts down, studying his phone. His waves more pronounced now that I can see the top of his head. I knock on the window. I don't tap, I don't gently pat the glass. I am suddenly on a mission and I beat that glass with a rap so hard, I'm lucky it doesn't break.

Dean jumps in his seat and slaps a palm over his heart. If there wasn't hot lava raging through me at the moment, I would have laughed.

I drum my nails on the glass and motion for him to unroll the window. He does, staring out at me, eyes wide.

"Hey," he says. "You—"

But I interrupt anything he thinks about saying. "What kind of shoes am I wearing?"

"Ah," his forehead wrinkles, "your shoes?"

"You said you liked them? So, what are they?"

One brow lifts and he scratches the five o' clock shadow on his chin. "Black Converse, high tops."

I nod. "And what is a wirehaired pointing griffon?"

He pauses, with a look that says—*are you crazy, lady? Do I need the pepper spray?* "It's a dog," he tells me.

You'd be surprised how many people answer that question with something like—*a monstrous beast from the Lord of the Rings.* My eyes widen with his correct answer. "And how do you feel about your grandmother?"

"My grandma?"

"Yes. You have one, right?"

"Uh, yeah. She's great." Dean gives a lop-sided grin. "She lives too far away. I don't get to see her enough. And!" he says, a surge of excitement in his voice, "She makes the best chocolate chip cookies—no joke. Plus, she loves to watch me ski. She makes me send her all my videos." He's staring off and for a hot minute I think he might cry because he misses his grandmother.

"Great," I say, tossing my camera bag through the open window. "You can take me to Evergreen."

TWO

Iris

"Oh, we're trusting each other now?"

"Sort of," I say, shutting the passenger door behind me and holding up my pepper spray.

"Ah." Dean shifts his car into gear and we start off. No looking back. "Why the change of heart?"

I breathe in through my nose, holding the breath for a second, Shelia and Travis, and my Hazel home alone all swirl in my head. Then, I speak. What do I care if this stranger knows? He's some random man who I'll surely never see again... Huh? It might even release some built up negative mojo inside of me.

"I'm a photographer."

"Yeah?" His eyes scan to the bag on my lap, then up to my face before turning back to the road. "Nice camera bag."

"You should see my camera," I say, but it sounds a little flirty —which doesn't mix with the pepper spray in my hands. So, I clear my throat and change my tone back to serious. "I'll be taking pictures of my cousin's wedding next month." More like in three weeks—but that's a small detail that Dean doesn't need. "I'm meeting her and her fiancé at a restaurant called..." I have

15

to think a minute. Though Ebony and I grew up in Ft. Collins, just a couple hours from the mountains of Evergreen Colorado, I've never been there before now. "Ah, Willow something or other."

"Willow Creek?"

"Yeah." I point at him, pepper spray in hand and Dean flinches, like he's ducking a soccer ball aimed at his head. "Oops. Sorry. Anyway, yeah, I think that's it. I'm meeting her and her *future husband* there. It's been in my calendar for months now. Meet and greet with Shelia and mystery man—a few candid shots pre-wedding and of course I'll scope out the venue." I use the blunt end of the bottle of pepper spray to rub my temple—this night is giving me a migraine. "What Shelia so conveniently forgot to tell me all those months ago is that she's marrying my ex."

Dean hisses, breathing in through his teeth. "Ouch. That's not cool."

"Right?" I twist in my seat to see him better. Dean's hand flinches upward, blocking the right side of his face with the movement of my loaded mace can. "Oh, shoot." I lay the pepper spray in my lap. Surely, I'd have time to pick it back up if he tried anything—he's driving. "So yes, very *not* cool. Things with Travis did not end pretty. I always hoped that the next time I saw him he might be buried… beneath a pile of maggots… or something along those lines." I've only pictured it a few dozen times.

His nose wrinkles and his lip curls. I instantly regret my confession. Someone like Dean—the guy I saw in all those Instagram posts and the guy who told me he likes helping people—does not understand a statement like that. Or someone like me. Someone who names their camera and naps with their dog. I am as desirable as his grandma.

I'm not enough for men like Dean or men like Travis.

Just like Travis said.

"Maybe I'm the one who needs the pepper spray," he says.

I huff out a breath and face myself forward. "Never mind."

"I was kidding, Iris," he says my name like he knows me. Then slides a glance from the road to my face, I see him—trying to make eye contact—but I pretend I don't. "Come on, you mention burying some guy in maggots and I'm not allowed a cringe? If he deserves it, I'll help you buy the maggots. But... yuck."

I flick my gaze to the roof of his Jeep. "I'm not buying any maggots. I wouldn't be the one to bury him." My hands flail with my explanation. "It's as if I came upon him and he was *already* buried and then—"

"You just leave him there, begging for your help."

"Exactly." I smile—happy thoughts.

"Did he cheat?"

"No."

"Lie?"

I shake my head. If anything he was more honest than I would have liked—*You just aren't enough for me anymore, Iris. I need someone who excites me. And that isn't you.*

"Okay, help me out. Because, I truly want to hate this guy and invest in maggots, but I'm on the struggle bus."

"I told you, I'm not buying—" I groan and cross my arms. "Never mind. I don't want to talk about this anymore." I can't actually repeat Travis's words out loud—even to a stranger who doesn't care about me. They're too awful. Too telling. Why relive it? "Tell me about you?" I say, eager to change the subject. "Is your last name living-out-loud or is that just your social media name?" There's a whine in my tone that even annoys me.

"I'm guessing by that groan that you aren't a social media fan."

"Everyone in everyone else's business. No thanks." Maybe I should have paid more attention, followed more friends and family, actually cared to look at my phone. Maybe then, I would have known long ago about Travis and Shelia. "Ebony's always telling me to get online, to post more. She says it would help my business."

"It would. She's right." Dean doesn't ask who Ebony is. I'm used to giving out my little spill—*Ebony, why that would be my twin sister.... No, we aren't identical, but we still have twin ESP.*

"Maybe. But business is pretty good as it is." Well… it wasn't rotten. I could pay my bills. Sure, I couldn't eat out or go to Mexico. But Hazel and I never miss a meal.

We eat! Every single meal. So how about that brag?

Sure, it helps that I get to live in Great Aunt Frances' house for free. When she died and the title to the house went to Gram-gram, she offered it to me, and to Ebony. But my sister had to spread her wings and fly to Seattle for work.

Dean slides a glance my way and I can't help but notice how long his lashes are. Does he realize that women all over the world pay loads of money just to have eye lashes exactly like his?

"Well, congrats then. I'd love to see some of your photos… oh but wait! You haven't posted any."

I roll my eyes. "Ha. Ha. I'm going to start calling you Ebony."

Again Dean only snickers. He never asks about my sister.

"Ebony," I say, offering, since my brain is telling me it's time to share, "is my twin. Fraternal. We look like sisters, but she takes after our dad. I look more like my grandma when she was young —mom's mom. Ebony is brilliant and beautiful."

I stare out at the road, wishing my sister were here. She'd know what to do. She'd say exactly the right thing to Shelia without looking like an idiot.

"She sounds nice," Dean says, he watches the road too.

I breathe out, my chest feeling full and heavy. "She's the best." I blink back the tears that have suddenly come on and realize I need to change the subject—and, technically he didn't even ask about Ebony. I'm forcing all this emotion onto myself. "So, where do you live?"

"I'm in Evergreen."

"Oh! So, headed home." I hug my camera bag close. "Thanks for taking me to Willow Creek."

"How will you get home? I'm guessing Shelia and Travis are out."

My eyes go wide and my jaw tightens. Even if they offered, I wouldn't accept. I'd rather walk back to Ft. Collins than sit in a car with judging Travis and boasting Shelia for two hours. "I'll figure it out." I blink and look over at this man who was kind enough to save me tonight. "You don't need to stress. Uber and I are friends." I clear my throat, feeling too intimate with this stranger. "Thanks, Dean." The pepper spray in my hands might as well grow Ebony's head and start yelling at me that this man is a total stranger and I should be more on guard.

And she's right.

But I like him—I think.

————

WILLOW CREEK GROUNDS ARE GORGEOUS. It's no wonder Shelia wants to be married here. The outside walls are framed in windows from top to bottom and mountains make up the picture perfect background.

Dean pulls up to the front entrance, as far as he is able. "You sure you don't need anything else?"

I shake my head. This is something I have to do—and no one else can do it for me. I let out an uneven breath. "Thank you for the ride." I reach for the door handle, but turn back around, holding up one finger. "Oh, and for not being a psychopath who wanted to murder me."

He presses his lips together, his blue eyes glistening. "You're welcome. I usually try to avoid the psychopath route." He smiles. "Thanks for *not* using that pepper spray."

I can't stop the corners of my lips turning up. He's cute,

adventurous, *and* funny. And I am one hundred percent *not* his type. Not that I care… just an observation. My stomach has not flip flopped once over his chiseled chin. "You're welcome."

"Good luck, Iris."

I nod, square my shoulders, and start toward the door to the restaurant. Travis and Shelia. Here we go.

THREE

Dean

I watch Iris walk away, knowing she's miserable going. It feels so wrong.

I'm not a psychopath and I'm not a stalker, but I am someone who once upon a time needed a friend. Iris *was* that friend. Even if she doesn't recognize me. Maybe she doesn't even remember Dean Cooper. I lived in Ft. Collins for eleven months —with a pretty awful set of foster parents—I wouldn't blame her if she didn't. Iris was the only person who made life easier that year. She was my saving grace.

And I recognized her the minute she told me her Instagram handle.

So—I park my Jeep, knowing I have hours of video editing waiting at home for me, and head into Willow Creek. I don't have reservations, but I do have it in with the manager. I just want to make sure that Iris can get an Uber, that she will make it home okay. Surely, I owe her that. Even if she doesn't remember me. She is the only reason I survived tenth grade and I owe her this.

Lucky for me, I see a few empty tables and Darrin, my

manager friend, instructing a bus boy at the back of the room. I look right past the hostess—as if I am meant to be here—and walk straight for Darrin.

I wait for the kid, with the deer in the headlight eyes, to nod at Darrin and scurry away before tapping my friend's shoulder. "Hey," I say. "How's business on a Tuesday night?"

"Dean." Darrin claps his hand into mine and pulls me in for a pat on the back. "Where have you been?"

"The powder has been good this year. I've been outside. You need to take a day off so you can join me sometime."

Darrin laughs, but it's a tired sound, and looks around the room. "Yes, I do."

I know he's busy and I still need to scope out where Iris went. "Can I sit?"

"Pick a seat," Darrin says. It helps that I've endorsed Willow Creek without compensation a few times in my videos. That, and Darrin is just one stellar dude.

I scope out the seating—the room is large, plus there's seating on the terrace and the grounds. It's a cool night though and it only takes me a minute to find Iris's long wavy chestnut hair, it's golden brown with a few streaks of blonde shimmering through it. I don't remember the blonde when we were in school. But then, she doesn't remember my face.

I find a table right next to the one she sits at—facing two people who look like they want to eat her alive—there's a large wooden pillar, ceiling to floor separating our tables and I'm able to sit at her back with the pillar blocking me from view. Very— non stalkerish.

The guy—what did she call him again—maggot man? He twists the band at his wrist, making a show to look at his watch. What a peach. "You're thirty-five minutes late, Iris." He says her name with too much familiarity and I feel the urge to slug him— and not in the shoulder.

Iris's shoulders stiffen—I can't see her face, but I imagine her glower. "Yeah, that's what happens when your car breaks down out in the middle of nowhere."

"I'm just saying—not very professional." The moron puffs his chest—we're in the wild and he's proving his dominance.

"Thanks for offering to help me out. Aren't you both the chivalrous ones. "

Iris's cousin is a tiny thing with whitish blonde hair that Dolly Parton would envy. Her pale cheeks pinken with the reprimand. "We weren't sure you were being forthright, Rizzo."

"Ugh." Iris blanches. "Please don't call me that. I've never liked that nickname. And I'm not fifteen. Of course I was being honest. My car is on some lonely highway waiting for a tow that's going to cost me an arm and a leg. Not to mention I had to catch a ride here with a stranger! So again, thanks."

"A stranger? Maybe you are fifteen," Maggot Man says. He grimaces when he looks at Iris, like the sight of her pretty face causes him pain. "You should know better."

"Well, thankfully my ride was much more of a gentleman than you are, Travis."

Travis, that's right. Travis, the maggot man. I am starting to see why Iris wants to find him in a mass grave of insects.

"Oh, Iris," the girl says. "I'm sure it came as a shock to you. Me and Travis, that is." Shelia looks from Iris to the lanky man next to her. "I thought maybe you knew by now."

"Nope," Iris says, lifting the drink in front of her and downing it. "Convenient about that group of wedding invites that got *lost*; mine, Ebony's, Gramgram's, my parent's. *None* of us knew."

Shelia lifts one shoulder.

There's a short pause and then, Iris says, "As you so brilliantly pointed out, Travis, we're behind on time. Should we get down to it?" She's all business.

"Can we order? We've been waiting for *you*." Travis lifts his hand, calling over a waiter.

"You waited even though you didn't think I'd actually come?" Iris rests her elbow on the table, her chin in her palm.

"We ordered drinks," Shelia says, motioning to her wine glass —the empty one that Iris just downed.

"See, I'm more of a gentleman than you thought." Travis snuffs the air like it smells bad in Iris's direction.

"You mean, than I *remember*." Iris lifts her head from her palm and smacks her hand down onto the table with a loud thud. "And I'm not so sure of that."

"How is life, Iris? Fulfilling?" Travis's voice takes on a nasty tone and I want so badly to slug him right out of his chair. But I'm not here to embarrass Iris. And I'm not normally violent. I'm just here to make sure she gets a ride home.

"Actually, it's very fulfilling. Life is great, in fact. I have my own house, my own business. And I own the cutest wirehaired pointing griffon that would give you a sneezing fit if you came within two inches of her. She's perfect."

"A dog and a house. Wow. Sounds exciting." Travis's voice is full of mockery. I know his kind. He is a bully. Which always takes me back to sophomore year. If there's one thing I hate—it's a bully.

"It is," Iris answers. "My life has only gotten better since college. I left behind all my *regrets* and have made the most of life."

Travis snorts, as if to say how could he be a regret.

The waiter Travis summoned over arrives and peers from Iris to the couple across from her. The tension is palpable. I can only imagine what might happen if that idiot says one word about Iris's pup. The waiter shoves his pad of paper back into his apron and slinks away without anyone ever having noticed him.

Shelia sets a hand on Travis's wrist. "That's great, Rizzo. You've always wanted a dog."

"Are you seeing anyone? Or just the dog?" says Travis, the diabolical maggot man.

What is with this guy? I asked Iris all the wrong questions earlier. Maybe he isn't a liar or a cheater—what about a pig-headed jerk? That's a one hundred percent—*yes*.

But then, it's been so long since I've seen Iris and I'm curious to hear her answer. *Is* she seeing someone? It wouldn't surprise me. Why wouldn't she be? She never mentioned a guy on our ride over, though—just the dog and the grandma.

"I… am…" she says, but the words come out like a question. Even I don't believe her.

"Right," Travis says and Shelia offers her a pity smile.

"That's… *great*, Rizzo."

"I am!" Iris bellows. "I am, and he's on his way here. *He* refused to leave me stranded. Unlike somebody else I know."

"Great. We can make this a double date." Shelia pinches one of her long-nailed clawish paws toward Iris.

"Well, he is coming from a long ways away. A very long ways. So… most likely you'll miss him."

"Is he coming to the wedding?" Shelia asks.

"There is no *he*," Travis says, sneering down at Shelia. He sets his full toothy glaring grin on Iris.

"There is," Iris stands, her chair scrapping along the wooden flooring. There is so much confidence in her tone that I doubt my doubts from before. "He is sexier, smarter, and so much kinder than you, Travis Cheesebro. *And* his last name isn't completely ridiculous! Sorry, you're getting stuck with that one, Shelia."

"Oh, I'm keeping my own name." Shelia purses her lips, blinking up at Travis. "For *feminist* reasons."

Travis stands, towering over Iris, only the table between them —the two are starting to turn heads.

Iris sets her hands to her hips, but Travis's face has turned a beetish purple ever since she brought up his last name.

"You are a *liar*, Iris. I'm not surprised." His mouth turns down in a gloating smug grin. He is everything I dislike about humans.

Iris turns and I can see her profile, her throat moves with a nervous swallow. "I'm not. And hey... perfect... He's here." She grins, but the smile is forced. I'm not sure Travis can see it—I'm guessing that guy gets a lot of false smiles.

Then, Iris walks right up to my very *married* friend Darrin, standing at the doorway, and loops her arm through his. "Hi, honey."

FOUR

Iris

I string my arm through this stranger's. He's just walked past the restaurant's entrance. He's in a suit and tie and has kind eyes—Dean has kind eyes too. So, I'm hoping I can get lucky twice in one night.

Do insane people get to be lucky? Because it's possible my sanity has jumped ship. And swam to Africa. Then drowned.

Still, if this man will follow my lead and pretend, for even five minutes, to be my boyfriend I promise to never eat Oreo's in the bathtub again. I will stop wishing for maggots to claim Travis's body. Heck, I will never say another evil word about Travis Cheesebro. And I'll let Shelia call me Rizzo all throughout her wedding. *Please universe*, let him be a nice guy—and play along with me.

I am not giving up Oreos in the tub if he doesn't play along.

No way.

I flick my gaze upward. *You got that universe?*

The poor man I've linked myself to peers down at me with a horrified expression. I whip my other arm up and around him—

like I'm hugging him. But really I am just getting myself closer to his earlobe.

"Hey," I whisper. "I'm not crazy. Please play along. I just need—"

"Iris!" I hear my name called across the room. And then an unnatural—"Sweetie!" sings in the air.

I drop my arms from the man who has gone completely frozen in my grasp and turn for the person who just called me… *sweetie.*

Dean.

Living out loud Dean strides over to where my—if the universe would play along for once—fake boyfriend and I stand. And he's calling me sweetie? Why is he even here? I saw him drive away—at least I thought I did.

"I see you found Darrin," Dean says, his voice off—but then I am pretty off myself at the moment. "I'm so glad that you're okay!" His speech is loud and worse than Ebony's 6th grade performance in *The Princess and the Pea*. I'm guessing Travis and Shelia have no problem hearing him.

Dean snatches me by the hand and pulls me away from the man at the door—who, I have to admit, looks much more at ease now that Dean is putting distance between the two of us.

My tongue is suddenly swollen and paralyzed. I can't say a word. And somehow, Dean knows exactly what to say. "You must be Shelia," he holds a hand out to my cousin. Did I tell him her name? I must have. "And Tommy Boy?" Dean's eyes pierce into my ex's.

Travis's lips fold in on one another as he holds back his grimace and shakes Dean's hand. "Travis," he growls. His face has gone a deeper purple that makes him look a little like an Oompa Loompa. It's a beautiful sight. "So, *you're* with Iris?"

Dean slips an arm around my back and while it's foreign and not exactly comfortable, I leave it right where it is—over my shoulders, his hand hanging down like a limp fish.

I lean into him and breath in cedarwood and musk. "Yes. He is," I say with all the confidence my inchworm self-esteem can muster.

"Yes, I am," Dean says at the same time.

Shelia claps her hands as if this shock is the greatest news on the planet. "Sit!" she squeals, setting a hand to Travis's forearm. "Where? How long? What's the level?"

"Ah—" I peer at Dean.

Then, at the same time we answer her first question.

Only I say—"Dog park."

And Dean answers—"Skiing."

I pull in a breath, a nervous chuckle spills out with my exhale. "We were skiing at a dog park."

Travis's brows knit together—he'd argue, except that Dean is sitting right in front of him, proof that I'm not the liar (that I actually am) because my *boyfriend* is flesh and bone.

"Yeah. Well, I was skiing. Iris was walking Hazel."

"Hazel?" Travis says, his lips twitching with a sneer.

I could kiss Dean for remembering Hazel's name—like lay one on him—right on those full pink lips. My new friend is a bit of a hottie. Yep—I am *so* not his type. I just hope that Travis and Shelia will miss that fact.

Again we open our mouths at the exact same time. "My dog," I say.

"Her dog," Dean says like we are the most in sync couple the universe has ever created.

Yes! Thank you universe, I will keep crumbs and cursing out of my tub from this moment on—I promise!

Shelia giggles at our simultaneous answers.

I am a bit all over the place—distracted by the man sitting next to me, but it hasn't escaped my attention that Shelia is eyeing my "boyfriend" up and down. Okay, I noticed Dean's long black eyelashes. And yeah, I see the way his broad shoulders resemble small boulders. Sure, that T-shirt tells me there are plenty of abs hidden beneath it. But I have not conjured up a picture of them in my head—*no way*. I ignore all of that. Mostly, I have paid attention to the non-crazy side of Dean. You know that attractive part of him that equals not hunting me down and killing me in the night.

Shelia doesn't know him, but she wastes no time—checking out my *sort of* boyfriend, right in front of me! And her fiancé. *Nice*.

She bats her lashes and grins. "Yes, Hazel," she says, though Shelia has never met my fur baby.

I slide my gaze to Dean, who grins back at me—faking, but more at ease than the other guy I tried to convince to be my "boyfriend". Dean is cute—like *super* cute—he's not just eyelashes and abs. I probably shouldn't think about it too much or I'll get nervous. Still, I lean a little closer, breathing in Dean's cedarwood scent, just playing my part.

Shelia waves her hand, telling me to continue—she had other questions. *How long?* How should I know… *What's the level?* What does that even mean?

So, I deflect. "This is Dean. Dean—" Why did I do that? I start talking like I'm about to full name him, when—*duh, Iris! You don't know his full name!*

Dean holds out his hand—again, "Dean Cooper. And I've heard all about the two of you! When is the big day?"

Whew. Thankfully my fake boyfriend is smarter than me.

But then—*Cooper*? I know that name. I guess it's not as if it's uncommon.

Still, I study Dean. But stop myself, before it appears as if I'm studying him. He is my boyfriend after all. I have definitely seen him before today—no doubt about it.

"Three weeks," Shelia says. She's fine with our unanswered questions as long as the topic is on her.

Travis however hasn't stopped staring at Dean's hand around my shoulders. His judgmental, laser beam eyes make my sweat glands work overtime. I'm certain he can see through every lie

I've told tonight. All adding up to Iris not being enough in the end.

I feel a trickle of sweat slide down my back, and I hope that Dean can't feel the nervous perspiration through my sweater. I cross my legs and create an inch of space between myself and my stranger boyfriend.

"Uck. Iris, what are you wearing?" Travis's nose wrinkles. Can his judging laser beams *see* the sweat pooling in every crevice of my body?

"What am I…" I peer down at my gray and white chunky striped sweater. I've always liked it with my denim skirt.

"You're shoes. Geez, Iris."

"My Converse?" I wrinkle my nose. What in the world is wrong with my shoes? They're my favorite—and I'd wage that Travis remembers that.

"Yes. You can't be a lady for once in your life?" Travis smirks, like he's made a joke rather than insulted me in public.

Dean stiffens next to me. "Why do you care about her shoes?" he says, and he's more protective than a stranger should be.

I jab him with my elbow. But I don't know why—his acting just keeps getting better and better. Still, I don't want any more of a scene than we're already causing.

"I love her shoes," Dean says—not dropping it. "She is a sexy little sass in those tennis shoes."

I can't help it—it's like a reflex and I elbow him again. "I am not a sass."

"Well, not a sass, but sexy. Look at those legs."

My eyes go wide.

"Or don't. That's not cool. Hey," Dean points at Travis, his acting skills heading right into the toilet, "you shouldn't look at another girl's legs. You're engaged."

"Can we please talk about the wedding? Please." I look from Shelia to Dean and avoid Travis all together. "*Please.*"

"Yes." Shelia pipes. "You're coming, right?" She's talking to Dean. "You can meet the family and be Iris's assistant." Shelia chuckles.

Dean lives in Evergreen—I mentioned the wedding was here. I stay quiet. He can answer this one. I could fake one more day... I think. But I won't make him.

His lips puff out with air. "I wouldn't miss it."

I don't even realize I'm holding my breath until it deflates from my chest. "Of course he'll come!" I sit straighter and Dean drops his arm from around me, setting his hand on the table. As if we've been doing it for years, I slide my fingers into his, only to realize I am a clammy sweaty mess and now my sweat juices are covering the inside of his palm. Ew. Yes—I am one sexy lady, just like Dean said.

"Perfect!" Shelia beams, clapping her hands in front of her. "One little change, Rizzo."

I swallow down the bite that so badly wants to rip from my mouth with her nickname. "Yes?"

"We've decided to tie the knot in Tahoe."

"Wait. What?" I drop Dean's hand, smacking my sweaty palm to the table top.

"Lake Tahoe. You know—water and sunshine. It'll be perfect. Travis has an aunt who runs a resort there. She said we could have a dozen rooms, three days, and a wedding right on the beach."

"But, but, but—"

"Spit it out, Iris," Travis says, all smiles again.

"The wedding is in three weeks. What about your guests? What about the arrangements here?"

"Momma is switching everything over." Shelia shrugs, looking like a spoiled three year old. "It's fine."

Ugh. My poor aunt Sandy.

I say nothing—nothing kind or coherent comes into my head. Tahoe isn't even near us! What is she thinking?

Shelia sighs, like it's been a long night. *For her.* Yet, she isn't switching all the arrangements over. She didn't break down on the side of the road. And she hasn't been putting on a show with a fake boyfriend! "You were super late Iris," she says, "and we need to go. Busy. Busy. But Dean, you're still coming right?"

Dean just stares at her.

"Right? Right? Right?" she says, again and again.

Dean swallows, and his Adam's apple is like the strength tester at the county fair—up and down. "Uh, right," he finally agrees.

"I've got a room for Iris, Ebony, and Gramgram. But Grandma can't drive that far and who knows if Ebony will come, now." Shelia rolls her eyes. Cupping her mouth she says in a hushed, but not quiet voice, "She's kind of the prodigal son of the family. She's a *writer*," her eyes widen, "about things like *football.*"

"She is not the prodigal son," I say—Shelia will not talk about my sister. "She's not even a son!" My hands flare out. "She's brilliant. She's spreading her wings and—"

"Anyway," Shelia says, not hearing a word I've said, "so there should be plenty of room for you. Here's the agenda." She takes a fat envelope from her purse and hands it to me.

"Shelia!" I bellow. "This is crazy! All of your plans, your guests, your arrangements—"

"I told you. Mom is taking care of it. I want a beach wedding, Rizzo."

"What about tonight?" I pound the table with my fist and my voice rises louder than I intended. "I thought we were taking pictures. You said you waited for me to order dinner."

Her face pales and her eyes can't quite meet mine. They didn't wait. That was just a story they made up to make me feel guilty. *Oh yes—you're some gentleman, Travis.*

"Why would I want pictures here?" Shelia's brows cinch.

"Wedding's in Ta-hoe," she says slow and silly—like I might be too dense to understand.

I sigh. I suppose right now I have bigger problems. Like the stranger sitting next to me.

Travis stands, ready to go. "See you then, *Dean*." He says Dean's name as if it were made up. He knows. Somehow Travis knows that I am a big fat dateless liar. He doesn't believe a word we've said. He doesn't believe Dean will make it to California.

And somehow—I am going to prove him wrong.

FIVE

Iris

S o, my logical brain knows that I should be thanking Dean. He sort of saved me—again. But the emotional part of my brain, which is definitely in charge right now, is on the defense.

"Why did you do that?" I bark, jetting away from Dean's side the minute Travis and Shelia have left the building. They're like Elvis—they have *left the building*—and now chaos has broken out. "I had everything under control!"

Dean stares at me like I might be speaking Mandarin… and he can't compute any of my words. "If by control you mean hitting on my *married* friend and scaring him to death—then yeah, you were doing great on your own."

Married? Oh joy. I am so on a roll. "What are you even doing here?"

"I was worried you wouldn't be able to find a ride home."

"Oh," I grouch, crossing my arms. "Well, that's really nice of you."

"Yeah, well I got in a little deeper than I planned." The

annoyance that sprinkled his tone has gone. He doesn't even sound upset—just surprised.

I chew on the skin of my bottom lip. Yes, I'm guessing he didn't plan on leaving this night *attached*. Crap. What if he already has a girlfriend? Why wouldn't he? And here I am yelling at him. Why am I yelling? Because somehow it's easier than apologizing.

I push the water glass in front of me to the middle of the table and rest both elbows on the table top. This is a mess. I can't actually ask this man to go with me to Tahoe. Nor can I bear the thought of going alone, listening to all of Travis's snide remarks.

After an entire sixty seconds of silence, Dean speaks, "I can see why you'd like to bury that man in maggots."

"I'm not burying him, I just come upon him—" I shake my head. "You know what? Never mind. It doesn't matter."

"So, when do we leave?"

My gaze flutters up to meet his face. "We? *We're* leaving? You'll still come?"

He shrugs. "I can't imagine leaving you alone with those two vultures ever again. But I don't have to come. If you'd rather I didn't—"

"No. No. Wait. Just let me think." I swallow and lick my lips. This is a really bad idea. Ebony and Gramgram will not approve. Hazel probably won't approve. I clear my throat and look into Dean Cooper's face. It really is a nice face. His eyes look like the ocean in Mexico—so blue. They stand out against his dark lashes and brows. I decide to trust those eyes. "You cannot stay in my room with me. No matter what Shelia says."

"Of course."

"Okay then, you're really in?" I peer at him, waiting for him to point at me and yell something like—*You've been punked, Iris McCoy!*

"I'm in." He smiles and it makes me totally suspicious and a little swoony.

36

I'm a smart single woman—well usually I am—so I listen to the suspicious part of my insides. "Why?" I point one finger at him.

"Because I've never kayaked, snow skied, and sailed all in one day. I'm pretty sure we can do all three, in the month of May, in Tahoe."

I crinkle my nose. "Huh. Okay." I mean, that answer matches his Instagram feed. I make a mental note to not tell Ebony about this scheme. Maybe Shelia's right and she really won't make it to the wedding. And I can magically avoid telling her anything about this horribly embarrassing situation.

Who am I kidding? I'll be lucky if Shelia doesn't talk to Ebony before I do. I'll have to tell her. She is my other half. She might already know of this whole situation through our twining brain waves.

"So, you'll want a day for that," I say as I unseal Shelia's envelope with her new itinerary. I read in my head, humming and mumbling a few notes out loud. "Rehersal dinner is May 4th, wedding May 5th, a day for Dean to ski and sail and whatever else, May 3rd."

"A day to fly in—" he says.

"Oh, we'll be driving."

"Driving?" His brow furrows and he pulls out his phone. Two seconds later he says, "It's almost fourteen hours in a car."

"Yes, but Hazel can't fly."

"Hazel? Your dog?"

I nod. I don't care if I seem crazy to hottie, adventurous Dean. Not when it comes to my Hazel. I can't leave her for days.

"Okay then a day or two to drive there. So, we leave on the first or the second." He breathes out. "That gives us three weeks."

"Three weeks? For what?"

"We've got work to do. If you're going to convince your

family that we're dating, you're going to have to do better than you did tonight. No more attacking married men."

"I didn't—" But I did latch on to Dean's friend pretty quickly. Maybe we need an extra day to get my head checked out. I clamp my mouth shut, swallow, then say, "What kind of work?"

———

I CANNOT LIE to my grandmother. She's my favorite person in the whole world—besides Ebony—and I just can't do it. I have to tell her about my fake boyfriend. I can't lie. That, and she lives right next door to me. Surely, if I had a boyfriend, Gramgram would know.

When Dean dropped me off, I pointed to my house for a full minute. "It's the violet one—or the *iris* colored one," I'd told him.

Dorky, I know—an iris colored house for Iris. But Gram had it painted when she found out I'd taken her up on her offer. Our two little houses look just alike except that mine is a blueish-purple and Gramgram's is her favorite—bright yellow. I couldn't have him knocking on Gramgram's door tomorrow and startling her. So, I had to make it clear.

"Got it," he said. "I'll see you tomorrow." Dean is certain that we need to prep and prepare to make this hoax work. And I just keep thinking—why is he so invested?

I stand outside Gramgram's house, anxious to see Hazel, but dreading what my grandmother will say when I tell her my news. She'll probably lock me away and tell the whole family of my sham. I wouldn't blame her. Still, I have no choice but to tell her —she'll find out one way or another. And she'll never believe I've been seeing someone.

Mom and Dad won't be difficult to convince, they're in Nepal for the next two months...so my hope is they will never know. I might get Ebony on board, but Gram—I don't think so. That woman points out everything male we see, just to see if my eyes light up. They don't. She will not be okay with *fake*.

I tap on Gram's door, with one glance back at Dean—he's waiting for me to go inside. I really couldn't have asked for anyone more chivalrous to stop and pick me up on the side of the road. I got lucky. Thanks, Universe.

I tap again, just to let Hazel and Gram know I'm here. I don't wait any longer, I open up Gramgram's stark white front door and shuffle inside. Leaning against the door I let out an audible sigh.

What a night. What a stupidly horrid night.

"Who's that?" Gramgram peers through a crack she's made in the sheer curtains. She's watching as Dean's white Jeep drives away.

I gulp and try out the words on her. Gram always said a band-aid was better ripped off. "That would be my boyfriend."

Her gray brows knit. "Iris Elaine McCoy get your booty in here and explain yourself."

It isn't until I take another step into Gramgram's living room that Hazel finally acknowledges me. She's always a little grumpy when I leave her for more than an hour. She stands from her perch on Gramgram's couch and leaps to the ground, stretching her legs, and taking her merry ol' time.

"Hazel," I say in a sweet voice. I wouldn't like being abandoned for hours either. She trots over with my coo and I squat to the floor to give my fur baby some love. I run my fingers through her wiry curls and nuzzle my cheek to her bearded chin. She is the cutest. She's tall for her breed and when I sit on the floor like this she can see over the top of my head.

Hazel licks my chin—I am one hundred percent forgiven.

"Iris!" Gramgram says, interrupting our reunion. "Boyfriend? Explain." My grandmother's tone is all business—which is a little hard to buy as she sits on her couch in her feather slippers and

Johnny Cash pajamas—top and bottom The Man in Black's face covers her body.

"Shelia called before I got to Evergreen tonight." She was lucky I was already driving and that Ebony talked me down—sort of—or I might have done exactly what Travis expected and chickened out. "Have you met her fiancé Gram?"

Gramgram shakes her head. "Only her mom has. How was he?" She dips her head, conspiratorially, as if now I'm in on a big secret. "Do you have an opinion yet?"

"Oh I have an opinion, all right."

Gramgram waves me on—I'm not making any sense. I mean, to anyone else. But then, Gram knows this about me. She knows I start from the top and trickle down when it comes to—oh—everything. So, she listens, knowing I'll get to the "boyfriend" part of my story eventually.

"It's Travis."

"What's Travis?"

"Her fiancé, Gram. She's marrying my college boyfriend."

Gramgram sits straighter. Johnny smoothes out over her large bust. "That boy who made you feel like you weren't worth a nickel in a dime store candy shop?" There's a growl in her voice that comes whenever she's ready to pounce.

"I was talking to Ebony, telling her about Travis when my car broke down thirty miles from Evergreen."

"Out there? On that road? In my little Volvo—" she sighs.

"It's fine Gram. They're towing it to the shop."

Her eyes bug. "Do you have any idea how much a tow from Evergreen is going to cost."

I swallow down my tears. "More than half what Shelia's job is paying me." I blow out a breath and push onward. "Anyway, this man, Dean, he stopped to help me." I sort of leave out the part where Dean drove me the rest of the way to Evergreen. Gramgram might lock me inside, at all times, if she knew I got into a car with a strange man. "He was nice. He sat from a distance waiting for the tow with me. I think he didn't want to scare me. Anyway, I sort of told Shelia and Travis that he was my boyfriend."

Her brows cinch. She's trying to connect pieces, but I've left a lot of the story out. My start from the beginning and get every detail of the story in, is lacking tonight.

I swallow. "I'm so tired. I can explain more tomorrow. But what you need to know right now is that Shelia has decided to get married in Lake Tahoe." I hike one brow up to my hairline, waiting for Gramgram's reaction—because it will be similar to mine. No doubt.

Gram's jaw falls open.

"Yes, Tahoe. She's says she knows you probably won't go, others too, but she doesn't care. She wants to get married—to Travis—on the beach."

"And this Dean is going?"

"How—" I shake my head. How does she know that? I purposely left that part out.

"You wouldn't have even brought him up otherwise, Iris."

I nibble on my bottom lip. "Yes. He's going."

She breathes in. "All right then. I am available tomorrow between the hours of two and six. I can quiz him then."

"Quiz?—But Gram—"

"I've said my part. Two and six, Iris."

Two and six? She has all day. And I don't know Dean's schedule. Maybe he's busy from two to six. I'll message him, so we can "get to work" as he said, whatever that means. I might know by now if I hadn't pretended to sleep the entire ride home. I just couldn't face him. The horror of my day and situation all caught up with me and I couldn't have another conversation. I'll have to face him tomorrow, though. And he'll have to face Gram.

But, ugh. I do not need my Gramgram's approval for a very fake relationship…

Who am I kidding? Of course I do.

SIX

Dean
_____

I haven't stopped thinking about Iris McCoy since I dropped her off last night. I haven't seen her in ten years, since we were fifteen—just kids. So, I can't be offended that she didn't recognize me. It took her name—just her first though—for me to realize who she was. She looks the same—only better. So much better.

The girlishness is gone from her face—and her legs. Iris always had nice legs—not like an athlete, Iris was never an athlete. Just feminine, and time has only improved them. Her eyes are still bright, still excited. Though, last night they may have been bright with anxiety. How did Iris ever end up with a punk like Travis? And from the way she spoke—he's the one who broke things off.

How is that possible?

My mind reels for a minute. None of that makes sense. Iris dated Kenny Norton when we were in school together. He was cool—nice *and* a jock. Not a combination you find every day. He didn't seem to care that Iris couldn't tell the difference between a football and a basketball. He never had much to do with me—

but then no one did back then, other than Iris. He was just a decent human. I heard him talking to his friends once, about Iris. He was respectful.

So, how did she go from Kenny to Travis? It doesn't make sense.

I messaged Iris this morning, but I haven't heard back from her. I wouldn't blame her if she blocked my account and never spoke to me again. To her, I am a stranger.

Although, I think she really does want my help. And I *want* to help her. Somehow—I could do what I never thought possible and pay her back for all the kindness she showed me during the worst year of my life.

I'm headed out for a hike... I need some fresh air. And time alone. Maybe, I'll even leave my phone at home and—

The device pings with a message, as if it knows I'm thinking about leaving it. Even though I probably won't. I need the camera.

> @iris_me: Why are you up at 5am? What's wrong with you?
>
> @deanlivingoutloud: It's almost six.
>
> @iris_me: Now. When you messaged me it wasn't.
>
> @deanlivingoutloud: Don't you have silent mode on your phone?
>
> @iris_me: I've never needed it until now.
>
> @deanlivingoutloud: Well... since you're up? Hike?
>
> @iris_me: I'm carless, remember? Besides you're almost two hours away.
>
> @deanlivingoutloud: Oh. Right.
>
> @iris_me: By the way. I never said thanks. For driving me home.
>
> @deanlivingoutloud: You did.
>
> @iris_me: Yeah, but you drove me home and then I just said—bye and thanks and I didn't even

consider your two hour drive back to Evergreen.
I'm not usually so selfish.
@deanlivingoutloud: You were under duress.
@iris_me: Still. Thank you.
@deanlivingoutloud: You're welcome.

I need to tell Iris that I know her. But in some twisted way I sort of like her not remembering that pathetic kid from tenth grade who wore the same jeans every day and traded between a handful of T-shirts. The kid who hid welts beneath his long sleeves, didn't know how to stand straight, or look another human in the eyes.

My stomach knots as I take myself back to that boy. I left him behind a long time ago and I haven't looked back.

@iris_me: So, you wanted to meet up? Work on
    things? I'm not sure what that means, but my
    grandmother would like to meet you. Can you
    come over today?

She adds,

@iris_me: Between 2 and 6 if possible.

With an eye rolling emoji.

@iris_me: I can help with gas. Sorry—just no car.
@deanlivingoutloud: I get it. You don't need to help
    with gas. Not yet. I'll let you when we drive to
    Lake Tahoe.
@iris_me: More than fair.
@deanlivingoutloud: Two works. You sure you don't
    want to take an Uber over? I know the perfect
    morning hike.

@iris_me: By the time I get there, it won't be morning.
@deanlivingoutloud: Sure it will. You pointed out how
nice and early it is. Hazel would love it.
@iris_me: No Uber would allow Hazel in their car.
@deanlivingoutloud: Oh. Right. See you at two, then.

Suddenly I have more built up energy than I should. I need to do some jumping jacks or run five miles. Instead, I grab a protein bar and head out for my hike.

———

IRIS SENT HER ADDRESS AGAIN, but I don't need it. I remember the way. I'm pretty thankful I'm the one who found her that night—what if it had been some creep? And now, he knew where she lived. My shoulders shiver with the thought.

I'm a little early, but we have plenty to talk about—more than just meeting Iris's grandmother and dog. I cross through the gate, it's a short little fence that encloses the entirety of Iris's front yard. I walk right up to her lilac colored house and rap on the sunshine-yellow door—it's the same color as her grandmother's entire house.

Iris calls something through the door that sounds like —"Mmm-am." I study the door—was that an *enter*? Again she calls and this time I swear I hear, "Mmmm—in."

Come in? I shrug and turn the knob.

Iris's front room is small and almost bare besides the couch and one end table—and of course, Iris. She sits on her hardwood floors, across from a large curly-haired dog with a brown head and a gray body, they each have one end of a rope in their mouths.

Iris's cloth shorts are *short* and her baggy sweatshirt slides off of one shoulder. She has puffy pink socks on that end at her ankle. Between the ankle socks and short shorts, there is a lot of leg stretched out on that hardwood. Her hair is piled on her head, with strings of it falling around her face. And truly—if it weren't for the rope between her teeth—she'd look adorable.

Who am I kidding? Even with the rope in her mouth she's somehow captivating.

Her gaze slides up to me—and those piercing blue eyes tell me I wasn't whom she expected. The dog across from her yanks, and the rope slides from Iris's dropped jaw without any trouble. The wirehaired pup, with the craziest coloring I've ever seen on a dog, goes tumbling backward, falling onto her hind legs.

"Hazel!" Iris bellows, scrambling to her knees, she reaches for the dog that at this angle seems almost the same size as Iris. She slides Hazel over the hardwood floors and against her, then scratches behind the pup's ears before giving her a kiss on the nose.

And then, Hazel decides to say hello. She's awkward and playful as she bounds toward me, her front paws landing on my thighs. I scratch the top of her head. "Hello, Hazel."

Iris scrambles to her feet, her face flushed a pretty pink, with her porcelain thighs blazing bright. I can tell her shorts are never this short out in public—those thighs haven't seen the sun in probably a decade.

I'm not sure why—they are sleek and unbidden, and hard to keep my eyes off.

"You're early," she says, her words a little breathless. Her right hand pats the ball of hair on top of her head.

"Yeah, I thought we might as well get started."

She swallows, her eyes darting from Hazel back to me.

"Did you want to explain?" I point to where she and Hazel just sat facing one another on the ground. I'm proud—I'm not even laughing, though I can't keep the wide smile from my face.

Her body goes stiff. "No, I do not."

Hazel hasn't relented our introduction yet. Her long tail sways back and forth as her head attempts to inch closer to mine.

Iris nibbles on her bottom lip and my eyes linger there too long. I'm not in tenth grade anymore, I'm not that kid who knew he never had a chance, and it's easy to linger on Iris's pouty lips.

"Hazel," Iris finally says, "you've said hello."

Still, Hazel is certain we're going to be best friends. It isn't until Iris walks over and physically lifts the dog's paws from my waistline that she relents.

Iris breathes in, "She likes you." And I'm not sure why, but it feels as if I've passed some sort of test in this. "Go find Patty," she tells Hazel. "Go on."

Excited, Hazel's feet slip and slide on the hardwood floors— almost like I'm watching an old cartoon of a coyote running in place. She takes off down a hall and Iris and I are left alone.

"So, no call to let me know you'd be an hour early?"

I shrug, the tips of my fingers sliding into my jean pockets. "I don't have your number. I sent a DM on Instagram when I left."

"I missed it." She scratches at the nape of her neck. "Can you give me a few minutes?"

"Sure." I step over to the couch. Iris's rope lays next to it and I pick it up. "Iris," I say, holding it out to her just before she leaves the room. "You know my imagination is probably going to concoct something much worse than the truth."

"It's just tug-o-war," she says, yanking the rope from my hand. "Hazel doesn't like it when I use my hands."

My brows hike to my hairline. "Hazel doesn't like it?"

"No. She thinks it's unfair."

One corner of my mouth lifts in a grin. I hope it doesn't say —*are you crazy?* Because even though this dog may have made her a little loco—she is adorable. She doesn't offer any more of an explanation and then she's gone.

I take a seat on the couch and peer about Iris's place. The room doesn't hold a lot of furniture—and now I know why—it's the tug-o-war arena. But it does have photographs on every single wall. Pictures of people on one wall—I recognize two, Iris and her sister. Pictures of Hazel on another wall, colored and black and white, in the sun and in the snow. Hazel could be the star of ModernDog magazine. The third wall has scenery photos, they're beautiful and make me believe that Iris is more of an adventurer than she's let on. The wall with the couch has a long oblong mirror above it and nothing else. It's an interesting room and could hold my attention—studying each photograph for a time, except that… Hazel is back.

Her long legs remind me of a young antelope just learning to walk. She bounds into the room and at first I think there is a dead rat hanging from her mouth. But a rat wouldn't wear an apron. Hazel brings the ratty thing right over to me—a rag doll, missing one eye, half its brown yarn hair gone. I can't help the cringe that comes when I look at the thing.

Hazel sets the doll in my lap and instinctively I push the nasty thing off of myself. A snort and a shake of the head tells me Hazel doesn't agree with my reaction. She scoops the doll back up and again drops it in my lap.

"I don't want it. You keep it," I tell her—attempting to talk to her just as Iris did—sweet but assertive.

I pick the doll up by one of her mangled dirty hands and dangle her up—maybe she wants to play fetch. The word *Patty* is embroidered on the apron. "Patty," I say aloud, looking to Hazel for confirmation—which makes me think that I might have gone a little crazy in the seven minutes I've been inside Iris's house. I toss Patty across the room and Hazel skids along the hardwood floors after her doll.

There. Fetch with Patty. I lean back into the couch—it's old but comfortable and fits the room. I've just settled in when Hazel returns, Patty in tow. She climbs up onto the couch, laying her large body next to me and placing her head in my lap. Patty is clamped between her teeth and once again on my lap. This time, I don't think she's going anywhere.

I lift my hands unsure where to place them, but then settle my arms across Hazel's shoulders and back when it's clear she doesn't' plan to go anywhere.

"I guess Iris isn't crazy. You really did tell her that tug-o-war isn't fair when she uses her hands. Because I'm pretty sure you just told me that I need to hold Patty and if I won't listen, you'll just make it happen. That's fine. I can hold Patty. Though, she's a little off putting, Hazel. You know that, right?"

"She doesn't. She loves that ugly little scrap. I've tried to replace Patty. Hazel won't have it." Iris stands in the doorway, one hand on her hip. She's changed into jeans and a green sweater that looks like something my grandma would have crocheted. The pink fuzzy ankle socks still adorn her feet, but her hair is down, falling in waves over her shoulder.

My heart thunders in my ears. Yep, I am more attracted to Iris McCoy than I ever was in the tenth grade—tug-o-war and all.

SEVEN

Iris

We walk through the gate from my front yard and start toward Gramgram's house—I lead, while Hazel and Dean trail behind me.

"Iris," I hear Mrs. Walker call from across the street. She's stepped outside her house and waves hello. "Who's your friend?"

I look at Dean, my lips clamped shut. He gives me a waggle of the brows and I assume that means—*go for it. Try out the words on your unsuspecting neighbor.*

I squint in the sun. "Ah. This is Dean. My. Boy. Friend." I sound like a robot—but I get the lie out.

Mrs. Walker tilts her head, studying Dean. She slides her glance to me and looks more confused than ever. "Really?"

"Yes really," I bark at my older neighbor. She's got to be close to Gramgram's age. "You think he's too handsome and fun for me? Because. He. Is. Not." All of my lies come out like each word is it's very own sentence.

Dean smothers a laugh with his fist and Mrs. Walker's eyes bug, startled with my outburst. "No," she says, "I've just never seen a man at your place. I just assumed—"

"Got it!" I holler. "We all get it. Thank you, Mrs. Walker." Yes, thank you for telling Dean that I am a dateless loser.

My face is hot in the ten seconds it takes to reach my grandmother's door. I stop before walking inside, Hazel sits next to me and I turn to face Dean. I'm almost as tall as him, standing on the one step in front of Gramgram's house. "Listen up," I tell him. "I am not a weird-o."

He tilts his head, studying me. "Debatable."

"I'm not some crazy cat lady."

His gaze slides to Hazel. "Clearly."

"And I am not desperate. I may *not* invite men back to my home but that is because I don't want them there. My choice. Got it?"

He nods, his sapphire eyes like moon beams, staring intently.

"And!" I say, while I've got his attention and the height advantage—*almost* the height advantage. "My grandmother is *very* important to me. Be nice to her or your ride to Tahoe leaves without you."

I go to turn around, ready to enter, but Dean snatches me by the wrist, sliding his warm fingers into my hand. "I never assumed you were crazy or desperate. And, I think we both know you are not just my ride to Tahoe."

It's honest and I deflate a little with his bluntness. He is helping *me*. He hasn't stopped helping me since the night before. Not the other way around. I need to eat some humble pie and accept that. I clear my throat. "I do know that," I say, feeling as if I'm in a sauna with his closeness.

Dean drops the hand holding mine and slides it into his pocket. "All right, let's go meet Gramgram."

I tap on the door once and step inside my grandmother's house—cluttered with fifty years of lived in love and use. Gram's house is laid out like mine, but we've set them up very differently. We walk into her Johnny Cash sitting room. There are trinkets, pictures, records, and so much more covering the woman's should-be living room. For Christmas I gave her a life-size card-board cutout of The Man in Black and you would have thought he had stopped by for a visit. She cried, she squealed, she peed her eighty-one year old pants—luckily Gramgram is a firm believer in preparedness and "feelings". She had a feeling to wear her *Depends* on Christmas morning.

"Gramgram," I call, looking past that life sized Johnny in the corner to her hallway entrance. I hear the television in her make-shift TV room. AKA Mom's old bedroom.

"What the—" Dean says as he walks through the strobe light flashing on and off of a Johnny Cash bust made of copper.

"It's her thing. Okay?"

"I think obsessing may run in your family, Iris."

"Shh," I hiss at him. I reach back and snatch his hand as if this will shut him up. But it doesn't and it only makes me feel awkward. I haven't known Dean that long, yet I snuggled up to him in a restaurant and now I'm holding his hand.

"It's impressive," he says, peering around the space, "to say the least."

I hush him one more time before walking back to Gram's TV room. "Gramgram?" I say again. She's sitting on her floral couch, in a muumuu with print reading: *You can choose love or hate, I choose love.* It's her favorite Johnny quote, she had this dress specially made and it cost her a small fortune. I know because I helped teach her how to use her credit card online. *Whoa.* Talk about a big mistake, her collection has doubled since that day.

She lifts her gaze for a second, then her eyes are back on the screen. "You're early. I said two o' clock. My program isn't over yet."

"Oh, I'm sorry," Dean says, his blue eyes shifting to me. He's the one who came early, after all.

Gram sighs. "It's fine. It's too late now." She holds out her remote and turns the television off.

"Remember Gram, it's streaming. You can go back and watch it later."

"Oh, Iris. It just won't be the same. It'll be all over the net."

My brows furrow. *As the World Turns* probably won't be spoiled for her online, at least not where she's searching.

Hazel hops up on the couch and Gram turns the TV back on. My pup rests her head on top of her paws, and watches the screen as it lights up with a couple kissing on a boat dock.

"Now, let's head to the kitchen. I've made some treats." Gram stands, her large bust bouncing with the movement. "This must be Mr. Dean Cooper."

"Yes, ma'am. It's nice to meet you." Dean holds a hand out to my grandma and she pats the edge of his outstretched hand.

"My name is Georgia, but you may call me Gramgram. Everyone does." She smiles at him. "Well, what about you? Does everyone call you Dean?"

"They do," he nods. "I mean a few people in school called me by my last name—but that was a long time ago."

I tilt my head. *Cooper*? I know that name.

"And? What about yourself?" Gramgram says.

"Ah. About myself?"

She nods, not making herself any clearer.

Dean grins at her, and he is swoon-worthy gorgeous—just like one of Gram's soap men. "I walk the line," he says and his brows bounce with how pleased he is with himself.

Gram's face splits into a wide grin—Dean just quoted her favorite Johnny Cash song. She pats his chest as she scoots her way past him. "I've got a good feeling about this one," she says, making her way out to the kitchen.

This one? She says it as if she's met a bunch of my boyfriends. She hasn't, because there haven't been any to meet.

EIGHT

Iris

After eating monster bars with Gramgram, Dean explaining to her that his job is all about getting people to watch his videos on YouTube and Instagram, and listening to Gram's Johnny Cash concert experience, we say our goodbyes and start back for my place. A solid hour and forty minutes later.

For an hour of that time I didn't speak. While Gram and Dean chatted, I pulled up my dusty Instagram app—well, dusty until last night when Dean had me using it—and I stalked the man enthralling Gram with his stories.

I watched a few videos the night before, but today I went back *months*. Dozens and dozens of hiking, skiing, boating, and rock climbing adventures. Dean is daring, energetic in a toddler type way, and kind of amazing. He has women into the hundreds commenting on these posts. He never replies—maybe he saves that for his private messages. But then, he doesn't seem like the kind of person who would do that.

I open the door to my home, the lemony candle wax I have

melting in my scent pot teases my nostrils the minute we enter. It's clean and happy and smells like home to me. Hazel stretches her front legs, halfway through the door.

"Lazy girl," I say. "How can you be ready for a nap after watching soap operas at Grams?" She ignores my question and curls up on her dog bed in the corner, her snores will soon be our background noise. I lick my lips, feeling like this is a very strange and long first date. "Have a seat," I tell Dean. "Would you like some water?"

"Sure," Dean says as he sits on my hand-me-down couch. It's comfortable and even if I had an extra two grand to buy a new one, I wouldn't.

Before snagging the water bottles from my fridge, I go to the bathroom and rake through my long hair, check my teeth for any remnants of Gram's monster bar, and remind myself—"This isn't a date, Iris." One—I hardly know Dean Cooper. Two—Dean Cooper would never date a girl like me.

I hand Dean his water, kick off my shoes and take the very opposite end of the couch—as in making sure there is an entire body's worth of space between us—and not a skinny body, but an extra-large, tough guy body. I pull my legs up under me and sip from my own drink

"Thanks." He grins and it seems to showcase the little U shaped scar on his chin. "I like your grandmother."

My lips tickles. "Yeah? Me too. She's real."

The corners of his eyes crinkle with his smile. "She is." He holds out his arm. "You wanna pinch me? I'm real too."

"No," I push his arm down. "I just mean, she's herself, without any care or reservation. And she's wonderful. I envy that."

He leans forward, resting his elbows on his knees, his eyes never leave mine and make me feel warmer than the seventy-one degrees my house sits at. "You *are* like that."

"Right—*fake boyfriend*, I am so sincere with who I am."

Dean huffs out a breath and sits back, his laser beaming eyes still on me. "Okay—fake boyfriend aside—or heck, even with the fake boyfriend—you are, Iris."

I blink to hold back the sudden moisture in my eyes and soon my blinking resembles batting my eyelashes at him. *Smooth, Iris.* Thankfully he doesn't seem to notice. I turn my gaze and my crazy, tearing eyes down to Hazel, whose snores make sure we are never left in silence.

"Okay, come here." He pats the large man size space I've left between us.

I raise my brows and stick to my seat on this side of the couch.

"I told you, we have work to do."

I clear my throat and look at the space.

"I don't bite. I promise. I will be the most gentlemanly fake boyfriend you've ever had." He crosses his heart with his pointer finger.

I scoot an inch closer to him and he slides right up next to me, pulling out his phone. He brings the thing to life and holds it out—selfie style.

"What are you doing?"

"*We* are taking a picture. A very normal couple thing to do."

I slap on a grin and Dean snaps a quick photo. He grins when he looks down at it, then opens his Instagram app. I watch over his shoulder as he types.

> @deanlivingoutloud: Hey peeps. I'm not on a
> mountaintop today. Just hanging with my girl, Iris.
> I'm one lucky fella.

I watch over his shoulder as each word appears on the screen. "Fella?"

Then, he clicks post.

"Wha—" I snatch the phone from his hand, but it's too late. It's out there. In the world. Saying my name. "Why? Why? Why did you do that?"

"This is how the world—including your family—are going to be convinced of this relationship." He shifts one brow above the other. "*Instagram.*"

"Instagram?" I repeat and my tone speaks to how convinced I am—*not at all.*

"I'm serious, Iris. Social media is a powerful tool. This is what we need to do. We'll take pictures of us on different adventures, dressed in different clothes and we'll post them."

I study his phone, my forced smile shining back at the both of us. "I don't think three weeks of posting pictures are going to make it seem like we've been dating for *months.*"

"Lucky for you, you are fake dating a hacker."

"A hacker?"

He winks. "Well, a mediocre hacker. I do happen to know how to back-post on Instagram." His brows bounce. "And three years ago when I first started all this, I had a private account and a public account. I stopped using the private account a few months into my journey though. So, we'll back-post a bunch on my private account. Not many pay attention to that account anyway. Then I'll introduce you to my adventure world."

I pull in a breath and it hisses between my teeth. "Didn't you just do that?"

Dean chuckles. "Yep, I guess I did." Bobbing his head to the side, he says, "Also lucky for us, you have *two* Instagram friends." His eyes widen at the number. "And two posts. Will those two notice a sudden influx in posts."

"Aw, yes. They most definitely will."

"Who are they?" he says it like it's for research, and I guess it is.

"My sister—my twin sister. And our mutual college friend, Coco. I haven't seen Coco in more than a year though…"

"Okay," he nods. "We can work with that. The truth will probably come out to Ebony anyway, right?"

I can see the mental notes typing out in Dean's head. I'm surprised he remembers my sister's name.

"So, we'll do some back-posting. You can start to friend other people and wa-la, *boyfriend*."

I swallow, an anxious lump forming in the back of my throat. But then, I was the one who started this. I might as well jump in with both feet. Right? Or in more Iris fashion, I will slip, slide, and tumble my way in. *Whatever.*

I tap in my passcode and hand Dean my phone. "All right, boyfriend. Work your magic."

Dean holds out my phone, so that I can see the screen. He clicks on the small heart in the upper right hand corner and I watch, as he accepts his own follow request. He winks and my stomach flips. Standing from the couch, he walks around to where Hazel lays and crouches down next to her sleeping body. He snaps a couple of photos. He stands and a popping noise produces from his knees. I watch him, like he's one of Gram's nightly television programs. He walks to the wall of my favorite scenic photos and snaps a shot of three of the framed pictures.

He plops next to me—not bothering to leave that extra-large man space between us and shows me my own phone screen. His fingers run over the screen and soon I have four new posts— although according to the dates, they aren't new at all.

"Ready?" he says, speaking for the first time in ten minutes.

I blink—*for what?* Slow—as if he's asking permission, he wraps one arm around me—instantly his masculine—trees and musk scent surrounds me. I breathe him in and the sensation produces flutters in my still flipping stomach. He holds out his other hand, phone in his grasp and says, "Smile, Iris."

I watch the two of us on the screen, hold my breath—Dean's

scent is making me dizzy—and grin. He presses his cheek to mine and warmth floods my body, just before he snaps the photo.

He looks down at my phone before drawing his gaze up to me. "Perfect, Iris. It's perfect." He types on *my* phone, on *my* feed, and then he clicks post.

NINE

Iris

"So, where are we going?" I ask.

"I know this hiking trail that's perfect."

"A hike?" I say and I can't hide the skepticism in my voice. "I don't often hike."

He tilts his head and peers at me. "Iris, no one will believe that I'm in a relationship with someone if we don't spend some time together outdoors."

"What about a dog park?"

"Iris," he says my name again, but this time with a laugh. "I've seen the photographs in your living room. You spend time outside—more than just at dog parks." He's excited and ready to go and with that declaration, he charges four feet—from my kitchen to my living room, until he's standing in front of the framed photos on my wall. "This—" he says tapping the wall next to the picture I took at Rocky Mountain National Park. The sun had just gone down and the sky had turned the prettiest shade of violet. "This is outside. You had to get here."

I clamp my teeth down on my bottom lip. "I drove to the visitor's center, walked a ways, and used a great zoom lens."

"You *walked*. It's the same as hiking—sort of. Come on! We're bringing your camera, Hazel, and your best walking shoes." He claps—like he's saying, *go team! Get moving!*

So, I do. I grab my black Converse and sit on the couch to put them on. The thought of this awkward day has about given me hives—but Hazel and pictures. Those are my two favorite things. I think I can do this. "Hazel is going to love this," I say— much too giddy for fabricated poses with my fake boyfriend.

"Whoa—those are your best walking shoes?"

I look down at my favorite pair of Converse. "Yep."

He huffs out a breath. "Okay… we won't walk too far. Let's go."

Hazel tends to go a little bit loco when I pull out her leash. She just gets so excited. She also likes to bring it to me—ALL the time—in a not so calm fashion. So, I hide it from her. Today it's on top of my refrigerator. "Let me grab the l-word."

Dean's thick brows cinch while his mind works it all out. "L word? Her leash?" he says and Hazel bolts for him. Her long legs pounce and her front paws hit Dean right in the chest. He goes down—luckily with my couch right behind him. My hardwood floors would not have been very forgiving to his backside. Hazel's paws are on his shoulders and she's bathing him with her tongue.

"Hoo—" he grunts, pinned to the couch, assaulted by my dog.

I'll help him. I will. But first I pull my phone from my pocket and snap a picture of the two of them nose to nose. I press a hand to my mouth—attempting poorly to suppress my laughter.

"You're taking pictures?" he says, dodging Hazel's next kiss.

"You said today was a photo-shoot day." I smile down at him, enjoying the moment. "No one would ever believe that I'm in a relationship if I weren't taking pictures like this one," I say, throwing his words back at him. It's delightful.

Ten minutes later we've got a super excited Hazel in Dean's Jeep and we're ready to go.

Hazel sits in the back, but stands on Dean's backseat and pushes her head between us. I'm nervous—and maybe even excited. And yet none of it's real—it's a weird mix of emotion. Still, I pull out my cell. "Should we start now?"

Dean shakes his head at Hazel butting in between us, but he's grinning. I'm not sure how he feels about her, but she is half in love with Dean Cooper. Maybe someone needs to inform Hazel that this is a *fake* relationship—we aren't keeping him. Still, Dean moves his head in and I do the same. Hazel—as if she were trained in the arts of modeling—practically smiles at the camera and I snap a selfie.

"You're so pretty," I tell Hazel, looking up at her. I nuzzle my forehead to hers. But something has caught her attention and she jets backward, scurrying to look out one of the back windows. My head, pressing next to hers keeps moving forward—of its own volition—until it bumps right into Dean's. "Ow!" I cram my eyes closed and press two fingers to the spot on my forehead that knocked into his.

Dean grunts too. "You okay?"

I smell him before I see him. Blinking my eyes open, my heart patters at his nearness. Dean's eyes are on my head. He takes my face in his hands and peers at my forehead, the spot where we collided—and I think—*What's up there? Zits? Dog slobber? How's the view?*

It's hard to think straight at all when Dean's mouth hovers so near my face. I smell the mint on his breath and zoom in on his mouth for half a second. I give myself one more half a second, because it really is a very nice mouth—full lips that peak in the center. And then, I shoot backward, away from his touch.

"You aren't allowed to kiss me," I blurt. This isn't real and I can't be played with.

"Why would you think I'd kiss you?" He drops his hands to his lap.

"I don't know. Because. Just because. I don't know the rules

62

when it comes to fake boyfriends. But the thing is, I don't really know you... and we aren't a real couple... and you're not allowed to kiss me. Okay?"

"Okay. I won't kiss you." His grin reminds me of a mischievous little boy sneaking candy. "I mean, unless you ask me to. Then, I'll think about it."

The sleeping butterflies in my stomach come to life, fluttering wildly and forcing me to hold my abdomen. "Ha." I bark, but it's not as confident as I'd like it to sound. "Fat chance." But... there might be a small chance.

Riverbend Ponds are fifteen minutes from my house. Not a long drive. Still, I try to do the math—how long have we been gone? Five minutes? How long ago did Dean post that picture of the two of us?

Because my sister has already seen it. She texts me—knowing that I don't normally use my Instagram app and that I normally would never check it for DMs.

Normally—Dean isn't a normal in my life.

Ebony texts:

> What is happening?
> Who is that?
> When did you start using Instagram?
> Have you been hacked?

I slide a glance at Dean who has one hand on the wheel and one bent back so that he can scratch under Hazel's beard.

I type out a quick response—

> Why would anyone hack me? I have zero
> followers, besides you and Coco.

Ebony is a writer and her typing skills are incomparable. It takes her an entire three seconds to respond.

> And some dude named @deanlivingoutloud. Is he the one in that picture with you?

"Everything okay?" Dean asks, his gaze leaving the road to study my face for just a second.

I type out a quick text to my sister—only able to concentrate on one question at a time.

> I'll explain later.

And then, my phone rings. I clear my throat and a nervous laugh bubbles from my mouth. I press ignore and look up to Hazel and Dean both peering at me.

Dean's gaze returns to the road, but he extends another quick glance my way. "Iris? You okay?"

Another ping from Ebony:

> Did you just ignore my call?!

"Umm, yes. I'm fine. My sister saw the picture you posted."

"Aw… Well, good. At least we know your posts can be seen."

I chew on the end of my thumb nail and think of all the ways Ebony is going to ream me out. For the first time in three years, I am grateful she decided to move to Seattle instead of in with me. She can yell at me over the phone instead of in person.

"It'll be okay, Iris," he says.

"I know. I'm just not… this isn't like me." My heart plummets into my stomach for the billionth time. What must Dean really and truly think of me? "I'm not pathetic." But the more I say it, the more pathetic I sound.

"I never said you were."

"And I'm not desperate."

"Iris," he squints, thinking. I suppose he did already assure me that he knew I wasn't desperate. But I don't believe him. How could he not believe that? "You forget," he says. "I was there last night. I don't believe you're desperate. I don't blame you. In fact, I've already started investing in maggots to bury Travis in."

"I'm not—"

"I know. I know," he says. "You aren't the one burying him. You just happen to find him that way and leave him." He sighs. "Who says I'm not the one burying him?"

I smirk.

Dean gives one shoulder a shrug. "I'm pretty sure it would feel fantastic to dump a bucket of maggots over that guy's head."

"That's just not me."

"No." Dean grins, eyes on the road. "I don't think you'd leave him buried, either. I think you'd help him out."

I probably would—but that doesn't make me feel like a good person. It just makes me feel like Travis will always have the upper hand. He'll forever be able to make me feel like a piece of used tissue. "Can we talk about something else? You live in Evergreen, did you grow up there?"

Dean clears his throat and for the first time, he looks a little uncomfortable. "Ah no, a few different places."

"Was your dad in the military or something?"

"No," he says, eyes completely focused on the road. "No dad in the picture at all, actually."

"Oh." My voice goes small. I can't help it. "Did you ever know him?"

"Yeah. I mean, I met Carl a few times when I was in elementary school. He just wasn't interested in a relationship with me. Last I heard he was spending some time in jail." Dean clears his throat, his tone and body telling me how difficult this topic is for him.

"It's okay," I say, and for some weird reason, it is. He's honest at least. It's not his fault. "You didn't do anything wrong. I'm sorry he treated you so poorly."

Dean's shoulders relax and he takes a left turn—a dirt road. I don't have my pepper spray, but I'm not stressed. There are cars and people around. Dean is smart and polite enough not to take me out to the wilderness alone. "We'll park over here. And then we can walk around the pond, if that's okay."

"That's good. We should probably keep talking, too. We need to get to know each other." I want to keep talking. I need to know the person helping me and showing up in my Instagram feed. And if I'm being honest, I *want* to get to know him better. He's interesting and new and I haven't had interesting or new in my life for a while. "So, you grew up with your mom?"

"Yeah. Mostly." Dean clears his throat and doesn't spare a glance my way, then parks in one of the many spaces. "Here we are."

I've been watching him so closely, only giving the people and space around us slight glances. I haven't paid close attention until this second. I laugh. "Look! There are people canoeing."

"Yeah," he says, a crooked grin plays at his lips. "It's pretty popular over here. You've never been?"

I shake my head. Crazy, but I haven't.

"You grew up here." he says it more like a statement than a question. But how would he know?

"I did. Clearly, I haven't explored enough."

Hazel is doing her best to pace in the backseat—mostly she turns from left to right. She's long for the small space.

"You ready, Hazel?" She barks with my question.

"That is the funniest dog," Dean says, peering back at Hazel. "I've never seen another act like her."

"She's the sweetest. Aren't you the sweetest?" I say and even I hear the sickly sweet tone in my voice. Hazel licks my cheeks, the whiskers from her chin tickle my skin and I beam at my fur baby. I love her—I can't help it.

But then… it's as if someone has blasted me with a warm spot light, Dean is watching me. Not casual, but dissecting. He is studying me.

I clear my throat and throw open the passenger side door. I snatch Hazel's leash which is still attached at her collar. "Come on, girl."

Without reservation, Hazel hops into the front seat, her curly-haired bottom knocking right into Dean's face. She leaps from the car and any creature within two or three feet better look out, because Hazel's tail will knock them right into Wyoming.

I peer up to see Dean wiping at his face. "I'm not sure I care for that end."

I suck in a breath. "Sorry. I didn't mean to—"

He shakes his head and pulls another Hazel hair from his chin. "It's okay." He steps out of the Jeep and walks around the vehicle. Behind him is a pond with cattails and tall grass—we haven't walked one step and already I feel inspired.

I nibble on my bottom lip, but hand him the leash. "Here," I say and he takes it without question. With my camera bag still in the Jeep, I pull out my phone, and hold it up, my picture app already opened. "Do you mind?"

His brows raise in curiosity, but he doesn't question me.

"Set your foot on that boulder," I say, pointing. "And look down at Hazel."

Dean follows my directions and I suddenly think I'd like to be his personal photographer. He is long and lean, like a chiseled piece of art. He's adorable in the shot of Hazel mauling him and he's close to perfection standing on this gravel road. In fact, this camera phone isn't good enough.

In three seconds, I have Snappy from the car and I take another picture with my two thousand dollar camera.

He looks up at me. "Good?"

I nod, nibbling on my lip and swallow. I need to simmer and I really need to stop thinking about Dean as a piece of artwork. "Thanks."

Dean keeps ahold of Hazel's leash and I follow him through a few feet of brush to a walking path around the ponds.

"Tell me about Hazel."

"Hazel?" I can't say her name without smiling. "What do you want to know?"

"Well, you sort of light up like a new mother when it comes to your dog. So everything. Clearly she's important to you."

I let out a long breath and ignore the fact that I find my fake-boyfriend hunkier than I should. I will answer his questions—without any reservation because fake also has its advantages. "So, the weird thing about this all being false," I point from myself to Dean, "it's a little liberating. It's freeing. I can just tell you *every-thing* and not really care. Because you aren't real. I don't have to stress about your opinion of me."

"Gee, thanks."

"No, I mean, you aren't going to wake up in the morning and decide I'm not enough for you—that you need more—that I'm too weird and nowhere near exciting enough." I blow out a breath with my honesty. "Because I'm not really yours." It doesn't matter how stupidly cute Dean is—the words are freeing and true and I know it the minute they leave my mouth.

"That's true. I wouldn't do that to you." Dean watches me while we saunter along the path, Hazel trotting along, letting us know she'd be totally okay if we chose to pick up the pace a notch... or ten.

"Whoo," I blow out a breath and begin. "I got Hazel after Travis crushed my heart into tiny little pieces." I press my hands together as if to demonstrate. "I didn't really think about him when I got her. But all of the emptiness, all of the crushing loser projections I placed on myself because of his words, they went away. Hazel loves me for me. She doesn't care that I wear fuzzy socks or have disastrous effects when I drink too much caffeine. She ignores my bad hair days and loves when I sneak an extra muffin—because I always share with her. She likes it when my music is loud and she doesn't complain because I want to stay in rather than go to a party."

Dean laughs—and surprisingly it isn't a—*wow, you're such a dork* laugh. He laughs *with* me. He pauses his steps, and Hazel stops with him. He pulls his phone from his pocket. "Do you mind? Your eyes kind of sparkle when you talk about her."

I swallow and heat flushes to my cheeks. I finger a stray hair behind my ear. "You must think I'm a weirdo."

"I don't." He moves so that one of the many ponds in this area is behind me. "But even if I did, you've already made it clear that it doesn't matter—which is a good thing. Just be yourself, Iris. You don't need to be anything you aren't. For anyone." He watches the screen of his phone and there's something about the fresh air and my liberating speech that frees any anxiousness I should be feeling. I smile for him, and there's nothing forced about it.

TEN

Dean

_____

I ris's eyes are shining beacons in the night sky. It's pretty obvious how much she loves her dog. I snap the photo and study her face inside my phone. Is it creepy if I add this one to my personal favorites?

A woman walking the opposite direction on the path stops when she approaches us. "I can take a picture of all three of you," she says. "I'm Gail."

I look at Iris for confirmation.

"Ah, sure. Yeah," she says to the lady, that Hazel-smile still blossoming her on cheeks. I hand the woman my phone and move to stand by Iris. We line up, side by side, Hazel posing between us. This dog is a curious one.

The older lady tilts her head to the side, as if to look at us at a different angle. The joy has left her voice and her nose wrinkles. "Ah, maybe move closer."

We inch a little closer together.

Gail waves all five fingers on her left hand at us—her tone still unapproving. "Put your arm around her," she says to me. I do, but it's awkward with the pressure of Gail judging us. She taps her chin. "Huh. Okay." She must take the picture, because she peers down at the phone. "You want to try another one?"

"Can I see?" Iris says. She walks over and peeks at my phone in the woman's hands. "Yeah, see the lighting is all wrong and horizontal you don't see much of Hazel. Turn it this way. And Dean and I will stand over here."

Hmm, Hazel and photography, it's like the two bring Iris to life. They are *her* through and through, and when she's just being herself and not trying so hard, she shines. She moves me and Hazel to the other side of the path—we both listen intently by the way. I'm every bit as behaved as Hazel—but she's the only one who gets a pat and a kiss on top of the head. Then, Iris positions the lady. Gail moves her hands with Iris's instructions and holds the angle just so.

"Ahh!" Gail says as if she's had an epiphany. "I am going to take the best picture of my grandson next time I see him." She giggles. Then, holding her hands, almost as if she's afraid to move them from where Iris has placed her, she nods Iris away.

Iris jumps into the shot next to me and I set my arm around her shoulders, but it doesn't feel quite right—almost like I'm saying hello to a buddy, definitely not my *girlfriend*. Her lip is clamped between her teeth when she peers up at me and says, "Try this." She moves my hand down her side, so that my arm is diagonal across her back and my fingers sit at her waist.

"Much better," says our gray haired friend, Gail. She takes one picture—I assume, because she's studying the screen again. But her stop-sign hand held up tells me she isn't quite finished yet. Gail is loving her newly learned skills. Iris, Hazel, and I have become the models who do her bidding.

I slide my gaze down to Iris, whose lips press in a flat line, holding in her laughter.

"Yeah, that's better. Dean?" she says my name like a question to Iris.

Iris nods.

"Back up a little, honey. The sun is kind of making you look like you're a vampire."

"Oh—" Iris starts.

But I'm obedient. I back up one step and then two. And then —I back up right into the Riverbend pond. Mud and muck slosh beneath my foot and find its way inside of my shoe. "Ahh-crap," I mutter, lifting my foot—which isn't the best idea, because the minute I stand on one foot—a foot that's standing on a bed of moss covered mud, I slide. I'm down. I'm out. My head is under the murky water of the three foot pond.

I hear Iris yelp and wonder if she's gone down with me or if I've just scared her.

But neither is true. When I emerge from the dirty pond water, blinking the moss from my sight, there is Iris, Hazel, and Gail looking back. Iris has a gleaming smile plastered across her face and her phone is up and in position. She's taking my picture.

"Not that far back," Gail moans, a grimace on her face—like this is all my fault.

Iris couldn't hide her joy if she tried. "I don't know, Gail. I think this is the perfect shot."

I hold a hand out to her.

Iris stands straight, hands on her curved hips—I don't remember her having those curves in high school. "I don't think so," she says. "I've seen this movie. You hold out your hand, I try to help you up and you pull me in. It's not going to—"

But before she can finish, Hazel jumps in after me—to save me or to play with me, I'm not sure yet.

"Hazel!" Iris cries as if a shark that only eats wirehaired pointing griffons might be lurking in this pond.

The dog paddles around me like we're just having a fun dip and there's nothing to worry about. Ugh. My Jeep. This isn't going to be a pretty ride home—or a sweet smelling ride. It won't just be wet dog and wet man, it's pond dog and pond man. Hazel and I are going to reek.

A hiss escapes Gail's mouth and then the coward makes her escape. "Well, kids, I've gotta run. Nice to meet you both."

I rise from the pond, thinking I *should* pull Iris in, then we'd all be in this predicament together. But then my Jeep would need to air out that much longer. I flick my hair back, leaving a wake of water in front of me. Iris squeals with the cold droplets that have just rained down on her—totally worth it. Then not without effort, I trudge my way back onto solid ground.

"Gail is never allowed to take our picture again," I say, from the ground, on my back, and out of breath.

"Agreed," she says. One of her pretty brows—who knew eyebrows could be pretty—quirks above the other. "How about a selfie?"

I huff, get to my feet, and shake out my hands. "Why not?" I say, knowing exactly the pose I plan to create. She laughed at me, she wouldn't help me out—she deserves this. I snicker to myself.

Iris steps over next to me, making sure the light is in the right spot and holds out her phone. Only, I cross behind her, wrap my wet arms about her waist, hug my dripping torso to her back, and place my chilled cheek right against hers.

I imagine her squealing again, laughing as she pushes me back into the pond—huh, maybe I didn't think this through. I just want to see that laughter glint in her eyes once more.

Her body is warm and soft and fits with mine in exactly the right places—so when she doesn't squeal, when she doesn't push me backward, it's hard not to notice *everything*. She sets her left hand across my two, latched about her waist, and grins.

I'm not sure what kind of alien possesses my body, but I press my cold lips to her cheek right before she snaps the photo, then smile as she takes another.

Her breaths feel a little haggard and I'm certain she's about to ask why I'm still holding onto her when she says, "Dean."

"Yeah?" I say, the warmth from her body and sweetness of her voice distracting me.

She wrinkles her nose. "You smell."

"Yeah," I groan, let go of her, and back away. I clear my throat and swallow. "Sorry about that." I point to her face, to her pink cheek. "It—it was an accident."

Iris wipes her left palm down the thigh of her jeans. "You *accidentally* kissed my cheek?"

A long breath leaves my throat as I watch her, trying to decide on the best answer. "Yes."

She nods. "I guess, you're lucky you didn't accidentally kiss my lips or I would have pushed you back into that pond." She holds out my phone—I'm grateful I gave it to Gail before my dip in the pond. Then, Iris pats her thigh once. "Come on, Hazel! Time to go."

ELEVEN

Iris

I'm not exactly sure what happened back there. Dean cuddled right up to me—and I let him. Why did I let him? Why for ten seconds wasn't it weird? Of course—those ten seconds ended and then it was most definitely weird.

We postpone the rest of our outing for tomorrow. Dean and Hazel need to bathe.

Dean lays out a blanket for Hazel in the back seat of his Jeep and thankfully her swim has worn her out. She'll curl up and sleep for the ride home, rather than drip over every inch of Dean's back seat.

"I can vacuum out the mud when we get back to my place."

"It's okay. It's easier if it dries first anyway." He watches out the windshield, at the road, and I wish I had his excuse.

My eyes can't decide where to land. Where should I look that says: *I'm not still feeling the sensation of your body close to mine.*

"Did we get any good pictures?"

Sweet—I can stare at my phone. I open my picture app.

"Check mine too," he says, passing his phone over to me.

"You're pretty trusting, aren't you?"

Dean laughs. "Not exactly. But I do trust you, Iris."

I do not understand his declaration. I have no idea why I would be more trustworthy than any other stranger he met yesterday. But I take the phone and open up his photo app as well.

I stare at the first picture Gail took. "Huh."

"Huh, what?"

"Well, we look like strangers. Or maybe cousins. Or maybe really bad actors in a toothpaste commercial."

"Tooth—what?"

I hold up his device and he glances from the road to his screen. "Huh. Not exactly bursting with chemistry," he says. "Yeah, that's not going to be enough."

I feel a blow to my gut with his words. I know what he means —this picture isn't going to convince anyone that we've been dating for months. I can look at it and say that with honesty. But Dean looks great—seriously how do some people get all the pretty genes? I look—*lacking. Not enough.*

I feel smaller and smaller with my inner thoughts. *Not enough.* Man, those words will haunt me for the rest of my life. Rejection with a capital R.

"What about the others?" he says.

I open the last picture taken with my phone. The one where Dean surprised me by wrapping his cold, wet arms around me and hugging me close. The one where he kissed my cheek and I forgot for a minute that we weren't really friends.

I should have pulled away. Logic says I should have. I'm not illogical. And I'm not crazy. So, I list all the reasons in my head for not pulling away or being appalled by his affection—

One- he surprised me.

Two- I was still laughing at his tumble into the water.

Three- Hazel was happy. It's so hard to be appalled when Hazel is happy.

Four—

"Any good ones?" he asks, interrupting my mental listing. I am still staring at the photo of us—without actually letting my brain process it.

"Um," I look at my face—Dean is even beautiful wet, so it's my face that will make or break us—I look as if I should be there, wrapped up in his embrace. I look happy, maybe even *pretty*. "This one is better." I swallow. I'm a photographer. This one is actually great—natural, in the moment, and exudes joy. It's perfect. I know that—it's my job to know that. Gail saved us with her bad directions from a series of crappy line up photos.

I hold it up for him. Dean's mouth parts—like the red sea—into a beautiful smile. "That's a winner."

Dean's focus goes back to the road and I scroll through the rest of the pictures on my phone. Dean kissing my cheek—his eyes are closed tight and though his lips are puckered, he seems to be smiling too. I'm not sure how that's possible, but he's doing it. I don't even appear to care. In fact, I look as if I'm enjoying his touch. And... maybe I am.

But—*come on, Iris, get some backbone*. I told him no kissing and twenty minutes later the man kisses me.

On the cheek—I remind myself. My uncle kisses my cheek too. Maybe that's why I had no backbone. Or didn't need a backbone. I don't know. Just trying to find a scenario where I get to keep my backbone *and* use this picture.

I scroll to the next one—Dean in the water, drenched while sprinkled with moss and dirt. His smile is forced—it says *why are you taking my photo right this minute?* Which is pretty natural, ironically. Hazel swims just behind him—happy as can be. My insides warm.

"You're smiling way too much over there," Dean says.

"Oh. Just found my favorite photo, that's all." I hold up my phone for him to see. Dean sputters and rolls his eyes—but he laughs too.

It's still early in the afternoon when Dean pulls up in front of my house.

"Do you mind if I shower here?" he says.

I blink, my eyes wider than they should be.

"It's just home is almost two hours away and I'm still pretty wet."

"Oh. Um. Okay." But all I can think is—stranger Dean, hunky Dean, kind Dean is going to be *naked* in my house.

We head inside and I find Dean a towel. I tell him with a dramatic stupid high pitched tone that I don't mind at all if he uses my $28 dollar shampoo, and then shut him up in the bathroom with a slam of the door. "I'm going to Gramgram's!" I yell —no, more like bellow through the bathroom door, though I am standing right next to it. "I'll be back in twenty minutes."

Hazel's asleep and smelly on her dog bed—no way Gram would appreciate my wet, stinky dog prancing through her Johnny Cash museum. So, I leave my baby and skip-jog over to my grandmothers.

I don't tap the door announcing my arrival, I just burst on through. Gramgram is standing with a cocktail in her hand, swaying to Folsom Prison Blues in her Johnny muumuu. She pauses mid sway, "What'd you do?"

I point at myself. "Nothing. I didn't do anything. Dean might be naked in my bathroom right this minute. But I didn't do it."

"Well, that escalated." She sets her non-cocktail hand to her hip. "Iris, why *might* Dean be naked in your bathroom."

"Because people usually shower naked," I say unable to keep the panic from my voice.

"And why is this *supposedly* fake boyfriend of yours showering?"

"It's not supposed, Gram. It's fake! But he fell in a pond and he smells like fish and moss and…ick. His drive home is long, so —" I shrug. "Shower."

Gramgram nods. "But his clothes are wet?"

"Oh shoot." I chew on my thumb nail. "Yes, his clothes *are* wet." And dirty and stinky. My eyes turn to headlights. "Dean Cooper cannot walk around my house in nothing but a towel for who knows how long."

Gram's turned down smile says—*why not?* She exhales a long breath. "Your grandfather's closet is still full. Go find him something."

"Grandad's closet? You are a genius." I kiss her cheek and haul back to my deceased grandfather's closet. Thankfully, Grandad did not share the same full figure as Gramgram, his khaki's may be a size too big for Dean, but they'll work. I snag him a Johnny Cash T-shirt and a flannel shirt too.

Wait—underwear? Grandad's underwear for Dean? *Blech*— that would be too weird. Even more weird than this situation already is.

"You probably need to leave them in the bathroom for him," Gram says when I exit her bedroom.

"I am not walking into the bathroom while he's in the shower. Grandma!"

Gram looks as though I've scolded her—and I suppose I have. I never call her Grandma. When Ebony and I were toddlers we'd follow after our grandmother wherever she went. Ebony would spout GRAM! Then I would yell, GRAM! They said we were like little echoes of each other—Gram! Gram! Gram! Gram! Eventually Gramgram stuck and that's what we all call her now.

"I'm just saying," says my eighty-one year old grandmother, "if I had a chance to peek at that boy, I'd take it."

"I cannot believe you just said that."

Gram lifts one shoulder, then settles onto a kitchen stool next to the counter. She pulls over a mug and the Johnny Cash on the front goes shirtless the minute she pours hot liquid from her coffee pot into the cup.

I hold grandad's clothes close to my chest, my heart thumps against the garments and my hands.

"He's a keeper, Iris. I like that boy." She nods—as if her saying so makes it a fact.

I walk past her and toward the front door. "Well, I'm glad you're fond of the stranger I found on the side of the road last night. But you can't keep him. So, get over it."

Gram rolls her eyes as if I'm being dramatic. But I am not being dramatic, she is being ludicrous! *Take a peek at him!* What is she thinking? Besides that, she's had one conversation with the man!

"Goodbye!" I bark and walk right out her door.

Inside, Hazel is still on her bed. The wafting smell of pond fills my living room with her damp body, but I won't be able to bathe her until Dean has finished up with my one bathroom.

Now… for the real problem, do I set the clothes inside the bathroom? Do I knock? Do I leave them outside of the door? Do I wiggle my nose, like Samantha Stevens, and zap the clothes into the bathroom?

Which option is less likely to give me a peek? Or more likely? Gramgram has my head muddled. No—I definitely do not want a peek.

I wait until the running water in my bathroom turns off before leaving the safety of the living room. I knock once on the bathroom door and yell, "There are clothes outside the door for you."

And then, I sprint back to the safety of the living room and Hazel.

Ten minutes later, Dean enters the room—shoeless *and* shirtless! What is he thinking? No shoes? No shirt? No Iris! I purposely made sure I wasn't peeking! And now, he's parading.

Grandad's khaki pants are big and hang low on Dean's slim waist, so much that I can see an inch below his navel. The shirt I brought him has apparently gone missing, because he doesn't have it on. My eyes rove from that show-off of a navel up to his abs—they're washboard. I know what that saying means now, because I have no doubt I could wash Dean's dirty clothing on those things. Slowly, I move my way up to his pecks—which only makes me blush, I sort of want to cover my eyes with both fists, as if I've spied something inappropriate with this *peek*. I move my eyes all the way up to his collar bone and shoulders which look a little like they belong to a sculpted god.

My vision starts to blur as I stare at him. "Where… where is your shirt?" I run a hand over the back of my neck. It's warm in here, I'm suddenly sweating.

"This shirt is *bedazzled?* I'm not sure I can wear this." He grimaces and holds out Grandad's Johnny Cash tee. Sure enough, Gram has bedazzled fake jewels all around the guitar that Johnny holds.

I pinch my lips together. "You'll look great all jeweled up. Now, please stop being naked in my living room."

"Naked?" He looks down at himself and my betraying cheeks turn into heating pads. "I'm not exactly naked." He's holding the shirt by its ribbed collar, his arm stretched out.

I snatch the thing from his grasp and throw it at him. "Close enough. Just get dressed. *Please!*" I storm down the hall, I need to splash some cold water on my face. But I have to hold my breath the closer I get to the bathroom. Dean's pond clothes are making my house reek—well, his clothes and my wet dog. Still, I pick them up by the hem and walk them straight to my washing machine. I toss them into the machine and dump inside an entire cup of my scent booster beads.

I blow out an exasperated breath.

Next, Hazel.

I call my pup and she comes running, meeting me at the bathroom door. Hazel is one of those strange dogs who actually enjoys taking a bath—it's just like a dip in the pond to her. I run the water and before I can even plug in the drain stopper, Hazel is in the tub.

I fill the tub and scrub Hazel's curly fur and body—all the while trying not to let my head think about what Dean might be doing in my living room. I hum Hazel's favorite song, *Girls Just Want to have Fun,* and move to the music as we wash.

After ten minutes, I reach over Hazel, balancing on one foot so that I can reach the drain to empty this icky water and fill the tub again. "So long nasty pond water."

"Do you always talk to your bath water?" Dean's voice is playful—like he's been silently laughing.

I gasp in a breath with his sudden presence and spin—on one foot—with Hazel pawing at my shoulder. I must be moving in slow motion because in the three seconds it takes for me to spin and fall back into a tub of yucky water, I see Dean's face. He's smiling at first, shock registers as he reaches out one hand to me, and then pure amusement fills his expression. I see it all in those three seconds.

Water soaks into my shirt and waistband. I feel the fishy pond on my face and in my hair. *Ew.* I knock my head back against the tiled wall behind my tub.

Dean's face contorts, his brows lower and his lips fold in on one another—I know that face, he's trying not to laugh at me. He succeeds. He doesn't laugh. But he does pull his phone out of his pocket and aims it at me.

I glare.

"What?" he says, rocking Grandad's bedazzled T-shirt. "It's your turn. You know you deserve it." He beams at me. "Smile."

I shut my eyes and do not smile. But when I open them he's still there, staring down at me, phone at the ready. "I'm not helping you out until you give me a smile."

"I don't need your help!" I press one hand to the bottom of the tub—my feet flailing up have no bottom to touch. Hazel rests her dripping chin on top of my head. "Hazel," I moan.

"Oh, that's it. Way to work it, Hazel."

I snort out a spiteful laugh and Dean snaps a picture.

"As your fake girlfriend," I say, "I demand you delete that!"

Dean just stuffs the phone into his back pocket and holds out a hand to me. Between Hazel and my awkward feet in the air, I have no leverage. Dean grabs both of my slippery wet hands with his and yanks. I fly up from the tub, all but my legs drenched.

"Whoa," Dean says, when I keep flying. He holds me by the elbows, but my chest still bumps into his. "You're a tiny person, aren't you?"

Tingly chill bumps spread from my neck to my knees. "You're just big." I tap his chest—it's rock hard with chiseled curves that my brain will obsess over later tonight when it should be sleeping.

"Should we take a picture?"

"In my bathroom?' I shake my head, annoyed that not only will I be dreaming about abs when I should be sleeping, but now I need a shower too.

"Sure," Dean smiles. "In your bathroom, with your dog, in my dashing bedazzled Johnny Cash shirt."

"I thought you didn't want to wear it."

He tilts his head, looking down at the diamonds that trace Johnny's guitar. "It's growing on me."

I flick my gaze upward.

But Dean takes the phone from his pocket. "A relationship has real every day moments. Right? Not just picture perfect poses by the pond."

"Sure," I huff. "Although, the one of you in the pond was pretty perfect."

Dean laughs. "Yeah," he says, agreeing with me.

I'm so aware of his arm, wrapping cautiously around my waist, his cheek lowering to touch mine, his warm skin pressing next to mine. I swallow past the lump that's formed in my throat. My pulse quickens—my nerves are shot and I can't decide, is it having a fake boyfriend or the way the fake boyfriend makes my heart speed up whenever his skin touches mine?

Which is insane because I've only known my fake boyfriend one *day*. So, it has to be all the pretending. I cannot be hot and bothered by some man I've known for a glorious twenty-four hours.

Dean's thumb rubs a small circle over my lower back. I am so aware of the pressure through my shirt and I have two spontaneous thoughts at once—*why would a fake boyfriend do that?* And—*I need to call my sister!*

Just then—as if to cool me off—Hazel shakes her wet body, sending droplets of bath and pond water all over the place.

"Hazel!" I wipe water from my once dry face and peer at my sweet girl, then back to Dean. "Okay!" I say and my voice is too loud for the tightness of the bathroom. "I need to shower now. Hazel needs to rest. And I... have... things. Surely you have *things*. So..." my head bobbles in a shake as I press my hands to his chest and inch him out of my bathroom, "bye."

"Oh." He nods, but his *oh* sounds disappointed—which is dumb—because he's not. Why would he be? I just freed up his night. I must be hearing things. Add *going crazy* to my list of downfalls. "Sure," he says, peering past me where Hazel's wet tail wags, making it rain inside my bathroom. "See ya, girl."

Hazel barks in response.

Once I've shoved us both out of the room, I shut the door. There's no sense in bringing Hazel's wet suds into the hallway, but this only makes her moan. "Sorry, I should get back." I shoot a thumb over my shoulder to the door Hazel cries behind.

"Yeah. Of course. Do you want to get together tomorrow? We still have pictures to take before I can get everything up and dated correctly on Instagram."

"Right. Um, tomorrow I have a photoshoot in Laramie at two. Oh shoot!" I slap a hand to my head. I'm supposed to go to

Wyoming tomorrow. A university soccer mom is paying me to take these photos. "I don't have a car."

"I'll take you."

"No," I moan out, sounding whinier than I ever should. "I can't ask you to do that. It's too much. Gram gets back from Pilates at two, maybe she could leave early and I could take her car."

Dean chuckles and it's a gravelly sound. "Gram cannot miss her Pilates class. It's no problem. We can road trip and photo-shoot along the way."

Sweat pools at my neck. "O. K." I say and once again my robot voice turns on. I never knew I had a robot switch until I met Dean.

"Okay," he repeats—that perma-grin making his cheeks swell like plums.

Hazel moans—saving me. My hand grapples at the door knob behind me and I back my way through the crack I've opened up. "Bye," I whisper as he watches me slip through. Inside the bathroom, I lean against the back of the door and exhale. Hazel's smiling at me from her perch on the ground.

"Iris," Dean says through the faux wood. I slap a hand over my heart and hold the breath I've just taken in.

Exhaling, I shut my eyes, but then, all I see is a shirtless Dean in my head. "Yeah?" I croak out.

"My clothes?"

"Oh," I spin to face the door, my hands pressed to the white faux wood. "They're in the washer. I'll bring them tomorrow."

"See you then, Iris."

I open my mouth—the word *why* on the tip of my tongue. Why would he do this? He doesn't owe me, he doesn't even know me. Is it really so that he can water ski and hike and whatever else he said in one day? That seems… unlikely.

———

HAZEL IS DRIED, fed, and napping. I have showered and washed my hair. And—it's barely dinner time. Still, I am mentally pooped. I lay on my bed, next to where Hazel is stretched out and call my sister.

"It's about time," Ebony says upon answering. "You post a picture of you with some guy I've never seen or heard of and—"

"I know," I groan. "You don't need to remind me. I know."

"Iris, what's happening?"

I stare at my ceiling, my phone laying on the bed next to me. I speed talk my way through a quick explanation. "Shelia dropped the Travis bomb and Travis was such a jerk. Somehow, I ended up telling them I had a boyfriend." I slap my hands over my face—as if she could see me and the pathetic being that I am.

"Iris?"

"I'm here," I say, cracking open two fingers to peek out.

"How did the real live actual man come into play?"

I hiss—knowing she won't like my answer. "He picked me up on the side of the road after my car broke down." I keep going—might as well barrel through, rip off the entire band-aid. It's hilarious that for a few minutes I thought I might actually be able to keep all of this from my sister. "Then after I asked his married friend to pretend to be my boyfriend, he stepped in and played the part for Shelia and Travis. Shelia invited him to the wedding and now we're taking pictures and posting them to make it look like we've been dating for months."

A strange squeak sounds over the speaker of my phone. I roll over and look at my cell, wishing my sister could step right through the screen, but she is more than an eighteen hour car ride away. Curse her fantastic sports journalism dream and the big fancy paper that hired her. Still, she says nothing—just a squeak and I start to wonder if I've lost her. "Ebony?"

"Yeah," her voice cracks and I realize the creaky sound through my speaker is *her*. "Sorry," she says, "just trying to make some sense of it all."

I groan. "I am pathetic."

"You're not. Your situation is a little... odd, but you've never been pathetic, Iris. Don't listen to what that butthole Travis said about you. The dust under your hardwood floors knows more about life than Travis Cheesebro."

"*Butthole?*"

"Yes, butthole."

I don't care that my sister has turned into a vengeful seventh grader. Ebony is beautiful and smart and rarely wrong. She'd never lie to me. I'm not sure she's capable of lying. She could never have a fake boyfriend—she'd tell the world it was fake before the first picture was posted.

"But you think I'm crazy."

"I didn't say that," she says. "I think this situation is a little wacky. Tell me about the guy."

So, I do. I tell her everything I know about Dean—which I'm realizing isn't much. I only leave out the part where I may have drooled over his washboard abs. I need to ask more questions. I make a mental note—tomorrow I will be the best talk show host any fake boyfriend ever had.

When I finish, I wait for my sister's freak out. "Well?"

"Well, what? I called Gramgram. She already told me all this —most of it, anyway. I can't believe you fell into your tub with Hazel. I am going to need a copy of that picture."

"Wait—you already knew about Dean?"

"You wouldn't pick up my calls or text me back, Iris! So, I called Gramgram. She informed me that she approves of your not-so-real boyfriend. She said—he's delicious and trustworthy— she can feel it in her glutes. Whatever that means."

Delicious? Ugh. Gram! "So?" I draw out the word.

"So... be careful. Be smart. Also—I wasn't planning on going to Shelia's wedding, but there's no way I'm missing it now. I'll see you in Tahoe."

I groan—joy—an audience for my big acting debut.

TWELVE

Dean

Hanging out with Iris yesterday was the most fun I've had since I climbed Mount Elbert. I'm guessing that day could have been epic if Iris had been there. I'd forgotten how her smile sort of lights up a room.

I tap my toe—thinking about Iris—as I finish editing pics of my newest hike and upload the reel I made for Instagram, as well as a video for YouTube.

I've also tracked my total trip for the day—Evergreen to Ft. Collins, Ft. Collins to Laramie—I need three hours. I may need to start investing in gasoline—because while Iris and I are pretending to date, I may go broke… Not really. My influencer business is thriving. My job is literally about having fun and telling people all about the best places to hike, ski, sail, and fish.

Although, some days it feels like I have a million eyes on me —probably because I do—and some days it sends me into an anxiety attack. But Iris has no idea who I am, not just from social media, but she's forgotten me from high school too. She has zero preconceived notions when it comes to me, and I like it that way. Her eyes don't stare to see what I'll do next or how badly I'll crash and burn on the slopes. They see me with a blank slate. I'm not a daredevil influencer and I'm not that silent bruised up kid who sat behind her in English.

I'm just Dean... her fake boyfriend.

Huh. I thought that would sound better. But I've never been *fake*. I've always taken the good and bad as it came. My reactions are sincere—whether full of emotion or completely devoid. It's how I felt. But now, I am somebody's fake boyfriend and my feelings are fairly confused about the whole thing. Although—I do know that I'm not confused about wanting to help Iris. So even my fake feelings are sincere—which may only make sense to me.

I'd planned a hike to a natural spring today—ten miles in and ten miles out—but a trip to Wyoming sounds good too. I'm antsy and I leave early again. If I learned anything yesterday it's that Iris is still that kind soul I knew back in tenth grade. She'll forgive my early arrival and maybe we'll have a little more time together.

It's weird that I want more time, right? I know it is, and yet I don't care. Iris doesn't remember me, but I remember her. And I want some time with that tenth grade girl again.

So, Iris needs a fake boyfriend, and I know I can sell this using social media. That fact gives me more than just a few days in Tahoe with her. Besides, she'll be more at ease at the wedding if she knows me a little better and realizes that I'm a good guy—at least I try to be.

I'm pondering my life choices and emotions, when my phone pings with an Instagram message.

@iris_me: You're coming, right?
@deanlivingoutloud: Yes. I'm coming.
@deanlivingoutloud: You doubted me?
@iris_me: No

And then,

@iris_me: Maybe.

I chuckle at her answer.

@deanlivingoutloud: No worries. I'll leave soon.
@iris_me: Thanks, Dean.
@deanlivingoutloud: No problem.

I write the response like I'm not driving hours or postponing my own work adventures. I am happy to do it and I won't mention to her all the rescheduling I've had to do. It would only bring her guilt that she doesn't need. Besides this could be a boosting post too.

@iris_me: It is a problem. It has to be. In fact, after the
    wedding I will probably owe you a kidney.
@deanlivingoutloud: I already have two.
@iris_me: I still owe you one.
@iris_me: And I'll pay for your gas!
@deanlivingoutloud: It's not a problem.

My heart's thumping now. I'm anxious to see Iris. I'm anxious for her to see me—the man I've become. I know that doesn't make sense—unless I plan to tell her who I am and I'm not sure that I do yet. Does she really need to know? Do I want her to know? Would she even remember some guy who sat by her in English a decade ago?

The truth is—she probably wouldn't. And I can't decide how that makes me feel—relieved or saddened. No one saw me back then, no one but Iris and the thought of her forgetting me, illogically hurts.

What am I, a thirteen year old kid stuck in the drama of Junior High?

I shake my head and snatch Gramgram's bedazzled T-shirt from the shelf in my room. Time to go.

I drive five miles over the speed limit, trying to hurry my ride along. It doesn't work. It takes forever. And I find myself tuned in to a Sirus XM Johnny Cash radio. When I pull up to Iris's little violet house, I've got *A Boy Named Sue* on repeat in my head.

I step out of my vehicle and shake my hands at my sides, trying to rid my body of the nerves that are exploding on the inside. I've bungee jumped a four hundred foot drop without nerves. So—this is new.

Iris's grandma is standing on her porch waving what looks like a white flag at me. I grab her shirt—realizing that I've forgotten the pants—and walk past Iris's house to Gramgram's front yard. "Here's your shirt." I hold it out to her. "Thanks for loaning it to me."

"I'm guessing you looked pretty fine in that tee, Dean Cooper. It's yours." She sets a hand to her wide hip—she's in a jumpsuit today. The same beads that bedazzle my new T-shirt create a silhouette of Johnny's face over her heart.

My hand around the shirt tightens and a diamond bead presses into my skin. "That's so generous of you. Are you sure?"

"I'm sure. You're taking Iris to Wyoming today?"

"I am."

"Well, I appreciate you making sure I can make it to Pilates." She winks—as if we are conspiring with one another. But concerning what—I'm not sure.

I'm not sure what to say. I mumble something like, "Not a problem." Yep, my go to answer these days. I clear my throat and take one step backward. "Well, I'm going to see when Iris wants to head out."

She nods and my feet move on auto pilot back toward Iris's house. "Oh, Dean!" she calls before I reach the yellow door. "I've told Iris I like you. Don't do anything to make me change my mind." She smiles the entire time she speaks, yet it sends a shiver down my spine.

"No problem. Nothing to worry about here." I set my hand to Iris's door knob. "I promise," I chatter, and then, I let myself into Iris's house. On accident.

Except for Hazel, Iris's living room is empty. I consider going back outside and knocking, but then she rounds the corner, pink fuzzy socks on her feet and a funny smile on her face. The smile quickly changes to a frown when she sees me.

"Uh, Hazel let me in," I say, no doubt in my tone.

Iris looks at her dog as if she might believe me for a moment. "She did not."

"Nah. Sorry—your grandma was kind of giving me a passive-aggressive threat and I'm not gonna lie, it scared me a little. So, I let myself in."

"Passive-aggressive?"

"She told me she liked me and that I better not change her mind."

"Oh—well, that's just Gram. Not really passive-aggressive. She just means what she says." Iris nibbles on her bottom lip and I think this is what she does when she doesn't know what else to say. Either way, it draws my gaze to her lips... Every. Single. Time. "So, Laramie. You ready?"

"Yeah. If we have time I looked up a hike for the way home. Have you been to Vedauwoo?"

"Ah, nope."

I can't help but smile. It makes me excited, thinking about being the one to introduce her to a place that I think she'll appreciate. "You'll love it. You'll be glad you have your camera."

Her blue eyes glint with something playful. "Okay. Sounds like a plan."

"Good. We need to get some backdated pictures posted and then we can start posting presently. And you'll need to start accepting all those follow requests.

She wrinkles her nose at my suggestion. I've never met someone with such an aversion to social media—and a photographer, you'd think she'd love a place to post her pictures.

"Should we go?" I ask, ignoring her disdain—like I'm just a teacher handing out homework, knowing my students will complain.

Hazel stands from her seat at Iris's side and barks at me. And it's not a welcoming bark.

"What?" I say to her. "We're friends."

"I told her she can't come today. I think she's annoyed that you get to come with me."

I hike one brow—is she for real? Is this *dog* for real? "How does she know I'm going?"

"Um," Iris hums, looking at me as if I've forgotten how to speak the English language, "you literally just asked me if I wanted to go."

Hazel barks again, moving an inch closer to me.

"Just tell her you're sorry." Iris shakes her head. "I need to grab a few things."

"Tennis shoes!" I call at her before she heads out. Although that's literally the only shoe I've seen Iris wear—black Converse.

"Apologize," she calls back in answer.

I don't need to apologize to a dog—but Hazel doesn't move. She stares me down, her eyes don't even shift with Iris's departure. This is one odd pup.

"Where's Patty?" I say to her, but she doesn't look away. I reach out to pat the top of her head, but pull back when another bark shouts from her mouth. "Whoa. Fine," I whisper. "I'm sorry, okay? She needs a ride. I'm just trying to help."

Hazel's long tail picks up from the ground and starts to wag.

"Yeah," I go on, encouraged by her wagging. "I wish you could come. It's always better with Hazel." I'm scratching behind her ear now and her tail is attempting to fan the western states.

"You're such a *weird* good girl." I bend down, meeting her at eye level.

"Just like her owner," Iris says—back from gathering her things.

"Maybe—" I say. "I mean, in a good way. She's the most interesting dog I've ever met."

"That's a compliment, Hazel." Iris has a camera backpack over her shoulders and another bag in hand. "Gramgram will be by after your nap. Okay?" Another wag from Hazel. "Bye bye," Iris says, leaning down and kissing the wiry curls on top of Hazel's head.

We start for my car, parked where Iris's should be. "How long is your car going to take?"

Iris's chest rises and falls with breath. "They said if the parts come it shouldn't take too long to fix."

My brows raise. "Well, that's good, I guess."

"Yeah. I might still be in the negative after Shelia's wedding, but at least she offered to pay for my gas money to Tahoe."

"Yeah?" I say, opening the passenger door for her.

"Yeah. I think she was annoyed when I took her up on it." Her head lolls backward until she's staring at the inner roof of my Jeep. "But I can't not take it at this point."

I climb into the driver's seat and ignite the engine. "You should always have taken it—even just driving to Evergreen. This is your business. You are providing a service—and it's normal to pay someone for their service. Expected even."

"Yeah," she says, but it comes out like a groan. I pull onto US 287 and glance over at her. Her pretty pink lips are pursed and her robin's egg blue eyes blink—looking out as if she sees nothing.

"You're a great photographer, Iris. You should be making money."

"Yeah," she says—just as believable as the first time it came out.

"This job in Wyoming should be paying all right—yeah? It's the University's soccer team."

She scratches at the back of her neck and brushes back her long chestnut hair—exposing her slender neck and left earlobe. "Well, the girls are on their way to regionals or state or something —I don't know, my sister's the sports nut, not me. Anyway, they have this big game coming and they had to win a big one to get there…" She throws up her hands. "One of the mom's reached out to me. It's the University team, on the University field, but one of the moms set up the shoot. She's paying for this picture. So—" she tilts her head.

"So, you gave her a deal."

"She's so proud, Dean. And sure maybe some of the parents can pay high dollar for a photographer, but not the mom who called me. I just—the offer just came out."

"And let me guess—no gas money was negotiated in that deal?"

She peeks over at me as if I'm her principal about to lecture her. "It never came up."

"As your fake boyfriend, can I give you some advice?"

"Is it fake advice?"

"No," I say. "It's legit." And then I barrel in without her permission. "You are only worth as much as you value yourself."

"O-kay," she says, slow and low.

"And you're undervaluing yourself, Iris." I pounce again, needing to get this out. I need my tenth grade friend to see that she is worth so much more than she realizes. "I've seen your work," I say, trying to sound a little less creepy and invasive, "it's good. Like, *really* good."

"I know that I'm good at what I do, okay?" She doesn't look at me anymore. She keeps her eyes on the road, unblinking.

"Then why aren't you allowing anyone to pay you what you're worth."

"How do you know what I charge?"

"I don't." Except that I sort of do. I breath in and speak truth—"Your ancient website gives an hourly wage—a pretty low wage by the way—and then also says you're willing to negotiate deals."

"So? Hopefully that will attract business."

"Has it?"

She avoids my question, instead she crosses her arms over her chest and says, "And my website is not ancient!"

We're both silent the remaining thirty minutes of the drive. I think we may be having our first fake fight. It isn't until we get to Laramie, Wyoming that her phone speaks up with directions, telling me where to go to get to the UW soccer field.

It isn't a game day and the parking lot is empty except for two cars parked right at the field's entrance.

I clear my throat and finally speak up. "Am I still your fake boyfriend? I mean, here?"

"Yes," she hisses. "This is all about pictures and practice, right?" She doesn't look at me though—I have officially offended the nicest human on the planet.

"I wasn't sure if all that silence meant you had fake broken up with me or not."

Iris whips her head to stare at me, but a glint of humor flashes in her eyes. Her chin lifts and she says with new found confidence. "When I break up with you, it won't be fake."

"Huh," I say, grasping to that glint. "Wouldn't that mean I was your real boyfriend though? I think a fake boyfriend gets a fake break up, but I haven't read the rule book on this."

Her eyes flick up to the ceiling. "You can be my caddie. Here, take this." She shoves the camera bag into my hands. She's trying so hard to be serious, but there's a grin playing at her lips.

"Yes ma'am," I tell her, thankful that the tension I unintentionally built on our drive is melting away.

THIRTEEN

Iris

Awoman with wide hips waves at me from across the field—as if she thinks I'm trying to land a commercial airplane. Elbows in, I give her a short, curt wave back —I'm overcompensating for her dramatic hand signals.

"I think she might want us to go that way," Dean says, pointing with both hands like pistols toward the woman.

It's a nice spring day and Dean wears shorts and a short sleeved white button up shirt. His biceps seem to bulge today, like they're screaming *look at me, Iris!* Also—he *always* looks ready to have his picture taken. How does he do that? Does he even try? Or is it just a natural gift? –One that I do not have.

His tan muscular legs and that white Oxford shirt against the green of the grass field make me want to photograph him here and now. He could just stand like that, hand in one pocket, smile, and it would be a small masterpiece.

I blink hard once—why am I thinking those things, even photographic things, about my very fake, very made-up boyfriend? I nod once to myself—*oh, right! Because I am a photographer and my mind sees a great photo when it presents itself.* It has nothing to do with the bicep bulging from Dean's right arm or the sweet way he talks to Hazel.

"Iris?" Dean says, waving a hand in front of my face. Yes, I've been staring at his bicep since my mind shifted from soccer moms to pictures of Dean on this field.

"Sorry!" I almost shout out the word. "Just picturing where I want them." I hold my chin in my hand and look out at the field, as if I'm still contemplating the idea. I'm not, of course. I researched and planned a week ago where the sun would be, how many girls would be in the picture, and where I'd want them to stand.

We start toward Renee—the mom who ordered the picture, the woman waving me down like I have poor eyesight and might miss her signal. She meets us halfway, her hand held out to shake mine.

"Iris McCoy?" she says when I set my hand in hers. She gives it one stern shake then pulls the beanie hat on her head down past her ears. Her tight curls spring outward from under the hat. It's not that cold out, but Renee is dressed for the worst—full winter gear on.

"You must be Renee."

She grins. "Yes. Can you believe these girls are in shorts? Back in Phoenix it's eighty seven degrees today. It's only fifty-two degrees here!"

That's right—Renee flew over from Arizona for her daughter's big game.

Her eyes drift to Dean—who is also in shorts. "You apparently don't mind either, huh?"

I don't give him a chance to answer—this is my practice time and I'm blowing it. Can I really introduce Dean as my boyfriend and be believable? I suppose I'd rather find out with a bunch of strangers than my entire family.

"Oh! I'm sorry Renee. This. Is. My. Boyfriend." I smile and I can feel all of my teeth exposed to the cool air. "Dean. Cooper."

Dean wraps one arm around my shoulders. "Smooth."

I elbow him—a little harder than my intention—and he grunts out in surprise.

"Nice to meet you," Renee says, holding her hand out to Dean now. He drops his arm from around me and shakes Renee's hand, his face flushed from my jab.

"Happy to be here," he says through a cough. Come on, tough guy, it wasn't that hard of a jab.

Still—he *is* happy to be here and he doesn't have to be. I need to try and remember that. Which means—no more jabbing my fake boyfriend in the ribs.

"He's here to help out." I reach my hand out for his. It's messy and grappling—there is no way on this green and blue planet that it looks normal, but Dean extends his hand and takes mine.

We walk over to the girls and I get to work. Dean stands back, holding my bags, while Renee and I set up the team so that they stand with their backs to the sunshine and just where I want them. I'm not blind to these girls ogling Dean. But I just keep working.

The blue sky goes on forever behind the Cowgirl's soccer team and with the green turf at their feet, I know it's going to be a great shot. That is, if the girls will look at me. I drop down my wide angle lens. It's attached with a strap about my neck. I let it dangle so I can clap my hands. I've turned into an impatient preschool teacher.

"Ladies! I know that Dean is nice to look at, but I need your eyes on me right now."

They don't start to attention like the good little girls they should be. In fact, one gasps and then mumbles break out amongst the team.

Behind me, Renee leans over, the tassels from her winter hat dangling over my shoulder. "You're dating a celebrity?"

"What? No. He's—"

"They all know who he is."

"Dean?" I look at him and his jaw is clenched, his lips pinched in a line.

Then from across the field, one girl, one that I couldn't pin point if I wanted to, says, "You're Dean! Living out loud, Dean!" It's a question and a statement all rolled into one.

They do know Dean. He told me he had viral videos—but I'm not sure I knew what that meant.

My mouth drops and air escapes through an inaudible groan.

"Come on ladies!" Renee says, clapping behind me and making me start. "This is your photo, do you want drool hanging from your mouths or smiles on your faces?"

I hold up my camera, but too many eyes are still to the left of me—right on Dean. "Dean!" I whisper yell, beckoning him over with one jiggle of my head. He walks to my side and I look up at him. "They all know who you are?"

"I'm sure not all of them do." He lifts one shoulder in a shrug.

"This is so weird." I lift my camera, focus my shot, and with Dean next to me I have the eyes of each player—as well as swoony smiles from all twenty female soccer players. I take a few pictures and then readjust positions. Two more rounds of photos and new positions and we're done. The photo shoot takes an entire thirty minutes. Which means, minus gas, I've made a whopping fifty bucks for the day.

The girls have practice in ten minutes, which means they can't ogle at Dean for long. A couple brave players run over to say hello and take a selfie with him. I watch and wait—is this how it's going to be wherever we go? Did Shelia recognize him? Travis didn't or he would have said something.

"Here you are," Renee says, handing me an envelope after the last girl has run off.

"Thanks," I say, slipping the payment into my back pocket.

"Wait," Dean says to Renee. "Do you mind? Could you take our photo on the field?" He holds out his phone and she takes it.

We stand side by side—both of us remembering that lineup photo Gail took. It wasn't believable or pretty. We need to *look* as if we're dating—that's the entire point of all these pictures. So, Dean wraps an arm around my waist and I turn into him, hoping we look like we have at least known each other longer than three days. I'm not so naïve as to hope we look as if we're in love.

"A little closer," Renee says.

We each move in an inch until the white of Dean's shirt touches the soft pink of my cuff notched neck blouse.

Renee is suddenly a runway model photographer spouting directions and snapping pictures every two seconds. "Look up at him, Iris. Dean, you look down at her."

We listen and Renee snaps.

"Now give her a kiss."

I keep my smile intact, as if someone had painted it on my pale skin. "Don't you dare." I say through gritted teeth.

"Not until you ask." He smiles down at me.

"Go on!" Renee shouts.

"So?" Dean says, one brow raising.

"Not a chance," my ventriloquist lips get out.

"Come on guys," Renee says again—as if this is her job and she won't stop until it's done.

Dean's head lowers—closer to mine. He wouldn't... Still I stay put—frozen. I even shut my eyes, Dean's cedarwood and musk scent intoxicating me.

Wait, I closed my eyes... is that permission? Because I most definitely did not give—

Dean's lips brush over my cheekbone, his kiss like a butterfly's wings whispers hello.

My heart thumps in my chest and if I didn't feel as if I might pass out—I would be horridly embarrassed knowing that Dean must be able to feel the thar-ump pounding inside of my chest.

My senses return and my hand on his chest, slips down to his stomach, attempting to find some loose skin to pinch. But he's so stupidly fit, I come up with nothing.

Instead I pull away from him. "Geez, how many sit ups do you do in a day?"

"What?" he chuckles—probably believing that I just felt him up, chest to abs.

"Thank you," I shout to Renee. "I'll email you when I'm finished with my edits." I start off toward the Jeep, knowing Dean will have to grab his phone and make his way out through a sea of fan girls.

"Iris!" He calls, jogging behind me. "Wait up."

I huff out a breath and whip around. "What was that?"

"What was what? I'm playing my part. You don't want a kiss, I didn't kiss you."

I point to my cheek, my eyes wide. I hate conflict. I'm so bad at it. Even when I'm right I can't win. Besides, it gives me a stomach ache. I can't eat or sleep. I just lay in bed at night thinking about what I should have said.

"Iris," he groans and his hand clasps around my upper arm. "I'm sorry. I guess."

"Nice." I roll my eyes because I am a mature adult.

His hands flap at his side. "You want people to believe we're together, right? I'm trying to do that without making you or myself feel too uncomfortable."

Ugh.

It was a kiss on the cheek, Iris, not a make out session.

The only thing worse than confrontation, is actually dueling, and then being wrong. And I am wrong. Ugh. Ugh. Ugh.

I shut my eyes, my hand a visor over my eyes. "Dean—"

"It's okay."

My eyes pop open and my arm whips downward—forgetting that I was wrong. "I didn't apologize!" Ugh. I'm not sure why I'm so ready for a fight. I breathe out and my shoulders droop.

"But…" my jaw clenches, "I probably should have. This is strange and harder than I thought it would be. But that's not your fault. And I am sorry. I'm sure this isn't natural for you either."

"I'm not exactly good at *fake*," he admits, but there's no malice in his tone. "That's pretty clear from looking at our first picture together. But we're getting better." Dean's sapphire eyes sparkle when he looks at me. His expression is kind and soft and when he smiles, I feel it in my toes. "So, we'll just have to keep practicing," he says and I wonder for a hot second if my *fake* boyfriend is for *real* flirting with me. Or maybe he's practicing and he's fake flirting with me? Or maybe I don't understand the definition of flirting and he's actually just explaining how bad I am at this in a polite way.

Either way, I choose to make an idiot of myself. I laugh—like I'm watching Nick at Night 80s reruns and Uncle Jesse from Full House just quoted Elvis. "Good one," I say and then, I wink at Dean.

I wink.

I actually wink at the man.

On a sexy scale from 0 to 100, it's a negative ten. I click my tongue and shoot both my pointer fingers out like pistols—why? Because I'm on a roll, that's why.

Then, I climb into the cab of Dean's Jeep—where I will curl up and die.

Good times.

FOURTEEN

Dean

"Are you still up for an hour or two at Vedauwoo? I've only been once, but it's a pretty epic place."

"Uh-huh," Iris hums without looking at me. She hasn't looked at me since she winked at me and climbed into the car. She was so much more chill when we walked around the pond, but then Hazel was with us. Iris always seems to settle when Hazel is around. And then I fell in and she actually seemed to enjoy herself after that. I harumph out a laugh with my thoughts and Iris says—without looking over at me—"What?"

I clear my throat. "Nothing. You brought a shirt and athletic shoes to change into?"

She finally looks at me, brows cinched. "Um, no. I haven't gained any new shoes since last night. And I didn't think to grab another shirt. Do I need one?"

"That one's nice. You might not want to get it sweaty."

"Sweaty?" She wrinkles her nose. "We're getting sweaty?"

"Maybe."

She looks unimpressed with the idea. I'm hoping some sic rock formations and the great outdoors will change her mind. I just want to see Iris smile again and I don't know why—but I think this will make it happen. Not to mention, we need a lot more pictures so I can get conning all of Instagram.

"It'll be fun," I promise her—hopeful that I'm not lying. "The photographer in you is going to love it."

She blinks and her fight or flight eyes seem to soften. "Okay."

I'm not wrong. Iris has her big camera out before I've even figured out where we'll park. She rolls down her window halfway, the spring chill filters into the Jeep. She rests her lens on the edge of the glass and I hear her snap picture after picture.

"You've climbed these rocks?" she asks.

"Yeah." I can't help but smile, outside is my happy place. Climbing makes me happy. Introducing it all to Iris seems to make me utterly blissful.

"How does it work? You make a video and post it and—"

"And people watch it. Yep. I mean, there's a whole lot of strategery in there, some figuring to monetize and attract followers, but yeah, pretty much."

She nibbles on her bottom lip, drawing my eyes to her mouth. "Video how? Do you have a crew?"

I chuckle. "Nah. Nothing like that. Here I'll show you." I keep my tripod for my phone in the back of the Jeep at all times, you never know when an adventure may strike.

I grab my set up and toss one of the three shirts I threw into a bag at Iris. "You should put this on," I tell her. "There's an outhouse over there."

Iris sets her camera back in its bag and looks more closely at the shirt I've tossed her. It's only fair she should have to wear it too. She sets one hand on her hip.

"You love Johnny Cash." I haven't taken my eyes off her.

"And bedazzling," she says.

"Perfect."

She walks off toward the bathroom and in sixty seconds I have my travel tripod all set up. I attach my phone and look at the massive rocks before me. I don't have any gear on me, but the smaller of the two I can climb without a harness. I hit record and start toward the boulder.

I'm half way up when I feel the bead of sweat pool and swoop down my back. It's like a victory bead. I climbed. I conquered. I lived. When I get to the top, I sit and cross my legs —boulders are great places to meditate.

After a minute, I breathe and blink my eyes open. I see Iris— on the ground, camera in hand, her zoom zeroed in on me. I can't tell if she's wearing her grandmother's bedazzled shirt because she's got a blue sweatshirt overtop of it. When she sees me looking down at her she adjusts the camera, letting her blue eyes, like newly laid robin's eggs, peek out from behind. She gives me a small wave and a closed lipped grin as if she's been caught.

I wave back, but my wave quickly turns into a beckon. This isn't that high, it's not a hard climb, but the view is awesome. She'll love it. "Bring your camera," I holler.

I can see she isn't convinced, so I start to come down, but all the while holding out my hand—asking her to take it. Iris slings her camera around her back—step one. She's got to process things right—that's what she said. Step two—*move your feet*, I tell her in my mind.

"Iris!" I call and I truly can't help the smile that I know is plastered on my face. It's just there—the rocks, the air, the trees, they produce it without effort.

She takes two steps with my beckon. Step three—keep going.

I don't want my feet to hit the ground or I'm not sure she'll ever come up. "Come on, Iris," I call again. "You can do this."

She squares her shoulders—which is apparently step four because she's at the bottom of the boulder now, eyeing it up.

"I—I don't know how, Dean."

"Yes, you do. It's just like when we were kids. Did you ever play on the jungle gym?"

She gives a one shoulder shrug, which tells me she did and she doesn't want to say as much.

"It's just like that." I scoot down the boulder a little farther and hold a hand out to her. "Come on. I've got you. The view is worth it. I promise."

She lifts a foot onto the first rock and reaches out for me. Her fingers shake, but she's doing it. I snatch hold of her hand, stopping the tremor that's filing through her.

"Nice," I tell her. "Just a few more rocks and we'll be at the top of this first level. Okay?"

She nods. She's brave. Anson, my stepdad taught me about bravery—he called me brave when I most definitely didn't feel it. He taught me one of my favorite life lessons and I say it to Iris now—I hear it in my head in his gravelly voice—"Way to be brave."

Iris slides an icy glare my way as she clings to my hand for dear life.

I wait until she's taken another step and then another, until she's right next to me. I wrap one arm around her, making sure she's steady and finish Anson's mantra. "Brave isn't doing something dangerous or risky. Brave is doing something despite the fear you feel."

"Did you read that off of a cereal box?"

I laugh because I know it's the fear talking. "It's something my stepdad told me after I felt like a two-inch tall coward."

She's steady, so I let my arm drop, but I'll keep my hand in hers until she doesn't want it. Iris's hand is warm and soft and sends strange tingles throughout my arm and into my body—tingles that I'm beginning to desire hourly.

We climb, slow and steady, hand in hand. Iris steadies herself on the rocks with her free hand and I can see the tremor running through it.

We get to the top and she breathes in the air like it's cleaner and purer up here—though we're only twenty feet off the ground. There's so much more rock, so much higher we could go. But I won't push her today.

She stands, her feet steady and laughs delirious at the view. "There are so many more formations like this one."

"Yeah." I nod, but I'm not watching the rocks. All I see is Iris.

She wrangles her camera like a cowboy with a lasso and points in every direction, taking a few photos and then slings the thing onto her back once more. She teeters once and I reach out my hand. She takes it and smiles over at me, the breeze rustling her hair.

"Can we sit—or is that cowardly?" she asks.

"Sitting is great."

She lowers herself to the boulder floor, and I use my status as fake boyfriend to sidle right up next to her.

"Can I see your phone?"

She hands it over to me without reservation and I pull up her camera app. We're getting the hang of things, because our cheeks collide like ferromagnetic metals and I snap a few selfies of the two of us.

"Can I see?" she says. I hand her the phone and she scrolls through, all the way back to our pictures on the soccer field. "I'm sorry I got mad at you. I don't know what's wrong with me. It's like my emotions have been stuffed into a blender."

I nudge her shoulder with mine. "Don't worry about it. How are they?" I lean over and swipe back to our picture of two minutes ago.

"Okay," she says in that tone that tells me she isn't convinced.

"How would you have set it up? You know, if you were taking this picture of another couple."

Her brows lift. "Me?" And I can see in her face, she knows exactly how she'd do it. My eyes draw to her lips—again with the bottom lip. I can't remember Iris chewing on her lip so much when we were in school.

Her forget-me-not eyes trace the lines of my face but she

doesn't say a thing. She just motions with her hands, telling me what to do. She taps on one leg, shifting my knees outward and widening the gap my legs have naturally made. Then, Iris lifts herself overtop my right side to sit between my legs. She scoots back until her back is flush to my chest.

My breaths are short with her body, warm and lean, next to mine. Still I don't move, not until she moves me. Her hands, careful and artistic, take me by the right fingers, wrapping them about her waist. She does the same with my left. My face automatically cranes down next to hers, my breath warm on her chilled cheek. I'm so tempted to kiss her again, to feel her soft skin on my lips. But I don't—I don't want to jinx anything that's happening in this second. Instead, I breath in the strawberry and coconut scent that must be her shampoo and settle for my cheek brushing hers. She is tender and breakable, and holding her like this makes me feel like I've been doing it forever. Or maybe, like I'm supposed to do it forever.

Iris settles into me and holds out her phone. She smiles and I exist, afraid to move, that I might spoil the moment.

We're quiet for a moment, she takes the photo and drops her hand. But she doesn't move, she doesn't leave my hold.

"Why did you feel cowardly?" she says, her face shifting just an inch to see me better—it brings her lips that much closer to my own and I have a hard time making sense of what she's asked me.

"When?"

I feel the rumble of her chuckle—something I'm not sure I would have even known occurred if she weren't lying against me.

"You said, your step dad told you that you were brave when you felt like a coward."

I swallow—nervous. This is a story that could give me away. It's a story I don't like telling. "He was referring to a time before he knew me."

She's quiet. That isn't an answer and we both know it. She

just climbed a small mountain—so I guess that means it's my turn to bare part of my soul. Okay, I can play.

"A few months before I met my dad, my step dad, I mean, I was… in foster care." I swallow again and it feels as if I'm trying to get down the state of Montana and my esophagus just isn't big enough. I press on—remembering Anson. "It wasn't a good time for me. School was rough, home was even worse. I could have run away, but that would have made things worse. So, I showed up every day, even though I felt like an ant about to be squished every second of the day."

Iris twists in my hold, so that she's seeing me better. "Foster care?" she says and her eyes look far away. I wonder if she's adding it all up. "What do you mean you showed up every day?"

"You know—to school, even though people were cruel. And I went back to that foster home every evening, though everything inside of me wanted to run."

"Why?" she says and I swear her eyes are lasers that see right through me, right to my core.

I've only ever really talked about this to Anson. This is the me social media has never met. Heck, even my day to day acquaintances don't know Dean Cooper, weak and inferior foster kid. They know me, the man I am, the man I want to be, Dean Cooper *Hale*, son of Anson and Melissa Hale. Dean Hale is brave and adventurous. He's fun and you'd never guess he had a screwed up past.

"They weren't nice people, Iris." I don't say more than that and she must decide not to press because she faces forward and for a brief moment, she settles into my arms, like we didn't set up this pose for a picture—like this is just us.

Then, as if realizing her error, she jets straight up, sitting straight and rigid, so that no part of her body touches mine. "Sorry," she says. "I'm sorry. I was thinking and I—" she runs a hand down her face—I can't see her expression though, she's facing away from me. She hops over my leg and is out of my arms in half a second.

Clearing her throat, she smooths down her sweatshirt and lays back on the flat top of the boulder we sit on. Her legs are bent and her hands fold together over her flat stomach. I scoot down a few inches and lay back, my head next to hers, staring up at the biggest, bluest sky I think I've ever seen.

"This is weird, isn't it?"

I know what she's talking about, and sure, it's not an average relationship, but I'm not sorry we're here. "I guess," I say. "But I'd like to think we're starting to become friends."

Her eyes pinch to slits. "Sure. Okay." She swivels her head to look at me instead of our sky view. "But I don't know any friends that con other people into believing they're dating."

My mouth tickles with a grin. "That's because they're conning you, Iris. It happens all the time. You just don't realize it."

The lie makes her laugh and she peers back at the sky. We sit in silence for a minute that feels like it could be an hour. There's so much unsaid in that minute.

"Are you happy now, Dean?" she says into the quiet.

My hand twitches with the insane desire to take hers. No one is watching and we aren't taking a picture, but I still want to touch her, to take her hand and squeeze her fingers. Instead, I ball my hand into a tight fist and slide my gaze to her face. "I am."

FIFTEEN

Iris

Dean and I explored Vedauwoo for a couple of hours after our heart to heart on top of the rock. We took pictures and changed our shirts a couple of times to hopefully account for different days. I have no idea if this is going to work. Dean keeps saying it will.

We took a few more with Hazel when we got back to my house. Now, I'm making shrimp scampi and Hazel and Dean are laying on my couch—looking through pictures.

My head keeps swirling with what Dean told me, with his rawness and vulnerability. His eyes—always so bright and happy seemed so sad as he recalled his time in foster care. Sad and... *familiar*. I wanted to wrap him in a hug in that minute, but I'm already forcing him to sidle up next to me for multiple photo shoots, I won't force my affection on him too. He might tease me about kisses—but guys like Dean don't date girls like me. I don't need anything—not even fake dating—messing with my heart.

I turn on some music and dish up our meal. I can't go crazy and dance or sing in my kitchen like I normally would. I mean, there is a *man* in my living room. A social media influencer who college girls swoon over. Dean's already seen me with a dog rope in my mouth. He will not see me pretending I know how to dance like Shakira and sing like Beyonce.

I dish the noodles and shrimp I've sauteed into two bowls, slide in a couple of forks, and walk the two steaming dishes out into the living room.

"Here you go," I say. I hand Dean his bowl and the corners of his mouth lift.

"Wow, Iris, this looks amazing. You didn't have to cook."

"I did." I nod. He put up with me and my abnormal moodiness today. He took a few dozen pictures with me—all for me. "Hazel," I say—and I know how sugary my tone sounds. I can't help it though. She's my baby. "Dinner's in your bowl."

Hazel hops down from her perch on the couch, leaving a long griff body indentation on my couch—well except for her head, which was laid in Dean's lap.

"I think you've made a life-long friend," I say, sitting next to Dean on the couch. Hazel and Gramgram's approval kind of mean everything to me. I mean, I like Dean, he's nice. Sure, he makes my stomach flutter in strange, annoying ways, but he's genuinely a nice guy. Still, they both like Dean, and that means he can sit on my couch and put his feet on my coffee table and I won't freak out that we've known each other a very short time.

"That dog has more personality than several people I know."

"That's Hazel." I laugh, a fork full of noodles and shrimp hovering in the air, steam billowing up from the hot bite. "Can I see what you've accomplished?" I ask, setting my food on the table in front of us.

Dean holds out his phone for me to see, his Instagram app opened. "These two are for the present. My account gets too much traffic for us to backdate anything, but I've started back-dating on my private account and on yours. And once we're finished, you'll need to start adding all those friends who've requested to view your account." He shakes his head a little. "Don't look at me like that."

"Like what?"

"Like I'm asking you to go cliff diving."

My eyes widen all on their own. "I don't want to do that."

"Exactly. This isn't cliff diving—although that's pretty great. It's going to be okay. You can have a few followers. It might even help with business."

"I know. I know. You and Ebony keep telling me." I snatch the phone from his grasp and look down at the picture of us from today, sitting on that huge monstrous rock, twenty feet off the ground. The sky is behind us, and strangely, I look like I belong in Dean's hold. A string of my chestnut brown hair has blown onto Dean's forehead. His arms are tight around me and he seems happy to be there. It's like an out of body experience. He's used some type of filter that I'm going to have to ask him about and he's written:

> @deanlivingoutloud: We climbed a mountain today!
> We are invincible!

He's used a dozen hashtags—my name being one of them. I swallow past the nervous lump in my throat. And then I see how many likes the picture has. I sit up straighter, staring at his phone. "When—when did you post this?"

"That one?" he leans across the couch and me, peering at his phone in my hands and filling my senses with musk and pine. "About an hour ago."

"But—but it has four hundred likes already." My eyes bug out on that number—four hundred and eleven hearts. "Four hundred."

I scroll down to the picture Dean posted yesterday, there's two videos in between our photos. Dean in a kayak—when did he do that? And Dean surrounded by trees—I'm thinking he's in Evergreen. I don't click on either video to see what he's doing, but I find our faces from the day before, Dean wet from the pond, his arms around my waist. Eleven thousand likes.

I stand, I can't breathe sitting here, my lungs and abdomen are all scrunched up on this couch. I can't breathe! "Eleven thousand," I say aloud, my breaths are short and spotty and I feel like any second now, they'll disappear altogether.

Dean stands beside me and takes the phone. "Yes," he says. "Eleven thousand likes and one hundred and four comments."

"Comments?" I bend over. Yep—I am definitely hyperventilating.

"Iris," he says, and the word is stern, yet kind on his lips. "Iris." Dean sets a hand on my back. He dips his head and peers into my face. "I know. It's hard and it's scary having so many eyes on you. I *know*."

My eyes drop down to his phone. But I can't speak. If it's so scary then why does he do this? Why let so many people watch you all of the time?

"Iris," he says again and I know he's biding for my attention, trying to distract my gaze from the screen.

I let him. I peer up to him. He is swimming in my unshed tears. What's wrong with me? It's just one picture. It's just one post. It's just eleven thousand sets of eyes.

Dean grabs my arm and gently sets me straight. His hold tightens and he pulls me in, crushing me against his chest. His arms wrap around my back and he hugs me close—like I'd wanted to hug him. His breath warms my skin and his lips move at my temple. "It's okay," he tells me.

We stand like that for so long that I'm certain my scampi has gone cold. I feel ridiculous. I feel like a silly little girl. It's just social media—only every human on the planet is participating. So, Dean has a lot of followers. Won't that just solidify our story?

My breath returns back to *almost* normal. I pull away from Dean. I am so good at making a fool of myself in front of him. It should be noted on my resume as my special skill. *Hi I'm Iris, I take pictures and make a fool of myself in front of Dean Cooper.* "I'm sorry. I really don't know what that was. I just——"

"I think you had a panic attack." He stares down at me, his brows knit together.

"Me?" I scoff and return to my seat on the couch. "No," I groan out the word. Though I do feel shaky.

"Or yes." He follows after me, sitting closer than he had been before.

"Look. I'm fine." I look down at myself, my fingers clasped together. "What?" I say when he won't stop staring. "Did you squeeze the panic attack out of me?"

He lifts one shoulder. "Kind of. I think everything we're trying to do just became a little overwhelming. It's okay. It happens to everyone."

"Right—I don't see you having a panic attack."

"I love the outdoors. I love sharing what I do with others. But sometimes all the eyes, all the watching—it's a lot. Believe me, Iris, I get it."

I want so badly to believe him—to believe that I'm not a total weird-o, that someone as brave and strong as Dean could understand me.

"The good thing about social media, there's always something new popping up tomorrow. And!" He holds up his hand, three fingers together, his pinky and thumb folded down. He looks like a boy scout. "I Dean Cooper Hale promise to never post an unflattering picture of you."

I squeeze my fingers in and out of their fisted hold and laugh. "Well, that's a relief." My brows furrow. "Wait? *Hale?* Where did Hale come from? I thought it was just Dean Cooper."

"Oh." Dean rubs his palms together like they've gone sweaty. "It is Hale." He clears his throat. "It's both actually. A few years ago my step dad adopted me and I chose to take his name."

The nerves inside of my body settle with Dean's words. I just listen. And I want him to keep explaining. Dean Cooper Hale has layers—like Shrek, and onions, and delicious puff pastries. "Because…" I say, leaving the word hanging in the air like a dangling oxygen mask—I want him to grab it! I want him to explain.

Dean's eyes rise to mine and they pierce me—like ice down my shirt. "Because I wanted a fresh start. Because to be the real me, I couldn't be Dean Cooper anymore."

I lean back, resting my cheek on the couch, my gaze directly on him, studying him. I can't help it. "Why did you keep Cooper at all?"

"Because the real me is Cooper and Hale combined. I need to remember how far I've come." Dean sits back too, he watches me back as if I'll share some glorious secret—but my life is pretty dull compared to his. I have no haunting past and no adventurous present.

"How far have you come?" I ask instead.

His eyes narrow and I hold my breath, waiting for him to tell me more. "Maybe that's a story for another day," he says.

My pulse thumps in my wrist and neck. All this fake dating has felt a little like actual dating—except I know in the end there's no happily ever after, nor is there a messy break up.

Still, I'm going to feel his absence. I know it. Which is proof, once again, what a weird-o I am. How long have I even known this guy?

Ugh. Pathetic.

Twenty minutes later Dean has finished his meal and kissed Hazel goodbye. I get a nice, friendly wave. *Perfect.*

My tingly twin power vibes go off—yes sir, it's a thing—just as my phone buzzes with a call. I know it's Ebony.

"You have five new pictures on Instagram. *Five*, Iris."

I hit speaker and flop onto my bed. "Yes. I know."

"Five, only one is two months old. In fact, the earliest one of these pics you posted yesterday. All the others say a week ago or later. How is that possible, Iris?" She speaks in her journalist voice—she's asking me a question and, by golly, she won't stop until she gets an answer!

"Because," I say with a little too much moan and force behind the word—I'm whining. "Because Dean is a social media mastermind and he's helping me convince the family that we've been dating. For *months.*"

"Why again?"

"I'm not sure! Travis, I think." I moan and plant my Johnny Cash throw pillow—a gift from Gram last Christmas—over my face.

"Is it really worth spending all this time with some strange guy just to convince Travis you aren't alone?"

"Oh that sounds so pathetic. Thank you for that, Ebony." I wail my words, so as to be heard over the pillow on my face. Still, my words come out with a strained, whiny moan. "Sister of the year is going straight to you!"

"Do you even like him?"

"I…" I stretch out the word far too long, "don't *dislike* him."

"Iris!" Ebony hisses in my ear. "You *like* your fake boyfriend?"

"I do not!" I bellow, tossing the pillow from my face and glaring at my phone.

"Yes, you do. I can hear it. There's attraction dripping from every word you say." She sounds appalled and that only riles me up.

"Who cares if I do? What's wrong with that?"

"What's wrong?" she yells—and we're in a full on shouting match now. It's high school all over again. Ebony and I could go from shouting to hugging to crying in sixty seconds flat. "It's *fake,* Iris! You aren't allowed to fall for your fake boyfriend or the word fake doesn't apply."

"Sure it does," I say, and the crying part is close—only Ebony isn't here to hug me. "He'd have to like me back for it to be real."

The shouts go still and we're quiet. "Iris, you like him?" she says and this time it isn't the journalist asking, but my sister. She wants to know and she's worried about me.

"A little. He's nice. He's interesting. He's sweet with Hazel. But you have nothing to worry about. Dean Cooper Hale is way too adventurous for boring ol' me."

"What happens when he touches you?"

"What?" I lay on my stomach staring at my phone, giving Ebony the stink eye even when she can't see me. She can feel it. So I give it.

"I've seen the pictures. I know he's touched you. So what happens?"

"I don't know!" I sound like I'm eleven. Eleven and guilty.

"*Iris*," she scolds—just like mom.

I huff out a breath. "Um… It's not awful. Okay?"

"Iris, for the love of all that is—"

"Fine! It's… *nice*."

"Are you in the seventh grade?" she asks, upgrading me from eleven to thirteen.

"Maybe," I say, on the verge of shouting once more, "because when he touches me it's like someone has zinged me with a sparkler and those sparks spread to my stomach and my toes and they linger. They linger, Ebony! And all I want is for it to happen all over again!"

There's a short pause before she asks, "Has he kissed you?"

"No!" I bark. But the sadness is evident in my tone when I say, "I told him he wasn't allowed to kiss me."

"Holy moly, Iris, what if he likes you back? That doesn't exactly say friendly—*you aren't allowed to kiss me.*"

My throat hurts and my tear ducts decide it's time to go to work. "You know I'm not good at being a girlfriend. You know I'm not exciting and spontaneous."

"I know that's what meathead Travis told you."

"He might fake kiss me, but we both know I'd be real kissing him back. And then our fake breakup might do me in."

My sister sighs into the phone. "Oh, Iris. I wish I weren't twelve hundred miles away. You need a hug."

"Me too. Every day. Every hour! Every minute! Every—"

"Okay. Okay," Ebony says with a laugh. "I get it. I moved away. My bad."

"As long as you're happy, Ebs."

"I'm mailing you a hug. It will arrive tomorrow."

"Perfect," I tell her because despite how much I miss my best friend and sister, she likes Seattle. She loves her job. She's living out loud—just like Dean. And I'd never want to be the reason she stopped.

SIXTEEN

Iris

_____

Sitting at my kitchen table, I drink warm, spiced Tang from my favorite mug—the one that I bought when I visited Ebony last summer. This place in the mall took one of my pictures of Hazel and slapped it right on a mug. It's the cutest. She's smiling and has a ring of bows on the crown of her head. She'd just gotten back from the groomer. The minute after I snapped this pic, she made me take every single bow out of her hair, silly griff. But she's a good girl and at least sat for the photo, and now I have the mug.

I drink Gram's spiced Tang because caffeine might as well be hard liquor inside my body. I go all limp and loopy. It isn't pretty. So—no coffee, coke, or hot cocoa for this gal. No one wants to see a caffeinated Iris.

I'm a whole twelve days into my fake relationship, and mindlessly scrolling through the, now, two hundred and twenty-two comments on our Vedauwoo picture. We've taken more pics all week and Dean is a posting machine. But this one is intimate and close and has more comments than all the others. It's strange and surreal and a small part of me pretends that this is not a picture of me. Except that my name keeps popping up in the comments.

> @laurenJ: This is adorable.
> @melissa.hale11: Iris is beautiful!
> @blueberrypancakeadventures: You and Iris make the cutest couple.
> @rayandmolly2018: Congrats man, you deserve it!
> @bssymes5: Is this in Colorado?
> @krisco81: I love this!
> @easystreetsam: Where did Iris buy her sweater?

Ummm… Costco, how much would that disappoint her?

> @billpepperclimbs: Can't wait to see Iris cliff dive with you this summer!

"Sorry, @billpepperclimbs, that's going to be a very long wait."

> @wildtad: Does Iris have a sister?

"Not one that you'll ever know about."

> @alabama.jama: Any chance Iris is accepting new friend requests?

"Hard pass @alabama.jama." My eyes go wide and I shake my head. Is he for real? Social media is the weirdest.

> @mike-n-susie99: Beautiful area! We go to Vedauwoo every summer.

I keep reading. Does Dean know any of these people? And then, my throat closes. The big swig of Tang I just threw back isn't going to go down, nope—I sputter, but I can't stop what's about to happen. Tang spurts across my kitchen table. I cover my mouth, choking on the remnants that are still attempting to make their way down my throat and reread that last message:

> @shelia.holmes.327: aww. Looks like a cute place to
> propose! So happy for my cousin!

A short string of responses after Shelia's ask if Dean and I are engaged, how long we've been dating, and when our big day is.

I'm going to kill Shelia. Instead of taking her wedding day pictures, someone in a dank police station will be taking my mug shot.

I can't kill Shelia though—she's clear across the state and she doesn't know my boyfriend isn't real... He's just pretend. I went to a store and picked him out.

Instead of confessing all of my falsities to Shelia and Travis, I message Dean.

> @iris_me: How do you delete a comment from
> Instagram?
> @deanlivingoutloud: Why?
> @iris_me: You didn't see what Shelia wrote?
> @deanlivingoutloud: I don't usually read the
> comments. At least not all of them.

Stupid Dean and his popularity.

> @iris_me: Well start reading!
> @deanlivingoutloud: Maybe you could clue me in...
> @iris_me: Shelia!! She mentioned a proposal and now
> everyone is asking about us.
> @deanlivingoutloud: Wasn't that the plan?
> @iris_me: A fake proposal? Ah, nope!!!!!!!!!!!!!!!

My fingers speed over the phone and I can't seem to stop the exclamation points from appearing.

> @deanlivingoutloud: Whoa. I think you might be
> yelling at me.
> @iris_me: Seriously, Dean. I'm not normally someone
> who lies.

I slump in my seat, Hazel with her super dog senses, realizes I'm miserable and comes over to sit on my feet. She's the sweetest dog the world has ever known.

> @deanlivingoutloud: I know that, Iris. It'll be okay.
> @iris_me: So what do we do? What's the plan of
> attack? How do we strike?
> @deanlivingoutloud: Well, for one—we don't go to
> war. We ignore.
> @iris_me: I don't like that. What's plan B?

Dean clicks on my last message and sends it a laughing emoji. I'm not laughing, buddy.

> @deanlivingoutloud: Believe me ignoring it is the
> fiercest form of action.

Fierce. I like that. But…

> @iris_me: How is that fierce?
> @deanlivingoutloud: We are too cool, too grownup,
> too distracted with each other to acknowledge
> your cousin and her insinuations.

"I'm too grown up." I nod and sip from my warm Tang. "I'm

cool. So cool. Like *super-duper* cool." *Cheese and crackers*—I am distracted by hottie Dean. That's not a lie.

> @deanlivingoutloud: I'm posting the last of our
>   backdated photos today on your account and
>   then…
> @iris_me: Then what? Why the dot dot dot?
> @deanlivingoutloud: I'm letting the backdated photos
>   settle in before I tell you the rest. You cool?

I write out the words *super-duper cool*, but then delete them. For some reason, they just don't sound all that cool.

> @iris_me: Very.
> @deanlivingoutloud: Perfect. Now, time for the one
>   thing you've been talking yourself out of for the
>   past week and a half.

"Ugh. Not that." I moan and Hazel lifts her head to peer up at me.

> @deanlivingoutloud: Yep,

He writes, as if he's heard my spoken thought.

> @deanlivingoutloud: Yep, you must add followers
>   today. You don't have to go public, but all those
>   friends and family members asking to see your
>   profile are getting a big fat YES today.

He sends a series of thumbs up and I can't help it, I send back the red-faced swearing emoji—eight times.

@deanlivingoutloud: That-a-girl! Embrace it like a
  champ.
@deanlivingoutloud: I'm already in your account—I
  can do it for you. You don't even have to look.
@iris_me: No. I should do it.
@deanlivingoutloud: You got this! Rip off that
  band-aid.
@iris_me: Don't you mean shoot yourself in your own
  foot.
@deanlivingoutloud: It'll be okay.
@deanlivingoutloud: Promise.

Dean and I didn't make any plans today—which oddly makes my very normal Tuesday feel horridly dull and empty.

I push my phone away. One fake boyfriend and I'm suddenly lonely without plans. That's lame. "Hazel!" I bellow—as if she were at Gramgram's and not still sitting at my feet. "Should we do something fun and fabulous today?"

Hazel lifts her head from my bare feet, her dark eyes watching me, her head tilted to the side in that puppy-dog way. Holy cow, my dog is the cutest.

An hour later, I am showered, dressed in joggers, a baseball cap, my favorite Converse shoes, with my camera on my back, and I'm headed to the dog park. Yes—really living out loud now.

My car still isn't ready, so we walk. Which is part of the fun, right? I don't have to climb rocks every day to feel alive. I'm not Dean Cooper—err, Dean Cooper *Hale*. I keep forgetting the Hale.

Hazel's pads tap like a quiet base drum and I keep time with her. "We never had a dog growing up, Hazel. It's too bad too, because Ebony and I would have loved the heck out of a pup like you."

Hazel is the best listener. She never interrupts.

"That time that Charlie Melon stood me up for homecoming

—I wouldn't even have cared if I'd had you to come home to. Okay, maybe I would have cared a little." Hazel walks right next to me and peers up at me as if she appreciates my honesty. "I was only a sophomore, believe me I had two more years of home-coming and they were great! I started dating Kenny that year and he was a looker. Whew! He gave me my first real kiss. That was the highlight though. No one likes their sophomore year. You're still figuring out high school and your body is going insane and —*blech*. Just be glad you never had to go to high school, Hazel."

I'm talking and talking, but my mind continues to wander back to Dean. If I had never broken down on the highway that night, I would never have met him. My teeth clamp down on my bottom lip as I think about Dean all wet in the pond, climbing rocks, grinning at the sunshine like it's his very best friend, and sitting on my couch with Hazel's head in his lap.

I'm glad I met him—fake beau and all—I'm glad to know him. And sure, this is fake, and it'll all end once Shelia and Travis have tied the knot. But I think Dean and I are friends now.

I mean, I don't expect him to keep messaging me, to keep seeing me like we have been. I don't see any of my other friends as much as I see Dean... Besides, we've got our backdated pictures posted, so our daily photo shoots have come to an end... A shiver runs through my body. Ugh. That's right—

I take my phone from my pocket and I pull up my Instagram app. I don't think, I just click. Confirm. Confirm. Confirm. As long as I recognize the name—because surprisingly, there are suddenly a bunch that I don't know—I approve it. I don't know how many follower requests I accept, but Dean will be proud.

"Oof." My stomach rolls, that little number on top of my profile page tells me *exactly* how many—sixty-three. I just approved sixty new followers. The thought makes me want to barf.

SEVENTEEN

Dean

I'm on top of Brother's Lookout, when a picture of my dad lights up my phone screen. "Huh," I gulp, "haven't talked to Mom or Dad since I started posting pictures of Iris." They don't get on social media much. So, chances are they haven't seen any of our pictures—until now.

I'm not surprised at all when I answer and Anson's voice rings through my Jeep. "Who's the girl?"

"Hey, Dad." I can't help but smile—he gets right to the point and it doesn't surprise me in the least. Anson's always been like that—and he's honest. I knew at sixteen when he told me that he loved my mother—despite her issues, she'd only been clean for eight months at the time—that he meant it. The first time he saw me he told me I needed a shower, some red meat, and to get outside. He was right. I'd been drowning in depression and anxiety and in what had become of me while in foster care. Anson saw it and he didn't ignore it.

I can't tell you how many times I heard—"You're handling this like a champ, Dean!" Or "You're the rock of this family." Or "You're strong. You're brave."

I wasn't handling it like a champ, I was no one's rock, and I didn't know how to be strong. But Anson took me outside, showed me that there was a lot more to the world than the small hole I'd been wallowing in. He helped me to love myself and my mom again.

"Your mother wants to know why we haven't met her."

"Ahh—well," I run a hand through my hair, figuring out what to say, "she's new."

"New? Those pictures don't look new. I'm pretty sure you've known this girl a while."

Well—he isn't wrong. "Sort of." I run a hand through my hair. "Ah, Dad?" I say, sparked with inspiration. If anyone on this earth could be called a safe place—it's Anson Hale.

"Yeah?" His tone tells me he's all ears, I have his attention— fully. For a guy who didn't become a father until the ripe ol' age of forty-five—and then, his child started out at sixteen rather than an infant to learn, mold, and know—he's pretty perceptive.

I stare out at the view; trees, and rocks, and space, help to clear my head. "So, when Mom wouldn't date you at first, how did you convince her?"

It's not a fair question. Mom had only been clean six months. She was fresh out of rehab, had just gotten me back, and she didn't want any distractions. Thankfully for both of us Anson has always been more of a support than a distraction.

"I befriended her. I asked about her interests. I took up knitting." He grunts with a laugh.

A snicker hums in my throat. I still use a knitted afghan that Anson made and gave me when he proposed to Mom.

"And then of course I adjusted her shift at the station so that she and I worked together. It was handy being her manager and all. But I also learned not to push. She needed time and patience. I took time for you too—that meant more to her than anything."

"I don't remember it taking that long."

My stepdad grunts. "Well, it felt like a long time to me."

There's a short pause and then he says, reading me, "Dean, what's with the memory lane? I've seen your arms around this girl. Why are you asking how to win her?"

"Because I haven't," I say honestly. Iris was special ten years ago and she's still one of the best people I know.

"Your arms around her say differently."

"What's he saying?" Mom's voice may be background noise, but it's as clear as this sunny day. "I knew something was up. I'm his mother and—"

"Melissa," Dad says, a patience in his tone that says Mom isn't speaking a mile a minute next to him. "Did you want to talk to our son?"

"You're in the middle, just—"

"Dean, your mom wants to say hello," he says, interrupting her.

My chest rises and falls—unsure and unplanned what I'll say to her. I've thought about my role and my declarations for Iris's family—not my own.

"Dean?"

"Hey, Mom."

"Honey, how are you? When are you coming to see us? It's been two months. Well, I can see you've been busy and—"

"I'm never too busy for my mother. I'm sorry it's been so long. I'll come over soon. I promise."

"I know you will," she says and I'm punched with guilt. It's been too long. "Will you bring Iris?"

"Oh, um, maybe. It's pretty new."

"New? Your post said you'd been unwilling to share her the last couple *months*. Your father and I were engaged after two months."

I clear my throat—engaged? I'm not even sure if Iris will agree to be my friend once this is all over. "I—well, I reconnected with her... and I've been helping her. The pictures and posts are… newish." I don't even sound like myself. And this is my mother—she knows it.

"Dean Hale," she says—always avoiding the Cooper. It doesn't carry good memories for her. To her, Cooper represents her failures as my mother. She'd wanted me to drop it all together and forget the past. "What's going on with you? And why ask Anson all those questions?"

Was I on speaker? Geez—thanks, Anson. I puff out my cheeks, holding my breath—how to answer that? I blow out the air, squint at the scene ahead and run a hand over the back of my clammy neck. "Well, I'm pretty sure I like Iris more than she likes me."

"Not possible. You are my favorite human. You're the most handsome man—George Clooney has nothing on you. You're exciting and fun and kinder than Mother Teresa."

"Mom—" I moan, knowing how she gets—that, and it feels wrong to lump me in with Mother Teresa. I'm no saint.

"What?" she snaps "Prove me wrong, Dean? You just try, because I am right and you are—" She sounds as if she'll burst into tears any second—so I do what I've always done when Mom is on the verge of tears, I rile her up. It's a good distraction.

"It's just—who is George Clooney?"

My mother sucks in a breath, horrified, as if I've cursed straight in the Pope's face. "Where did I go wrong?" she says and that's when I know she's playing along with me.

"It must have been the lack of Ocean's Eleven in my life."

"Ha!" she shouts in my ear. "I knew you knew him."

"You're right. I do. And he is pretty dashing."

She hums a little in my ear. "He doesn't hold a candle to my Dean."

I laugh and on instinct pull up my messages—there isn't a new one from Iris, though.

"Dean," Mom says.

"Yeah?"

"Just be yourself, darling. Don't try so hard. You are the best and anyone worthy of you will see that."

"Thanks, Mom."

And then in my ear, she bellows, "Anson! Come say goodbye. Tell Dean he's wonderful."

"Bye!" I hear my stepdad yell. "You're gonna kill it, Son."

"Anson Hale!" Mom moans.

"It mean he's the best. It's what the kids say."

"They do not say that," Mom scolds.

"Bye," I call, my chest swelling with laughter and luck—I'm pretty lucky to have two parents who love me like they do. I press end as my mom continues to scold Anson on his use of the word *kill*.

EIGHTEEN

Iris

I'm staring at Dean's newest post, rocks and trees, even a few patches of snow. I'm trying to figure out where he is when a drop down tab tells me that Dean is messaging me.

> @deanlivingoutloud: I'm headed back up your way.
> Wanna grab dinner?

"Wait, is this a real date or a fake date?" I shake my head. "Why does it have to be a date at all?" I'm going to puncture my lip if I bite down any harder.

Iris, I say, pretending I'm Ebony, *do you want to have dinner with Dean?*

"I do," I say aloud—to my imaginary sister sitting next to me. Imaginary Ebony says—*Then, stop overthinking it.*

"Great advice, Sis."

> @iris_me: Sure. What time?
> @deanlivingoutloud: I'm going to the Humane Society
> at four. After?

@iris_me: Humane Society?

@deanlivingoutloud: I wondered how long that would
take you...

@deanlivingoutloud: Wanna come?

Goosebumps rise on my arms. I do. I *really* do.

@deanlivingoutloud: Hazel is invited too. You don't
even have to pose for a picture with me. This is
just for fun. So, do you want to join me?

I can't decide how I feel about that. In an awkward, I'd-
never-tell-a-soul way I like posing for pictures with Dean. But he's
inviting me somewhere, knowing no one else will learn about it.
It's not a picture to post. And I like that idea even more.

@iris_me: I do.

My reply hits way too close to Shelia's proposal comment and
now I want to crawl under that boulder I climbed and die. But
instead, I do what I'm extra good at—and make it more
awkward...

@iris_me: Want to go.

@iris_me: With Hazel.

@iris_me: And you.

@iris_me: She'll love it.

@iris_me: Thanks.

@iris_me: It's a date—

Whew. At least I catch myself before sending that last
message. Instagram really should create some type of—*they haven't
seen your awkward DM yet, go ahead and delete it*—button.

Dean doesn't acknowledge my ramble and I think... maybe it

doesn't look as ridiculous on his end as it does on mine. Maybe Instagram does have a filter for awkward girls like me.

@deanlivingoutloud: Pick you up at eleven.

I repress the urge to write back—gotcha, sweet, don't be late —you know, all of the loony things going through my head. Because why write just one? See? This is why I don't do social media. You say something stupid and people forget it or they think maybe they remembered it wrong. Or you can say—*I said nothing of the sort*—in a British accent of course, and they can't prove you wrong.

But, you type out your crazy thoughts and feelings, hit post and it *never* goes away! It's out there, showing the world how zany you are whether you want it to or not. Maybe you've changed your mind! Like the time I said Oreos dipped in milk was disgusting and left chunks of soggy ick in your drink. Did I make a huge, ridiculous fuss before actually trying it? Yes, I did, but now I can dip my Oreos in milk all I want—even out in public. There's no proof that I ranted.

A new message from Dean brings me back to the present.

@deanlivingoutloud: You might not want to wear your Converse. You don't want to get anything on your favorite shoes.
@iris_me: All of my shoes are Converse.
@deanlivingoutloud: For real? Not even a set of high heels?

Might as well be honest,

@iris_me: Not one.
@deanlivingoutloud: Interesting. Hopefully you have an old pair that you don't mind getting dirty.

NINETEEN

Dean

D id I call my friend who owns the Humane Society and set up a time to volunteer just so I could invite Iris to come with me? *Maybe.*

But our backdated pictures are taken and posted. I needed an excuse. And sure, we should be posting a photo every few days to keep up on our charade, but we didn't need one today. And yet, I yearn to see her. I miss her.

As I make the hour and forty minute drive up to Ft. Collins— again, I contemplate getting a cheap apartment there. I could afford it and it might be cheaper than gas. That's when I remember that my relationship with Iris is *fake.* It's temporary. It isn't something that she plans to continue.

I haven't had a girlfriend in three years. I've focused on my career, building my followers and giving them content to keep them coming back. A relationship hasn't been a priority or even on my mind really. Yet suddenly—it's on my mind all of the time.

The problem is, the imaginary silhouetted woman sitting across from me at dinner always turns into a pretty petite brunette with wavy hair and the clearest blue eyes I've ever seen.

Iris is back in my life—only this time I'm someone who might deserve her.

My nerves start to jolt, knowing I'll be seeing Iris soon. I'm anxious, and if I'm honest with myself, I'm hoping to impress her. Mom told me not to try too hard—but that's what I want to do, *try*.

Hazel must hear my Jeep, because her head pokes through the curtains in Iris's living room and I can see her tail wagging in the shadows. She knows I'm here.

Anson said he made time for me—he did, and I liked him almost immediately. He was so real, flawed and good, all at the same time. He worked hard and he made sacrifices. I've never seen him look at a bottle of alcohol. Having a drink was never more important than mom.

I make time for Hazel… she likes me. I'll sit on the ground and play with Patty or her rope… though it's not going in my mouth… I'm not as good as Iris. Still, Hazel likes me. Is that the same?

I'm still pondering this when a, "Hey you!" from next door startles me. I slap my chest and whip my head around to find Georgia, Iris's grandmother in black leggings, stretched thin over her wide hips, and a florescent pink T-shirt, the word Johnny bedazzled on the front.

"Oh, hey Georgia."

She scowls.

"Hey, Gramgram," I try again. I hoped I had her on my side too.

She grins, her dark eyes, so different than Iris's, beaming. "I've been watching you on the Instagram."

"Oh yeah?" I lean against the short front fence separating Iris's home from her grandmother's.

"Yeah. Don't tell Iris I got it. She'll only worry. But I like it. I'm following you and Johnny."

"Isn't he… uh—"

"He must post from heaven because there's a new one every day."

I nod. "Okay then. Cool."

Gramgram sets a hand to her hip. "You're a little daredevil, aren't you, Dean."

I shrug and stand straight. "I like the outdoors. I like wind and snow and sun on my cheeks."

"Daredevil and maybe a closet poet. You and Johnny would have been friends," she says—like it's a fact, and maybe she'll even introduce us if I'm lucky.

I just laugh—a little forced, because I'm not sure what else to say.

"I thought you two were taking a couple days off from fake dating." She gives the word fake air quotes.

"Oh," I run a hand through my thick hair, my nerves back to bungee jumping again. "Well, I'm helping at the Humane Society here and I thought Iris might want to come along."

"Ooo," she says, brows raised and voice low, "good one. She's also a sucker for ice cream—take her out to dinner, but make it ice cream and she'll be putty in your hands."

I clear my throat. Are Gramgram and I conspiring? Is this for real? Or a test? I'm not sure what the right response is.

She only grins, ear to ear. I can see her molars she's smiling so big at me.

Hazel whines inside the living room, able to see me through the window, but I haven't come in yet. It's loud and I'm hoping Georgia has heard it too. "Well, I should probably—" I throw my thumb over my shoulder.

Gramgram cups her hands around her pursed lips and mouths the word, *ice cream,* before waving me on. I nod once her way, and then, for the second time, I walk straight into Iris's house.

Iris stands in her living room, I think maybe watching me out the window with Hazel. "You really don't know how to knock, do you?"

"I—sorry, I was talking to your grandma, but I could hear Hazel and—"

Her not so scary scowl softens. My dad is a genius, I may have been the key for him, but Hazel is the key for me!

"And, yeah, I couldn't keep her waiting. Hey girl," I add, looking at the wiry haired pup. She smiles up at me and jogs over for a scratch behind the ear. I rub her head and her back leg starts to twitch. "That's the good stuff, huh?"

Like supersonic laser beams, I feel Iris watching me. "You're making me wonder if I should start locking my door. You might come over in the night and steal my dog."

I stand straight, brows pinched, and stare at her. Swooning Hazel plots forgotten. "You don't lock your door at night?"

Her pink lips purse. "I do."

"You better." I shake my head. "And during the day too. I'm the last person to be worried about. But you're single and alone and too attractive for your own good. There are creeps out there Iris." I can't help but picture the way she tripped over to my friend, Darrin, and declared him her boyfriend.

She studies me like she can't believe what I just said—and she probably can't. Did I just mansplain to her about creeps who prey on women? That will win her heart—no doubt about it.

We're staring at one another—and I have no idea how to talk my way out of this one when Hazel stands from her seated position in front of me and barks once.

My hand smacks to my heart again. Georgia called me a daredevil, but twice in the last ten minutes I've grabbed my chest like a kid inside their first haunted house.

Iris's lips pull up at the corners and she breathes out a small snicker. "Someone must be at the door."

And then a knock clammers at the front entrance.

"You startle easily," she says, a playful grin on her lips. She walks past me—her floral scent leaving a trail behind her. She doesn't even look out the peep hole before opening. And I am seriously tempted to give her another lecture on protecting herself.

A man in a baseball cap and holey jeans stands on the other side. My sudden urge to be Captain America whenever Iris is around has me moving right beside her.

"Door dash," he says, pulling his cap down low, his jeans are stained with something dark and brooding... Is that blood?

I've door dashed plenty—don't they leave it on the step? I don't trust this guy—with his dirty jeans and suspicious knocking.

"Ebony says—" he peers down at a sticky note attached to the box, "here is your hug." He holds out a bakery box. "I told her I'd write a note. She wanted it stated." He shrugs, waiting for Iris to take the pink rectangular box.

"Thanks," she says. "Oh, let me grab some cash."

I'm certain that Iris's sister already tipped this guy, but he's still waiting. This is exactly the kind of guy I'm talking about—some random dude knowing where Iris lives—not cool.

"I got it," I say, digging into my pants pocket.

Pretty blue gems beam up at me. "Thanks." Iris heads inside and I slap a five into the guy's hand, doing my best to grimace at him. Hazel stands beside me and I swear she grimaces too.

He shakes his hand, my slap harder than he expected. Good —I hope it stings.

"We both live here," I say to him pointing to me and then Hazel who is showing the delivery guy all of her teeth.

His shoulders stiffen at the sight of Hazel. "Cool," he says as he backs his way out. Hazel and I watch him until his backside hits the fence.

I shut the door behind me and take one long blink—what exactly just happened? Did I just threaten the door dash guy? *Nooo*, not threaten. Sure, I gave him false information, but Iris and I have been doing a lot of that.

I follow Hazel into the kitchen where Iris is cutting the biggest chocolate chip cookie I've ever seen in two. "Here," she says handing me half on a napkin.

"Oh. Thanks. A hug from Ebony?"

"Yeah." She smiles down at her half, her blue eyes shining with moisture. "She sends me things occasionally. Last week she sent me a hug in the form of caramel chocolate brownies." She sniffs, and I fear for a minute that she's going to start crying.

"Hey, you okay?"

"Yeah," she says again. Then swallowing, she peers back at me. Her head lilts to the side and a small sigh falls from her chest. "I miss my sister."

"I bet." I'd like to wrap an arm around her or both arms, really, as tight as I can, but we aren't taking pictures today. So, that might be unwelcome. No, instead we're friends—err—or at least I am attempting a day as actual friends.

Hazel whines at our feet and Iris peers down at her. "It's chocolate chip. You know you can't have chocolate." Her face is a guilty shade of pink, though. "I'm sorry, girl."

Hazel whines again.

"I agree," Iris says. "It was very rude of Ebony to not send you anything."

I cough on a laugh.

"What?" Iris says, as if talking to her dog like a child who understands every word is perfectly normal.

"Nothing."

One of her hands slides to her slender hip and I laugh again —though my eyes linger on Iris's curves far too long.

"You just understand each other better than you should," I say.

"We understand each other exactly as we should."

"Of course you do." I want to intertwine my fingers with Iris's, kiss her soft palm, and tell her that she is strangely adorable. But I don't—I'm not sure she'd take that as the compliment I mean it as, and there's a good chance she'd kick me out or find her pepper spray. So, I reach down and caress Hazel on the head, leaving her with a kiss between the eyes.

I stand back up and Iris stares at me like I've just saved a litter of kittens from a burning building. And I'm reminded—*Hazel is the key*. I guess it's a good thing I like Hazel and my instincts tell me if I can't hold Iris's hand for real, then I'll snuggle up to her pup, and use my excuse as her fake boyfriend to steal any moment I can.

TWENTY

Iris

Dean Cooper…Hale just kissed my dog and earlier, he called me *attractive*. My throat is tight and my nerves are bouncing off the bones inside my body as I recall his words, his worry over me. What. Is. Happening?

"Ready to go?" he says, but I'm frozen, staring, unblinking and lost in my own thoughts. "Iris?"

"What are we doing here?" I say, my head speaking out loud before my mind can think through the words.

The skin on his forehead wrinkles. "Uhh—Humane Society?"

"Right. Right." That's totally what I meant. I wasn't asking what HE and I are doing? I wasn't asking if all this fake dating was getting his head muddled—like it is mine. "Let me change my shoes."

He looks down at my feet. "Black Converse high tops again?"

I would be barefoot except that I've already been over to Gramgram's today. "They're my fav. I can't get them dirty."

"I think I could have guessed that," Dean says, his cheeks blossoming into cherries with his smile.

I scurry back to my room and change into my holey, gray, pull ons—still Converse—yes, I have a problem. I grab Snappy, snug in my camera pack, and start back for Dean. "Ready," I say, hoping he'll forget my odd question from before. I'm afraid I'm just a book to be read—a large print, easy-reader. Hopefully Dean won't want to pick me up and read. It terrifies me what he might discover.

But really and truly—I mean, deep down—I do not have feelings for Dean Cooper—*Hale*! I can't… it's been two weeks since we've met. I think I am a puddle of emotion because back in school I had a friend named Coop. I haven't thought of him in years, but since meeting Dean *Cooper*, Coop has surfaced to the top of my memories more than once. That—and Dean didn't introduce himself as Hale until recently. Weird right? Maybe it's just new. Maybe he isn't used to it yet.

Anyway—I don't have feelings for Dean. Forget what I told Ebony. I'm sure that I don't. It's just all these fake pictures and outings—they're confusing my head and making me think that I like him, that in some strange universe, he could like me.

"Iris?"

I blink waking from my thoughts, standing at the end of the hallway with Dean watching me. Yep—he's reading me.

"You're zoning out again—you okay?"

"Whew!" I blow out an exhausted cry-like breath. "You know, I'm tired. I didn't sleep great. I am a little zony today." What does that even mean? Zony? Does that word have a definition? Is it in the dictionary? How do you spell it? With an e? Or without?

"Do you still want to go?" Dean's head dips to see me better.

"Oh yeah! I'm fine!" I shout, because I'm doing it again. Zoning. I'm zony… Definitely no e. That, and I'm anxious. I have no desire to sit at my house and watch TV or convince Gramgram to play checkers with me.

I want to go out. With Dean.

"Are you ready to make friends, Hazel?" He pats Hazel's

head and she falls to the ground, as if she's fainted, belly up, ready for a rub down. Dean complies and scratches my griffy girl's belly until she's practically purring.

I crouch down and without asking or thinking—just wanting to preserve, I snap a picture. Dean's eyes flick up to mine. He doesn't complain or ask why. He just grins and I sort of melt inside.

Crap. I *might* have feelings for my fake boyfriend. All that crap about pictures and outings confusing my head was just that —*crap*. I am *not* confused. I'm pretty sure I'd be okay having Dean Hale's babies. Ugh. It's really bad for my sanity to have feelings for my fake boyfriend.

Five minutes later, we're loaded in Dean's Jeep and I'm breathing semi-normal. Hazel sits on the backseat—used to our outings by now, her head visible in the rearview mirror.

"So, how are we helping?" I ask—I need to occupy my mind with something else.

"We get to bathe the animals today. My friend, Dorothea, the manager, said that tomorrow is adoption day and everyone needs to be looking their best."

My lips part with a grin that I'm not sure I could stop. "This is so great, Dean. Thanks for including me."

"How could I not?" he says. And my mind buzzes—is that like, *you're so attractive and I like spending time with you*—how could I not? Or is it a—*I'm in your town and knew you'd be annoyed if I didn't* —how could I not? "Iris?" he says, and I realize I'm going zony again.

I have got to quit doing that!

"Well, thanks," I say, my mind blank.

The drive isn't far—so my head doesn't have enough time to get all tangled. Err—more tangled than it already is.

We walk inside the cement building and we're greeted by Dean's friend.

Dorothea is pretty much exactly how I picture a woman

named Dorothea—she's tiny, like she and Hazel could see eye to eye when Hazel stands on her hind legs. And she's got white as snow hair. It's in tight curls around her face and so short that when she turns around, it shows off the tattoo on the back of her neck—*okay, I did not see that coming, Dorothea.* Way to trip me up. Tattooed in a cursive so fancy I can just make out the words, reads: "The better I know men, the more I find myself loving dogs."

I slap my entire hand over my mouth, shoving down the laughter that bubbles at my lips as Dorothea explains what we'll be doing for the next several hours. Dean stands in front of me, but isn't blind to the squeaky noises escaping my mouth. It's better than full on laughter. He reaches behind his back for my hand, the one not covering my face, and I give it to him, weaving my fingers through his. He squeezes—like he's comforting me, as I'm about to have a laughing fit.

I trip two steps forward so that I'm right next to him.

Dean leans close until his lips are a breath away from my ear. "Be grateful you can't see her thighs today."

My eyes go wide and a chirping giggle escapes. I have no idea what's wrong with me. Except that now I am imagining all sorts of quotes on Dorothea's white thighs.

"Control yourself, woman," he says, but the playful look on his face can't be denied. He is loving my loss of control.

I squeeze his hand back to silently say—*shut up! You aren't helping!* But I think it must translate as, *this is fun—keep going,* because the man keeps right on talking.

"Both thighs actually. An elephant's behind on one and it's head on the other, put them together and it's quite the sight."

My eyes go wide and I stare up at him. Squeezing his fingers is not going to stop him, so I let out a small, "Shh," before clamping my lips shut again.

"She tells me her favorite tattoo is on her left butt cheek. But I have never seen that one."

I bump him with my hip and clench my jaw. This seventy year old woman does not have a tattoo on her butt. But then— Dean nods, his smile slanted and mischievous.

"Iris, you and Hazel can work with the smaller dogs—on this side," Dorothea has been talking a mile a minute, but it's my name that brings me back. She's pointing to the right side of the kennel. "Dean," her eyes glint as she looks up at him, "you get the big boys." Her little white curls bob to the left where six larger dogs lay in their kennels.

Hazel pokes her head between mine and Dean's legs and a few of the animals perk up with someone new to meet.

"Tubs and soaps are at the end of the hall. I'll clean out the stalls while they're with you."

I wait for Dorothea to slap each of us on the behind and yell, "Go team!" Instead, she just claps her hands together.

I keep Hazel on her leash and find a spot next to the metal tubs to keep her. I tie the handle of her leash around one of the spouts and like a good girl, she sits, tail wagging, waiting for my next move. "I'm going to grab Toby. Give me one minute. I'll be back." I nod at her and despite that Dean thinks I'm a little loco —I know she understands.

I peer back and she's watching me walk away. Dean already has Muffin—a mutt as large as Hazel, but a shedder—walking back to the tubs.

I'm not sure what Toby is, he's got the face of a Boston Terrier and the black and white curls of a poodle. He hops to the front of his kennel when I approach. "Hey, Toby. Ready for a bath?"

Dorothea is already cleaning out Muffin's shelter and I can't help but think that Dean and I are getting the better end of this deal.

Toby hops in place as I unlatch the lock on his kennel. He's sweet and young and I'm praying will get adopted tomorrow. He deserves a home—little happy Toby. I pick up the pup to walk him down to the tubs and he immediately bathes my face in kisses.

Crouching, I introduce him to Hazel. "Toby this is Hazel," I tell him. The two sniff one another for a minute and then I rise, ready to get to work and make Toby gorgeous. I set my pup in the tub, Dean already has his full of water and Muffin inside. But when I turn on the water, sweet Toby starts to whimper and Hazel paws at my ankles.

"I know," I say to Hazel. "I've got it." I pick up Toby and cradle him like a football while turning the water to warm.

"Do you need some help?" Dean peeks over at us.

Hazel is clearly concerned and Toby is shaking in my arms. "No, I think he's just a little nervous."

"Hazel, stop whining. I've got this." I turn the water off with only a few inches in the basin and carefully set Toby inside. He's still shaking like a fall leaf, so I kneel down and Hazel sets her paws up on the tub. "Hey, look, we're both here. You're okay." Toby hops his little paws up next to Hazels and they have another sniffing match. I rub him down with water and soap and he seems to relax, nose to nose with Hazel. "There you go. What a handsome guy."

"Oh man. We aren't going to come home with another dog, are we?" Dean says. How long has he been staring at us? "Or... *all* of the dogs?"

I let out a strangled laugh. "No. Of course not." Though a string around my heart squeezes. And I think to myself—*maybe*. If someone does not adopt Toby tomorrow there is an 87% chance that I will come back here and purchase him myself. And then a 52% chance that I will gift him to Dean. I'm not sure when a calculator was installed in my brain—but apparently it's in there. Still, Dean would be great with Toby. He's so sweet to Hazel. And Hazel likes Toby.

Not that we'd see the two of them much after Shelia's wedding.

I'm still giving Toby a little back massage when Dean walks down with his next dog. She is as round as she is tall and I have no idea how Dean is going to get her into this basin that's built into the counter and four feet off the ground. She gives a little snort and Hazel jumps to the side, closer to where Toby and I are.

"This is Queeny," Dean says, offering a formal introduction. "She isn't excited for what is about to take place."

One of my brows quirks upward. "Have you done this before?" Maybe Dean and Queeny go way back.

He clears his throat—a little nervous like—and says, "Uh, no. Dorothea warned me."

Queeny's face almost resembles that of a pig—in a cute way. Though—I'm pretty sure all dogs are cute. Ebony disagrees with me.

"So, I'm taking a tip from you, Iris, and I'm going to set the record straight, right off." He crouches down and I'm already pulling out my camera. "Queeny," he says and the sixty pound mutt snorts in his face. Dean wrinkles his nose, but doesn't wipe away any trace of how close they are. "I'm here to bathe you." Another snort. "I'd love for you to be adopted and you'll make a better impression if you're clean. Got it?"

Queeny doesn't have it. Five minutes, and around forty pictures later, Dean is possibly more wet than Queeny, but she is in the tub with water up to her little ankles. She's fought and splashed the rest of the water out of the tub and onto Dean.

For the first time, Dean glances over at me—where Toby, Hazel, and I watch him, my camera ready. He isn't impressed. I can see it all over his haggard face.

"One more," I tell him. "Smile this time."

"Smile?" His brows pop to his hairline "Are you serious?"

"Do it."

Dean sighs, sets an arm around Queeny, and smiles for the camera. I am brave and strong and hold in my laughter until

Dean peers back down at Queeny. "I really really hope you get adopted."

And then, I lose it. I snicker all through drying off Toby. Then, I take his very handsome picture and return him to his freshly cleaned kennel.

"This is fun," I say, setting little Lucky into the basin.

Dean takes the towel in his hand—the one meant to dry Queeny and whips my behind with a snap.

"Whoa!" Both of my hands spring to my butt cheeks. "What was that?" Even Lucky and Hazel stare at Dean.

"Just having some fun," he says and my cheeks warm with his grin.

I take Queeny's picture too. And that's how the next three hours play out. Wash, dry, picture, repeat.

While Dean is in the bathroom—cleaning up, he is a whole lot dirtier than I am—I show Dorothea the pictures I've taken.

"Ooo, look at Queeny. She's never looked so happy."

I laugh. "She'd just drenched Dean. I think she was pretty pleased with herself."

Dorothea continues to scroll through my photos. "And Toby and Lucky. Aw, look at Boomer. And little Molly." She oohs and awes over each of my pictures. "Iris, can I use these? For adoption day tomorrow? You've captured each of their personalities so splendidly."

"Of course."

Dorothea's jotting down her email for me when Dean returns from the bathroom. I've almost seen him more often wet than dry, I think.

"Oh, no," he says. "What are you two doing out here?"

"Dorothea is giving me the name and number of her tattoo artist."

Dean's eyes go wide and he blinks far too many times. "Um—"

Dorothea slaps a hand to her knee and laughs. She points at Dean. "She got you. She got you good!"

"Do you really have an elephant on your thighs?" I ask her.

The little woman stands, her hand on the button of her pants.

I press a palm over her working fingers. "That's okay—I can see it some other time. I just had to ask."

Dorothea laughs again. "You two." She sighs and wipes a tear from her right eye. "I like this, Dean. It's about time you found a nice girl."

TWENTY-ONE

Dean

"Do you still want to grab dinner?" I ask Iris, trying to remember every ice cream shop in Ft. Collins. When did I start taking dating advice from other people's grandparents?

We sit in my Jeep, all finished up at the Humane Society.

"Do you date?" Iris answers me with a question—that has nothing to do with what I've asked her. I'm getting used to this. It's a common occurrence. I'm pretty sure she's having an in depth conversation inside her mind and every once in a while I get to be privy to what she's thinking about. I don't mind—I want to know what she's thinking. And this thought surprises me.

"Uh," I hum for far too long. "I date."

Her stare feels like a heat lamp has been adjusted to sit right over my head. "Do you? That sounded unsure."

I turn the question right back on her. "What about you? Do you date?"

"I have dated."

"You *have* dated?" I'm not sure what that means.

She nods emphatically.

"Okay, who was your last date with? Tell me about him. Why isn't he sitting here with you instead of me?"

She purses her pretty plump lips and stares out my Jeep window—thinking again. "Michael. He and Hazel did not get along."

I hold up my arms like I'm the official X screen for Family Feud. "Oh, that's a big no."

She shrugs one shoulder. "Huge no." She tips her head back. "Before Michael, there was Marcus. He was way too into his coin collection. Like how many dates can we go on where you pull out your coin collection?"

"How many?"

"Three." Her eyes flick to the top of my roof and she bobbles her head in a little shake. "He probably thought that about Hazel, though. I brought her up a lot." She scrunches her adorable face and looks a little like a frightened kitten. "I never introduced them though."

"I mean, in your defense, Hazel is extremely sweet and lovable. Whereas coins aren't that exciting."

She turns, bending her knee up on the seat and facing me. "Right? Although, Marcus didn't really see things that way. And I am probably insane—I love Hazel the griff so much it's bordering on unhealthy."

"It's not. You're fine. And you aren't alone." I reach into my pocket for my phone. "Let me show you something." I pull up the search bar in my Instagram app and she leans closer to me. Roses and daisies fill my senses, drawing my body closer to hers. Everything about Iris is inviting.

"What is it?" she asks with my short pause.

"Hashtags. Have you ever used them? Or looked anything up?"

"Hashtags?"

"Iris, you are twenty-six years old, please don't say that word like you're Gramgram. Tell me you know what a hashtag is." I moan with the declaration, but really I find it endearing how old fashioned Iris is. She's sincere in her lack of social media love and knowledge.

"I know what a hashtag is, Dean Cooper. I've just never used them. What's the point?"

My name is Hale. I want it to be Hale. I love that it's Hale. Anson is the best thing that ever happened to me and Mom. But I love that Iris never remembers to add it. I know it's because I didn't mention it when we first *re*-met. But it makes me feel like a small piece of her remembers me. Dean Cooper—that quiet and sad kid who dressed poorly and probably didn't smell too great from her English class. And maybe that answers my question of —do I really want Iris to remember who I am... It has me leaning toward—*maybe*.

"Here's the point," I say, purposely sloping myself until we're so close that my leg brushes hers. I type in #wirehairedpointing-griffon and hundreds of posts fill my screen. Iris takes the phone from my hands, her soft warm skin sending sparks as it grazes mine.

She scrolls and scrolls, a beam lighting up her pretty face. "These people are as crazy as I am."

"Yes, they are," I say, not bothering to deny that Iris is a little crazy when it comes to her dog. I've never met another human who loves their animal like Iris does. I mean, she isn't one of those people setting a place for their pet at the table, but she talks to Hazel the same way she speaks to me. And Hazel seems to listen.

We sit there for fifteen minutes, Iris scrolling through and staring at my phone, me staring at Iris. Her hair is pulled back at her neck, but sprigs of brown and sun streaked blonde fall randomly around her face and all I want to do is scoop a stray back behind her ear and caress her cheek in the process. My eyes drop to Iris's lips. *Okay*—I'd actually like to do a little more than that, but that's another story.

"Dinner?" I ask again, shifting the Jeep into gear.

Her eyes lift to find mine. "Sure." She swallows and I hope I haven't pushed too much today—none of this is supposed to be real. Even if I have—I am going to save the day with ice cream. There is a Cold Stone Creamery maybe ten blocks from here.

Iris doesn't spoil the surprise, she doesn't ask where, she just keeps scrolling through posts about griffs, occasionally showing Hazel a picture.

I park, shut off my engine and wait for Iris to notice.

I know exactly the moment she registers where we are. Her eyes brighten and she lets out a joyful laugh. "Ice cream? I thought we were going to dinner."

"You've never had ice cream for dinner?" I scrunch my brows like this is a ridiculous notion. Like her Gramgram didn't give me the idea. "You aren't living."

Still smiling, she knits her brow. "Ah, what about Hazel?"

"We'll get it to go. She'll only have to wait a few minutes." I roll down my window halfway and turn to Iris's favorite living being before getting out of the car. "Hazel," I say, talking to her like Iris would, "we won't be gone long. Will you be okay?"

She sniffs my cheek.

"You can have milk bones for dinner. I don't care what Iris says." I scratch behind her ear and she licks my chin. "Thank you," I tell her.

Iris's gaze is soft and almost sad watching me talk to Hazel. She leans across the Jeep console, surprising me with a brush of her lips to my cheek.

It takes every ounce of my energy not to turn my face. Just a few inches to the right and her lips would meet my lips and I'd love to make that introduction. But Iris made me promise not to kiss her. And I joked that I wouldn't—not until she asks me to. But I'm seeing now, that declaration is no laughing matter. There's a good chance she'll never ask.

Iris slams her spine back into the leather seat, the look on her face screaming guilt. Though, I'm not sure what she did to feel guilty over. Then her door is opened and she's outside and jogging to the Cold Stone entrance.

"Be back soon, Hazel!" I bark and leap from the car. I want to buy Iris dinner. I want this to be more than two acquaintances hanging out for the night.

Iris is already in line and I have to cut in front of a kid with his grandma to stand next to her. "Sorry," I whisper. "My date." We're out in public, it's okay to be in character. Right? I slide in next to her—my shoulder brushing hers. "You okay?"

"Mmm-hmm—I just really like ice cream." Her cheeks are flushed a strawberry pink and her eyes are bright and glistening. There's twenty seconds of silence that aren't completely comfortable. Iris isn't saying something—but I don't know what.

I'm thinking about asking her when her phone chimes from her pocket. It's a facetime call and Shelia's name lights up the screen.

"Ugh." Iris groans and goes to shove the thing back into her pocket. I don't blame her for wanting to ignore her cousin. But—

"Answer it," I tell her. "This is perfect." We couldn't have planned it better.

She cringes, but pulls her phone from her pocket once more. "I really hate talking to Shelia. I mean, it wasn't fun before she was engaged to Travis, but now—"

She's going to miss the call, so I reach down and swipe to answer. Shelia's face is so close to the screen that I can just see her nose and eyeball.

"Oh!" Shelia backs away with a giggle. "You are home." Her eyes shift to me and widen. And that's when I see the white strip above her upper lip. "You *aren't* home." Her eyes shift from side to side like she walked into a crime scene and just now realized it. "Eep!" she squeaks and ducks her head out of view.

I look at Iris for help, but she's confused too. We hear a ripping, a crying, and then Shelia's platinum curls sneak back into view. It's clear she's looking at the tiny screen of herself and not at Iris or myself. I can't blame her. Her upper lip is free of the white strip, but it's now a bright red, possibly even bleeding.

"Shelia?" Iris says, her tone soft. "Are you okay?" To her credit she does not mock or laugh at her cousin—and I'd bet money that Shelia deserves a laugh. She's put Iris through the ringer and with Iris's "missing" wedding invite, I'd also bet money that a lot of it has been on purpose.

"I'm fine," Shelia says, pretending she didn't just rip each and every hair from her upper lip. "Just doing a little wedding day prep."

"Hey, Shelia," I say, standing so that I peek around Iris, almost cheek to cheek with her. I am in character after all.

Shelia smiles weakly. "Hey, Dean. I've been following you." She shakes a finger at the screen.

"Oh yeah?"

"Yeah." She must have something in her eye, because she's suddenly blinking rapidly. "You are a regular stuntman."

I wave a hand as if she's paid me a great compliment. "Nah. Just a guy who likes the outdoors."

"Travis did think it was a little strange you just started posting pictures of Iris." One of her painted brows hikes to her hairline.

Iris gulps next to me—this is what I warned her of. But we both knew we couldn't back-post on my public profile. The traffic is too high. So—I've prepared.

"Yeah, well, I guess I wasn't ready to share her with the world yet. I'm a little selfish like that." I'm tempted to nuzzle Iris's cheek or ear or neck... But then, she might smack me and ruin our cover.

"Aww," Shelia moans. Her eyes flick to Iris. "What about you? Suddenly I'm approved?"

"I..." Iris drags out the word, unsure what she's being accused of.

"Instagram, Iris!" Shelia squawks. "I asked to follow you a year ago."

"Oh." Iris licks her lips and my eyes linger on them longer than they should. "I didn't... I mean, Dean," she swivels her neck to look at me. I'm standing close enough to feel her breath on my cheek. I smell the sweetness of her hair and feel the warmth of her body. "He talked me into it," she says.

My skin itches, and I move a fragment closer to her. "Don't be offended, Shelia. It took a lot of convincing to get her to approve anyone." My mind is lost in Iris's skin, and scent, and lips—it's a miracle I came up with a response.

Shelia laughs and dabs at her red upper lip. "I was just calling to see when you two were leaving."

"Well," Iris blinks and her lashes brush my jaw, distracting me further, "the wedding is Sunday. So, Friday?"

"No. No." Shelia waves a hand at us. "You need to come sooner. Thursday at the latest."

"Sooner? But why? I can't ask Dean to do that."

"Sure you can," I say, putting the pieces of this conversation together. Pieces that equal time with Iris. "I can do it. Sounds fun."

Iris peers at me, though Shelia can see her profile. "Sounds fun?" she mouths to me.

I tilt my head and give a false apologetic smile. But I'm not sorry. An extra day or two with Iris is exactly what I want.

"I guess that... sounds... fun." Iris blinks, slow and long, with each word. "We will *maybe* be there." Doubt slams into me. She doesn't want to go. Why would she? Extra time *pretending* to have a boyfriend as well as more time with Shelia and Travis. But what if I could make it fun for her? What if we turned it into an adventure? I could do that, right? That's kind of my job.

"It's settled then!" Shelia claps her hands—her phone must be propped up somehow, giving her complete freedom to speak with her hands. "All righty! See you Wednesday!"

"Wed—" Iris's eyes widen. "Or Thursday!" she shouts just before Shelia ends the call.

"So… maybe I should have asked you before I agreed." I study Iris's face, trying to gauge her expression. But I can't tell what she's thinking—the woman behind us rolls her eyes as if to tell me I'm an idiot and I should have thought of that sooner.

Iris's long lashes flutter up, her azure eyes meeting mine. "I just hate to make you put up with this charade longer." Her gaze casts downward and she swallows. "I never meant for you to be stuck with me for so long."

Is that really what she's worried about? Being stuck with her? How do I say without scaring her—*I want this. I want more time. With you, Iris.*

The grandma behind us is clearly listening. One of her penciled brows hikes up and she stares at me, waiting for my response. Nervous, I rub the back of my neck and pretend the woman isn't there. "Iris, by now, I would hope you consider me a friend. An extra day or two in Tahoe with a friend sounds fun to me."

"Yeah?" her forehead wrinkles when she peers up at me.

"Yeah." I shove my hands into my pockets to stop myself from touching her.

A rough grunt sounds behind us—I'm thinking that means the eavesdropping grandma doesn't approve… or maybe she does. I have no idea.

Iris orders Oreo Cream while I indulge in Pistachio. We sit in the Jeep, Hazel pouting without her promised milk bones.

"She'll be fine," Iris says, pulling out a rawhide from her bag. "Here sweet girl. We'll be home soon."

"I should keep some milk bones in the car."

Iris laughs. "Really?"

"Well, yeah." I shrug and smile over at her. "Hey, I was thinking I could map out a few things for us to do in Tahoe—you could get some great photos, I'm sure."

Iris turns her spoon upside down in her mouth, and pulls it out clean. I watch, my eyes glued to the utensil at her lips. She's thoughtful, so focused on that spoon. "My Uncle Charlie saw the post you made of one of my framed photos—you know on my wall?" We're diving into Iris's personal thought conversation again. "He wants to buy it. Can you believe that? I'm not even sure he knew I took photos and now he wants to purchase one?"

"Oh yeah? I'm not surprised. If you opened up your account from private, to public, you'd get more offers. I'm sure of it."

"We both know I'm not ready for that." Her playful gaze narrows and her blue eyes glisten.

It hits me all at once and the answer is so obvious that I want to smack myself. "But you could make a separate account—one that's only photos for sale or services for hire and make that one public. Nothing personal about it."

She slides her spoon in, bottom side up again, drawing my eyes back to her mouth. *Why woman? Why?* For the love of all that is holy—scoop it in and pull it out. It's ice cream, not your long lost lover.

But then, it isn't Iris's fault that I can't keep my eyes and thoughts from her lips. And my mother would slap me upside the head for suggesting that it might be. Still, I'm too worked up and when Iris finally pulls the spoon from her mouth, I pretend—yes, I am that pathetic—that she's got something smudged on her face. Well, not just her face, but the corner of her lips, right side. "Here," I say and reach across the Jeep console to run my thumb over the space where cheek meets lip. I linger there a little longer than I should—I know it, she knows it, Hazel knows it. Still my thumb has a sudden mind of its own as I trace the line of her bottom lip. I clear my throat and attempt to control myself. "Got it," I say.

Iris's eyes are wide, though she doesn't exactly look at me. "You aren't allowed to kiss me," she says before clamping her mouth shut.

TWENTY-TWO

Iris

"Wait. I'm confused. Was he leaning in to kiss you?"

"No."

"He wiped chocolate from your mouth?"

"Yes."

"Iris," Ebony moans. "You aren't making sense. Why would you tell him—*again*—that he isn't allowed to kiss you? You kind of want him to kiss you, don't you?"

"I don't."

"You do."

"I do not," I groan. But I totally do. I just don't want Dean to know that I want him to. If he knows that I want it, he might do it—simply because he's a nice guy. That would be horrifying.

"Liar," Ebony says. "You are my TWIN sister, Iris Elaine McCoy. I know when you're lying!"

"So?" I bark as if she's accused me of eating all of the Oreos in my own house.

"So!" she yells back. "Stop telling him he isn't allowed to do it!"

"But, Ebony…" I flop back onto my bed, throw a pillow over my face and scream.

"Iris—stop yelling into your throw pillows and talk to me."

Man, she's good at twinning. Tears pool at the corner of my eyes. I don't want to speak the words aloud, but then, I'm not sure Ebony will let me sleep tonight if I don't. Her secret twin radar will keep me up all night until I've spilled all of my secret beans. "What if he kisses me and it isn't great? Or he does it to be polite?"

"What? Iris, are you for real? Sweetie—"

"I'm serious, Ebony! The last serious relationship I had was Travis. I've dated some since then, but no one has stuck. They all find somewhere better to be. I'm just not exciting enough."

"Stop it."

"It's true," I tell her and one tear leaks from my eye, streams down the side of my face and onto my comforter. "Dean is possibly the most exciting person I've ever met and Travis specifically told me I didn't *excite* him. He wasn't wrong. I've always been content with… dull. I'm a bit of a bore."

She's quiet a minute. She's thinking and thoughtful and using her writer mind to articulate what she wants to say next. And I am silent. Waiting for the wisdom of my sister to fix my irrational feelings and help me forget Dean Cooper—*Hale*. "Iris," she starts, her voice so calm and earnest. She should be on the radio, her tone is that beautiful. "Maybe you were content with dull because Travis wasn't exciting enough for you. This Dean—who I haven't met, and FYI have not yet stamped my approval on yet —makes you want to try new things. He makes you anxious for your next adventure. He encourages your work. He loves your dog, for heaven's sake." She huffs out a breath. "Maybe you weren't the problem in all those other relationships, but especially with Travis. Maybe they weren't exciting enough for you!"

I listen.

I take it in.

I don't believe her for a second. "Yeah. I don't think so." I'm the one happy to change into my sweats and listen to Johnny with Gramgram on a Friday night. I'm the homebody, the dog mom, the let's edit photos until the wee hours of the morning girl. "I just about had a panic attack when Dean suggested I climb a rock, Eb. It wasn't even the biggest rock there."

"Yeah. But you did it. That means something, Iris."

I mean, she isn't wrong. I wouldn't have climbed anything for Travis, even if he'd insisted.

"Now," she barks, "stop telling him he can't kiss you!"

Maybe she has a point. "Okay," I tell her. "I will not say that again."

She moans a little and suddenly I can hear the click-clack of her keyboard, she's typing. "Really, it's too late."

I sit up on my elbow and scowl at my phone. "What do you mean?" Because we both know that deep down I *do* want that kiss, even if I'm not willing to speak the words out loud. I'm just in denial. At least until you take the possibility away—*Ebony*—and then I might fight you for it.

"I'm only telling you this because you need to know. You've said it too many times. You want a kiss? Then you will have to be the one to kiss him, Iris."

"What? Like I will have to initiate it?" Just the thought sends my nerves into a frenzy.

"Yes." Her fingers click-clack over her keyboard. "And probably more than initiate it, you'll just have to lay one on him."

"I can't do that!" I sit up and wheeze in a breath. Hazel lifts her sleepy head from her dog bed on the other side of my end table. "What if he doesn't really want to be kissed and then I just force myself on him?"

"I don't know what to tell you, sister." She's in speed mode, now. How does she write and talk to me at the same time? Is that even possible? Is my fake boyfriend going to come out in the next sports story for the Seattle Times? "But before you go too far, remember I haven't met him yet."

"I know," I moan, I can't stop thinking about what she's said —me initiate a kiss with Dean? Can I even do that? I'm not sure I'm brave enough.

"It's the rule, Iris. I'm serious. You aren't allowed to give me a brother-in-law until I've approved of him as your twin."

"Oh my gosh, Ebony! You're trying to turn my fake boyfriend into my fake husband. Stop it." I run a hand over my head, sweat pools where my skin meets hair. My sister is stressing me out. "You're working and I need to go."

"Fine—but I never approved of Travis! I get my say this time," she shouts just before I hit end on our call.

I spend the rest of the night editing photos from the Humane Society. I email my favorites over to Dorothea and then surprisingly—I post a few on Instagram, three of the dogs, Muffin, Toby, and Lucky after their baths, and one that Dorothea insisted on taking of Dean and me. He's crouched next to Muffin and I'm stooped next to him, holding little Toby. We aren't posing— well, not in the sense that we have been. And our smiles are bigger and more genuine. I like this one. It's us, not pretending. I don't even think—I just tap a few times and the photo is now my screen saver.

"Whoa." I take one long blink. "Fake boyfriend, Iris. *Fake!* Bad girl!" Hazel lifts her head again and shifts to look at me. I've never once called her a bad girl. I wave a hand at her. "Me. Not you, Hazel. Me!"

Before I can change the screen, my phone lights up with Dean's face—yes, I sort of added a photo to his number two days ago. What can I say? I'm a photographer. I like pictures. It means nothing. It has nothing to do with the way my insides turn into a firework show when he talks to Hazel or smiles at me.

"Hello?"

"Hey, fake lover."

"Ahh…" I sound like a mouse. All I can do is squeak. *Lover?* Has he tapped my phone and heard every word I said to Ebony?

There's a short pause before he adds. "That sounded funnier in my head. Sorry."

I breath out a false laugh. "It's funny."

"I just saw the pictures you posted from the Humane Society." His tone changes with the change of subject. For a second I thought him embarrassed—something I'm not sure I can imagine.

"Oh. Yeah?"

"Yeah. They're fantastic, Iris. Dorothea will love them."

"I already emailed them over to her. She's using them for adoption day tomorrow."

"What if I helped you set up that business profile tomorrow?"

Tomorrow? We mentioned before he left that we could take a few days break from photos with the wedding so close. But then, this isn't a photo. Today wasn't about photos either. I decided to post these for me. I pinch my lips, reigning in my smile. "Um. Sure. I think that sounds great." I chew on the end of my thumb nail, thankful this isn't his normal Instagram facetime call. "Why don't I come to you? I'm picking up my car tomorrow."

"Great. It's a date," he says. "I'll see you then." And then he's gone.

He's gone. Leaving me to ponder his last statement. Is that just something people say or did we make a date? A *date* date? Not a fake date? Or just a—hey we have a date set… on the calendar… for our plans to work. I have no idea which one it is… but I'm pretty sure I'll lose some sleep attempting to work it out.

———

GRAMGRAM TAKES me to pick up my car the next morning. "How's my friend, Dean Cooper?" she says, brows raised.

"It's actually Hale. Well, Dean *Cooper* Hale." I wait for her reaction but she doesn't really have one. She doesn't care that Dean happened to leave off his actual last name when we first met. "I had a friend named Coop in high school." I don't answer her question, but Gramgram is a good listener. She won't care.

"Oh yeah?"

"Yeah. We weren't the kind of friends who hung out on the weekend or anything. And honestly, I haven't really thought of him in years. We only had the one class together. I probably wouldn't recognize him if I passed him on the street. But something about Dean is making me think about him."

"His name," she says simply.

"Yes. His name."

"And?" She peeks over at me—she's driving. She doesn't like anyone to chauffeur her around. She ain't no Ms. Daisy—her words, not mine.

"And... nothing else really. Coop was quiet and shy. He rarely spoke to anyone. I cannot imagine him being out in public like Dean is. But then, I knew him a long time ago and really, I didn't know him well."

"It's funny the things that bring back memories. The older you get the more triggers there will be and the more stories you'll have to tell."

"I don't have any stories." I smile and peer down at my lap. "Just someone I haven't thought of in a long time."

She nods. She's great like that. She'll voice her opinion night and day, but she can listen too. She doesn't care that I don't have a reason for my walk down memory lane, she's okay with me just voicing my thoughts out loud. I've always loved that about Gramgram. It's why I've often shared my feelings with her.

"And our Dean? How is he?"

I shift in my seat. "He's fine, but he isn't *ours*, Gram. You remember that this isn't real, right?"

"It feels pretty real to me." She smiles, like maybe she's had too much to drink or she's remembering something sweet. "I like him." She pulls into the auto shop. "I say we keep him."

"Gram!" I stiffen my back and glare over at her. "We can't just keep a person. That isn't how it works."

She chuckles and her very large bust—that I did not inherit, by the way—jiggles with her laughter. "Oh Iris." She wipes a tear from her eye. "I knew you liked him too."

"I didn't say that. I said we can't keep him."

"I heard, honey. I heard all the things you chose not to say too." Gramgram winks at me. She's parked and when I don't move, she nods her head toward the door. She'll wait while I give the mechanic one of my kidneys to get the Volvo back.

I almost hate sharing this next part with her—especially with her seeing right through me. It's one thing to tell her all the thoughts in my head, it's another for her to start guessing them. I hold to the open car door and shuffle my feet on the wet concrete —it rained this morning. "I'm going to Dean's house in Evergreen, now that my car," aka Daredevil, "is fixed. Do you mind having Hazel over?"

"She's not invited to Dean's?" The good thing about Gramgram, she doesn't gloat—at least not with something as sensitive as this.

"I don't know. I've never been to Dean's place. I'm not sure it's pet friendly. You know?"

"He wouldn't mind," she says, as if she's known Dean his whole life—she knows him, his house, and his desire for shoes on or shoes off.

"Well, I'll wait until he invites her."

"Okay. No trouble, honey. You two have fun plans?" Her eyes twinkle with mischief. I don't miss how her brows bounce with the question.

"No, Gram. We're just working. Dean thinks I should start a business profile." I shake my head. I'm still unsure.

"I thought your father mentioned that once too."

The nerves in my skin all start twitching. "He might have."

"And Ebony."

"Maybe."

"I'm pretty sure you ignored them." She taps her chin as if she's really thinking hard now.

I throw up my hands. "This is Dean's business, his livelihood. He knows a lot more than the rest of us. I just want to hear him out. I haven't made any decisions." I sound like he might be talking me into joining a cult and I'm a touch defensive about it.

"All right." Gramgram purses her lips as if she wants to say something but won't.

I don't ask, because right now I don't want any more of her insights. "See you tonight. Thanks for watching Hazel!" I shut the door before she can offer her own goodbye... and then I feel like a total jerk. So, I walk around to the driver's side.

She rolls down her window. "Forget something?"

"Yeah." I lean in and kiss her cheek. "I love you, Gramgram." I stand straight, feeling a little less like a heathen.

"Love you too, baby girl!" Gram yells. "Have fun! Go get him!"

A flush warms my cheeks. I'm warmer than a campfire in the desert. I scan the parking lot, but only a handful of people have heard her and they don't seem to care. At least no one is rushing up asking me if I'm falling for my fake boyfriend—so that's a plus.

My little Daredevil Volvo never looked so good! I think the guys in the shop may have even given her a wash. I slide into the driver's seat. She smells like a mixture of my rose body wash, the vanilla air freshener still swaying from the rearview mirror, and a strange musk that must belong to the guys who worked on her. "I've missed you, baby!" I run a hand over the passenger seat and for a moment I don't even care that she cost me everything Shelia plans to pay me plus a little extra.

I type Dean's address into my GPS and since he asked, I send him a DM.

@iris_me: Leaving Ft. Collins.
@deanlivingoutloud: Perfect. I'll be waiting.

"I'll be waiting." I nibble on my bottom lip and start out for I25. "I'll be waiting," I say again, glancing back down at the screen that has yet to go dark. "As in, you'll be here soon, Iris, and I won't ditch you, I'll be waiting right here for you." Another glance… but this time the screen has gone black. I tap the screen and it lights with Dean's message, still there, I haven't switched back over to my GPS yet. I glance once, then twice. I'm pretty sure if I keep looking at it, it will tell me more. It'll explain what he meant. "Or," I say, my voice almost a whisper—because heaven forbid the invisible people in my car hear me. "I'll be waiting… I'll be counting the minutes because I am anxious for your arrival. I've missed you, Iris." I shake my head, embarrassed, even though I'm alone. I tap tap again—I don't need to look at the screen though. I keep my eyes on the road and try to ignore my phone in its dashboard phone holder.

But my head continues to conjure Dean's voice. "I'll be waiting," I say, my tone as low as it can go. "I'll be waiting," I repeat, but this time I use a Latin accent. "I'll be—"

"Iris?"

I swerve my newly fixed, and very costly repaired, car right into the shoulder of the highway.

Dean's face lights up half of my screen. The other half is me. Instagram call.

How in the world did that happen? I hit my screen—did I answer a call? Maybe he didn't hear what I said. I blindly hit the screen again. Maybe I can hang up and pretend that we got disconnected.

But I'm driving and tapping and the next time I glance down

at my phone on the dash, I'm still there—only now I have a mustache.

A freaking mustache, Universe!

"Cheese and crackers!" I bark. I'm swerving and tapping and I can't hang up or get rid of my mustache.

"Iris," Dean says—his calm somehow loud above my chaos.

I stop tapping. I stop swerving. I grip my steering wheel like it's a neck for me to wring.

"So, what's up Ron Swanson?" he chimes, his tone much too giddy.

"Ron who?"

"You know—Parks and Rec? Ron Swanson."

I lick my dried out lips and avoid looking at myself. It will only make me feel worse. "Right. Yes. I know who he is."

"So…"

"So what?" I blurt.

"So, you're on your way and…"

"And?"

Dean laughs. "Iris, I have no idea why you called."

Wait, I called him? I called Dean. I called him, spoke in a Latin accent, gave myself a mustache, and then sat here suspiciously quiet. *Cheese and crackers!*

"I couldn't hear what you were saying before."

"Oh! Ummm, I was singing. To the radio. I didn't mean to call." I take one quick glance at our duo of faces and squeak. "Or give myself a mustache. It just sort of happened."

"Oh." He nods in my screen, a cheesy grin on his face. "Well, I'm glad it did. I've got a winner of a screen shot."

My eyes widen and I dart a glance at my dash to meet his silly smile. "You do not! You did not take a picture of me like that."

"Of course I did. My favorite photographer taught me never to miss a moment."

"When did I teach you that… or anything?" And then I realize I'm insinuating that *I* am his favorite photographer. I clamp down on my bottom lip and shut myself up before I say anything else incriminating.

Dean only laughs. "You taught me with your actions—not so much your words. I'm framing the picture of you in the tub with Hazel right next to this one of you getting your Swanson on."

I shake my head, but his words turn my groan into a laugh. I can't imagine such a thing. I glance back at him.

Dean points at me. "Eyes on the road, Swanson."

"You need to hang up," I moan, but my smile betrays me— it's ear to ear. How does he make me smile when I am in my most clumsy moments?

"Why me?"

"Because I can't! I'll just end up giving myself a mullet to go with my stash."

"Ooo, that sounds good. I'm gonna wait for it."

"Dean!"

His laugh rings through my Volvo. "All right! But only because I don't want you crashing. Goodbye, Iris."

"Goodbye, Dean!" I titter out the words, dramatic and annoyed—though I'm not annoyed at all. I'm just a little more twitterpated than before. How is that possible? The line goes quiet. Sighing, I shake my head. "Embarrass yourself, Iris and you end up liking him even more?" Gasping in a breath, every part of me goes still. "Oh, cheese!" I glance over at the phone, but he isn't there. He's hung up and my real feelings for this fake relationship are safe to hide another day.

TWENTY-THREE

Iris

Dean looks amazing in his plain gray sweatshirt and jeans—like he's about to do nothing and somehow he still looks ready for a runway. His dark hair is tousled and he's smiling as we sit at his table and he scrolls through different photographer's profile pages.

"See," he says, though I've been looking at his face, the way his lips wrinkle when he's holding back a smile and the way the sapphire in his eyes glows when he gets excited. "This one has different categories for story highlights. I do that as well. You could do that. It would help people find specific items more easily. But—" he says, lifting his gaze to my face.

I blink and force myself to look as if I've been intently listening to him.

"This profile would have to be public."

I swallow—pretending my thoughts are right with his. "Right. I get it."

"Great. Do you want to get started?" He stands and holds a hand out to me. I'm not sure why or where we're going, but I blindly place my palm in his—skin on skin. He can probably feel the warmth building rapidly over my skin. Any minute now Dean will ask me if I've caught some flu and have a fever—doesn't that sound kissable?

He walks me into his living room and we sit down on his fancy gray futon couch.

Dean's apartment is small, but the building is new and his space is clean and welcoming. There's a small round table in the dining area—right off of the kitchen. The space is open with only a bar separating the two rooms. The gray futon in his living room isn't like any I've seen before. It's oober nice. Like it probably shouldn't be called a futon. It faces the one thing on his walls—a fifty-inch TV. The whole space is cozy and homey—despite the fact that there isn't one picture on his walls.

"Do you have a business name?" he asks, interrupting my thoughts.

"Just Iris McCoy."

"That works. For people who find you and love you—it will be as simple as typing in your name. That's probably better anyway. So," he says, and he's typing. "Iris McCoy or Iris McCoy Photography."

"Um," I process. I take things one step at a time and sometimes each of those steps take me a week. So—when I see him type in the name Iris McCoy Photography on a brand new profile account, I don't think. I lunge. "Dean!" My fingers grapple around the phone in his hands. I crush him with the top half of my body, my feet no longer on the ground, instead they spring up behind me.

His grip tightens around my cell. "What are you doing?"

"What are *you* doing?"

"Remember?" He lifts one finger from around my phone, and since my face is only a millimeter from our grasping hands, he can easily tap my forehead with the pad of his pointer. "We're making you a photography account." He says each word slow, like I'm easily confused and he wants to dumb it all down for me.

173

"But, but——" I stutter, not willing to loosen my grip. "I should think about it."

His forehead wrinkles. "You should get started. We've been talking about it for an hour."

"But—the perfect name doesn't come in seconds."

"But the perfect name is Iris McCoy Photography. No need to bedazzle what's already perfect."

I whimper, but I don't move. If I let go, Dean will act. He is a ticking time bomb—he will blow, and I will end up with a permanent regretful profile name.

"Okay… How did you come up with @iris_me?" He peers down at me… you know, since my head is practically laying in his lap.

I flinch. I would cover my shameful face, but my hands are keeping Dean from hitting the detonator. "I meant to type Iris_Mc, but I typed me instead. I published my account before I realized what I'd done." I shut my eyes and let my head drop, my forehead knocking into Dean's thigh. Oh man, this is close, closer than close. I can smell the man's body wash as if I were the one wearing it. It's like someone smothered me in trees and musk. I'm just drowning in Dean smell over here. Really—not a terrible way to die.

"Do you not realize that you can change that?"

I lift my head. "I can?"

"Yes, Iris," he laughs and loosens his grip. "I could change it for you. Right here. Right now."

I sit up, though the side of my entire body is now flush to Dean's—and I don't remove my hands from his, which are around my phone. My lips pout out… because even though it was a mistake, I don't want to change my profile name. "I kind of like it now."

"Then leave it. But if you change your mind about @irismc-coyphotography we can always change it. You aren't married to it. Okay?"

My mouth has gone dry and I lick my bottom lip, feeling silly about my reservations. "Okay." I'm snarky—like I didn't just make a colossal deal out of nothing. "Who said anything about marriage?"

"Shelia, that's who," he says—telling me I spoke those words out loud and not just in my head. "Here, you hit the sign up button."

His release of my phone shocks me away from the marriage talk. "Me?" I yelp and drop my hands, jerking slightly away from him.

"Yes, you." He snatches me by the fingers and lays the phone we were just fighting over in my hold. "This is your business."

Dean's right. This is my work. My business—and it could be more successful. I want it to be. I can do this. I close my eyes—opening one to see what I'm doing—no more mustaches on my face. And hit "sign up".

"Nice!" he says, raising his fist for a bump.

My heart pounds. I did it! I breathe out, elated with myself.

All the eyes of social media terrify me. But I faced my fear and I took that step forward. I don't high five Dean like I should, I swing my arms around his neck—practically throwing myself at my fake boyfriend—and squeeze.

I would have been horrified by my forwardness, once it settled in—but then Dean squeezes me back. His nose and mouth grazing at my neck, sending sparks and tingles down my body. His arms are tight around my waist and I think I might be able to stay like this, wrapped in his embrace, all night long.

The voice in my head won't be quiet, though. In fact, it's given me a hundred reasons why Dean must be baffled by this joyous hug.

But then, it's Dean. I feel like I know him—after only a couple weeks of friendship.

Still, I'm pretty sure he'd embrace a toothless stranger in the grocery store if they needed a hug.

Slowly—as if I'm trying to get away with something—I move my head back, my cheek a centimeter from his. If I move slow enough maybe he'll forget how I grabbed ahold of him and forced myself on him. But then… this might be worse. His warmth, his breath, it's all so close—his lips, the ones I've told him half a dozen times are not allowed to touch me, are so close. They are a breath away, a flick of the head, a *whoops* I accidentally sat up from our hug and my lips landed on yours.

Ebony said I would have to kiss him. I would have to initiate. It would be so easy this minute. Only… I'm frozen… a frozen chicken… a package of chicken breasts straight out of the freezer section. Wait, what?

Oh yeah… kissing Dean. *Mmmm.* And ugh. What would he think of me? It took all of my will power to click on the words: "sign up".

I don't have the strength to see what kissing Dean might change. Then again, maybe I don't have the strength not to.

"Sorry," I whisper and Dean's head turns a fraction, so that somehow our faces, our lips, and our breath are closer than they had been two seconds before.

"Don't be." The flutter of his eyelashes beat against my cheekbone. "I get it."

But this throws me. I blink and jerk myself backward, officially out of danger. "What do you mean—you get it?"

Dean's hands have slid from around my back to just above my hips. The warmth of his touch seeps through my shirt and warms my skin. My hands still rest on his shoulders and we're like junior high kids dancing our first slow dance—on a couch.

The thought has me dropping my arms. I flatten my back against the couch, forcing Dean's hands from me. "Did you have a hard time making your account?"

I watch his Adam's apple bob up then down. "No," he says and it's almost a moan. His hands come together, elbows resting on knees, his head turned to peer at me. "But once I had a few videos go viral. My number of followers went crazy. I went from the average seven hundred followers—"

I blink slow and long, my head rocking with his words—that's average?

"To nine thousand in a matter of days."

A lump forms in my throat. "Nine thousand?" Have I ever looked at how many followers Dean has currently? I make a mental note to check later.

"Yeah, at first it was really exciting. I was able to monetize videos on YouTube and my social media platforms went wild. They just kept growing and growing. I was even on a couple morning news shows."

I feel myself inching closer to him—like Dean is the south end of a magnet and I'm the north end who can't keep away from him. "What happened?"

"At first I read every comment, every DM, I checked and compared likes daily. And then," he shrugs, "I think I broke."

My hand inches closer to his thigh with a desire to touch him, to take his hand in mine. Vulnerability seeps from every part of him and I just want to offer a little comfort.

Before I move any closer, he speaks again. "Suddenly, I had a hundred thousand eyes on me and it terrified me. I'd walk down the street certain that people were watching me. Judging me. Digging up my past. One little screw up on my end, and the world would know."

I blow out a breath, my chest tight. "Maybe adding a fake girlfriend wasn't the best idea."

He sits up, fingers folded in his lap—I study his strong, calloused hands, still wondering what he would do if I took one in mine. "I don't read the comments, anymore, Iris." He smiles at me, but it doesn't reach his eyes. It's a kind smile—sincere, but not joyous. "At least, not usually. Sometimes, I scroll through and find a friend's name and then I read what they say. I take anxiety medication—which I really should have been on a decade ago. And I like myself. Just as I am."

I smirk, unable to stop looking at him.

"I know it sounds dumb. But it's true. I no longer care what someone else says about me, my form, my outings," his brows bounce once, "or my fake girlfriend, because I like all of it."

I nod. "Me too."

His grin broadens. "This," he says, pointing to my phone, "isn't going to be easy or perfect. But it will help your business. And that's what you need to view it as. This doesn't define Iris." He taps the phone with my new photography page still lit up, on his coffee table. "This doesn't decide if she is good at what she does or if she is loved." His eyes seem to smolder as he studies me. "We already know the answer to that. Okay?"

I can hardly speak. I should have kissed him when I had the chance. I clear my throat, finding my vocal cords. "Okay," I say.

Dean's hand cups my cheek and I can't help it—I lean into his hold. His sapphire eyes hold mine as if we might be able to communicate telepathically. Then he leans in...cedarwood fills my scenes. This is it... he is throwing every—*you aren't allowed to kiss me* into the garbage can. I shut my eyes. My lips primed.

His mouth presses to my forehead... *my forehead*, and I blink my eyes opened, letting out a sigh. How sweet and chaste of you Dean Cooper Hale.

He sits back, his gaze roving over my face and for a minute. I'm sure he can read this simple, open book—*Jack and Jill went up the hill and Iris really wanted a kiss just now.*

"Do you want something to drink?" he asks.

"Yeah. Sounds good." And I need him to stand up, to walk into the kitchen, and to give me a tiny bit of space.

"Okay-give me ten minutes." Dean stands, slides his hands down his jean pockets and walks away. Wait—I was wrong. Come back. I don't like space. Come back!

I shake my head. I am going crazy. I snatch my phone,

huddle up on Dean's couch and send my sister a message, a DM through Instagram, it's open and fast and I know Eb will see it.

> @iris_me: I almost did it.
> @ebony_mccoy: I have no idea what you're talking
>   about.

I roll my head back and stare at Dean's ceiling. Ebony! I growl under my breath and huff out impatiently. Though I think I have time. I can still hear Dean in the kitchen. I'm in the clear. And—he said, *ten minutes*. What's he doing in there? Squeezing fresh orange juice?

> @iris_me: Where is your twin power now?

I very maturely send her a series of eye rolling emojis. She sends me back shrugged shoulders—eight of them. Half a second later, her super twin mind reader has turned on, and she sends a little yellow emoji face with its top smoking. Mind blown.

> @ebony_mccoy: You did not.
> @iris_me: So close.

I chew on my thumb nail.

> @iris_me: I'm not good at this. I should never be the
>   initiator. Of anything. Ever.
> @ebony_mccoy: Yes you should! You can do it!
> @ebony_mccoy: But remember, don't get too
>   attached.
> @iris_me: I know, I know. You get your twin approval.
>   Is that really a thing?
> @ebony_mccoy: It's a thing. You know it's a thing. It's
>   always been a thing.

@iris_me: Now what?

@ebony_mccoy: Kiss him already.

@iris_me: I can't!

@ebony_mccoy: Then tell him you've changed your
mind and he can kiss you.

@iris_me: He'll think I'm crazy.

She doesn't write back right away which makes me believe that she agrees with me.

@ebony_mccoy: He'll know what you want.

@iris_me: Yep. And think I'm crazy.

@ebony_mccoy: Do you want him to kiss you or not?

I feel as if she's shouting at me. A series of kissy lipstick mark emojis follows.

Dean appears in the doorway, even though it's only been six minutes, and walks back into the room. I yelp and juggle my phone as if it were a steaming hot potato. Finally, I catch the phone and hold it to my chest. It lays against me, screen out, and Ebony's name is at the top, but I cover our messages with my fingers.

"What's up? That was fast! You don't waste time, do ya?" I bark each word out, then click my tongue and point my finger like a gun at him. I really need to quit doing that.

His brows cinch—confused at my crazy behavior. Awesome —it won't be telling him that I want a kiss that convinces him I'm nutty. He's already thinking it.

"Yeah, I forgot I already had syrup in the fridge, so I just needed to squeeze the lemons."

My lips purse and I hold in a delirious laugh. I am going crazy. "You were in there squeezing lemons?"

"Um, yeah. It's my mom's recipe. Homemade sparkling lemonade. The simple syrup takes a few minutes on the stove top, but I already had some made up." He holds a glass out to me, but that would mean taking one hand from my phone and uncovering a conversation that I won't allow him to see.

"Thanks," I say, nodding toward his coffee table.

"Sure," he sets the cup down and his eyes go right to my phone. Crap! What have I shown him? "Did you post something already?" he asks.

"Me?" In a blink I flip the phone around so that anything incriminating faces my chest. "Yes! No! Um, I—I don't know."

"You don't know?" His thick dark brows lower, screaming suspicion. "Let me see."

"No!"

"Iris," he chuckles under his breath, "did you post a picture of me? One that isn't flattering?"

"What? No. Why would I—"

But then he's reaching for my phone.

"Nope!" I say, and the teenage girl living inside of my body drops the phone down my shirt. With my blouse tucked in, my phone passes by the girls, two little hills easy to climb, and lands next to my flat stomach, right at my belly button.

A slow smile creeps onto his face, but it isn't exactly friendly. "Iris?"

I shut my eyes and press my lips in on one another. "I didn't." It's all I can say and though my entire being drips with guilt.

He sits on the couch—the ultra-fancy futon. At this point, I expect the thing to fall backward, turn into a bed, and start talking—*she likes you, Dean. A lot. Don't let that "you aren't allowed to kiss me" talk fool ya.*

"You realize I can look on your feed—I follow you—and see what you've posted."

Why am I acting so darn guilty. There's nothing for him to see! I mean, as long as he doesn't make it into my private conversations and read my chat with Ebony. "Yes." I point at him. "Do that. I didn't post anything."

"Then why are you—"

"You have zero pictures on your walls, Dean! Zero. Like nada. That's weird. What are you hiding?" I giggle and it comes out like someone who should be locked up. It's official. Dean doesn't need a reason to think I'm crazy—I just am.

He looks at the wall across from us and the TV that's mounted on the wall there. "Okay, Johnnie Cochran, you can change the subject, but just know I haven't forgotten." He lifts one brow above the other, flashing me a stare down. "Oh," he points to the bulge inside of my shirt that is my phone. "You should grab that before you accidentally text someone something incriminating."

"Ha!" I force out a laugh—because I sort of feel like I've already done that. I dip my hand down my shirt, pray I'm not flashing him, and retrieve my cell. I lock it down—which is what I should have done five minutes ago, ugh—I am so bad under pressure! I shove the thing into my front pocket and grin like I've won the lottery. My nerves calm—a little—and I look back at Dean's blank walls around us. "So, tell me, no pictures—why?"

"Oh. Well, I just never knew what to hang."

"Really?" How is that possible? He has a family. He posts pictures and videos of all the places he's been—really Dean *is* a photographer of sorts.

His mouth turns down in a smile and he lifts one shoulder. "It feels so permanent and I guess I never wanted to commit."

"Aw, commitment issues. Every other man feels your pain." I tilt my head, still looking at the plain white wall.

He smirks. "Help me fix the issue?"

I dart my eyes his way, snapping my head around to him. "Your commitment issues?" I swallow. If I am a Dick and Jane storybook, Dean is a mystery novel.

"Yeah. I'll give you access to my pictures. And you can decorate my wall."

"Right now?" My jitters are going to start up again.

"Sure. You've got four days until we leave for Tahoe. Take all four."

I peer about Dean's living room, already sparked with ideas for this space and the rest of his home—that I've yet to see. Except, I'm determined to prove myself sane—so I'll work on the living room, just like he asked, and nothing else.

"You wanna come back tomorrow?"

My mouth twitches, but I manage not to bellow, *YES, I'm yours*. "Sure."

"Perfect—only, Iris, bring Hazel."

TWENTY-FOUR

Iris

W e leave for Tahoe tomorrow. Dean got invited to Breckenridge to ski with some friends. It's only an hour and a half away, and he's planned to spend the day. He gave me keys to his place—making me feel like an *official* fake girlfriend—and said I could decorate without him micromanaging me.

I never thought he would micromanage me, but Dean's absence does make me braver than before. I show up to his place with frames, photographs printed by my favorite one hour photo shop in Ft. Collins—the quality is still great—and... paint.

Yes, I know we said nothing about paint. But Dean and I have been hanging out for almost three weeks now—just about every day for three weeks. I've spent the last three days at his place, going through his videos and pictures and I feel pretty confident in Dean's style.

I'm no Property Brothers, but I do have an eye for what looks good.

I pop the lid from the paint can to reveal a soft, velvety green called Spring Morn. Even its name sounds like Dean. It's delicate and subtle and perfect for an accent wall in Dean's living room.

Dean said he'd be gone until nine or ten and Hazel and I should make ourselves at home. The word keeps racing through my brain, like there's a never ending track inside of my skull. "Home," I say aloud.

Hazel does make herself at home—she's already asleep on Dean's Futon couch. I stare at her. I stare at the couch. "Home." I clamp my teeth down on my lip and begin. I set my hands on the plush back and arm rest of Dean's fancy futon and push. Hazel lifts her head from her lazy lounge, but stays put.

Yep—Dean's going to come home to a brand new living room. But if his couch faced the east wall, adjacent to the window, he'd have a view of the outdoors and his accent wall. I'm not sure where he's going to put this big clunky TV because I'm certainly not putting it back up. Maybe it can go in his bedroom.

Once I have the futon and his overstuffed lounge chair moved, I get to painting. I need this wall to dry and get a second coat up before I can hammer in any nails.

Dean's apartment isn't huge, so it only takes me a couple hours to paint the accent wall. Hazel is appalled by the smell and has taken her day of snoozing into Dean's bedroom. I'm sure she's on his bed and I'm not looking... on purpose. If I don't see her, I won't have to lecture her that this isn't her house and that isn't her bed—or even my bed. And... I won't be tempted to look in Dean's closet and smell his flannel shirts. He smells so stupidly divine. Every man on the planet should smell like Dean Cooper. *Hale*. Dean Cooper *Hale*.

Geez. I'll remember one day.

I wash my hands, scrubbing the Spring Morn from my fingers. I wish I had more of Dean's homemade sparkling lemonade. I've been craving it at night. Dean said it's a family recipe and his mom might disown him if he gave it to me.

I pout, curling my lip and opening his refrigerator. What are the odds there's a glass pitcher inside that says—sparkling lemonade, for Iris? Not good.

There's bottled water and Gatorade. I grab a water and down it, not realizing how parched I am until I drain the thing. Painting is hard work. Dean better love it. I clench my teeth. I mean, if he doesn't it's not his fault. He told me to put up pictures, not complete a twelve hour home makeover.

But the wall is green now. It's soft and subtle. And man, does it look good. I'm not painting it back.

If Dean doesn't like it, he can fake break up with me and paint it back himself. I snicker at my own joke. But the truth is, I think it looks like him. I think he'll like it and I'm excited for him to see it.

I'm excited to give it to him.

Dean had this amazing photo of Bridal Veil Falls. I wished I'd been able to use Snappy to capture the scene, but he must have used some type of quality camera because I blew it up—big. He angled it just as I would have, with the falls on the right and the moss covered rocks crawling from the falls to the center of the photo. I can see the water running through the rocks as well. I've never been to the Falls, but this picture alone has made it a future goal. I'll get there before I'm twenty-seven! I've split the photo into thirds and blown up each piece in a vertical 18x32. I've printed them on canvas and I'll use velcro Command Strips on the back of each to attach them to the wall. They'll be easy to handle and simple to hang. But first I line them up on the ground, side by side, an inch between each photo—so that the pieces are separate but cohesive.

I love it. Eventually, this will be the only thing on my green wall. I don't want to cover up all that beautiful Spring Morn. However, I do have prints and plans for the white walls in Dean's living room as well as a few of the shelves.

I frame the rest of my pictures. The white walls get alder

frames. I have photos of Dean skiing—though I'm not sure I would have known it was him. He's wearing a helmet and snow is flying with Silverton Mountain in the background. I have a skiing wall, a hiking wall, and a water wall. I also have a small 4x4 photo of Dean with Hazel that I've framed to set on his one end table.

The second coat on my green wall goes on easily and soon I'll be able to hang the Bridal Veil Falls set.

I check my watch—it's almost six. "Time for dinner, Hazel." She's been kind of an angel—letting me ignore her while I work on Dean's house. She hasn't even tried to eat the bowl of jelly beans sitting on top of his table. Thankfully Dean keeps his butter in the fridge—or it would have been a gonner.

I fill two of Dean's cereal bowls for Hazel, one with dog food and one with water. Then, I search Dean's fridge for myself. Oddly—I don't feel out of place rummaging through Dean's cupboards and refrigerator. I find cheese and butter—and with bread on the counter, I make myself a grilled cheese sandwich.

I should feel awkward or maybe strange being here alone—but I don't. Dean's place, though majorly lacking in décor, is still comfortable and homey. I sit on his futon put my feet up on the coffee table and stare at the pictures I've already mounted on the white walls. I'm sleepy and I keep picturing the photo of us from Vedauwoo, on top of the massive rock formation on this hiking wall. It would look perfect right there.

I should have printed it.

I should have hung it… as a joke, of course.

I bite my inner cheek. Yep. A joke.

Because that's not weird at all.

TWENTY-FIVE

Dean

"So, who's at your house?" Andrew asks me as we ride up the lift. Andrew's a good buddy. We ski together every April—it's the best time of the year to visit Breckenridge. In town there's still live music and amazing food, but the traditional crowds have dispersed. Still—the snow is good, even in April.

Andrew and I talk skiing, hiking, white water rafting, but rarely real life. He has no idea what the names of my parents are or where they live. He wouldn't know if I had a girlfriend for a month or the last five years. I just happened to mention—on our last trip up the lift—that I was heading home to Iris and Hazel at the end of the day. At least I hoped they'd still be at my place. Either way, I wouldn't be staying the night, like normal. It was the first time I mentioned someone in my life by name and he noticed.

I like the idea of Iris at my place, making herself at home and including a little of herself in the décor of my walls. I will never look at the photographs on my walls and not think of Iris. I'm not sure what she's doing. I gave her access to every picture I'd ever taken or had taken of me, and free reign. I didn't even have to talk her into it. She was seemed excited.

"Dean?" Andrew combs his gloved fingers through his long red beard. His long hair—orange as a carrot—shoots out from the beany on his head and falls around his shoulders. His ginger brows are raised.

"Oh," I shake my head—in my own world...reminding myself of Iris. "Iris—"

"Your girlfriend." He nods—Andrew and I follow each other's social media platforms, but I wasn't certain he'd pay attention to a post about a girl, about something other than adventuring. "But Hazel?"

"Uh, that's her dog." And then I share—like Iris *is* real life and it's normal for Andrew and I to talk about things. "They're at my place today. Iris is decorating."

Andrew's face contorts—this is not a pleasant idea to him, his wrinkled nose and grimacing mouth tell me that without words. "Are you going to go home to tea pots and rose covered pillows."

"Nah. She blew up a few of my pictures from ski trips and hikes. She's a photographer. So, I told her to pick her favorites and decorate."

"And you don't' think you're getting rose covered throw pillows?" He curls his lip, staring at me. "Dude, you are."

I shrug. "Maybe."

"I'd never let a woman invade my bachelor pad with her pillows."

A chuckle erupts from my lips. "Yeah, well—"

"Well, you must be whipped."

"Nah."

"Yeah." Andrew gives me a disgusted eye—cluing me in to things I didn't know about him until now.

"Believe me, Iris won't go crazy."

"I don't believe it," he says, "send me a picture."

"How would that help? You've never been to my place. You wouldn't know what she changed."

Andrew grunts. "Just a picture of the throw pillows, then." He hops off the lift and starts down the mountain before I can argue that there won't be any pillows at my house.

I follow after him. I fly past trees, brush, and the world. Swish. Swish. Swish. Adrenaline pumping, my body fills with exhilaration and a loss of control that I need.

I am flying.

Though, in every shadow, every blink, every ray of sun—I see Iris. Her soft skin, her tender smile, the way her eyes light up when she's talking to Hazel or figuring out a project.

She can add all the throw pillows she wants.

When I reach the bottom, Andrew's waiting.

"You look different," he says.

"Different how?"

He points a gloved finger in my face and circles it. "Wipe that stupid love-sick grin from your face. I don't know, man."

I'm not love-sick. I'm not even smiling—anymore anyway. "Do you have a girlfriend?" Maybe Andrew and I should get to know each other better—more than our love for all things fast and outdoorsy.

He sneers. I've never really seen Andrew annoyed—we're always having fun together. But I think he's sneering.

Maybe I assumed prematurely. Maybe I've offended him. "Or a boyfriend?"

His eyes roll. "I have a life. I'm surprised you have time for a girl."

My eyes dart back and forth across the snowy ground. I don't even know him. I mean, we've gotten together every April for the last three years. We ski, we play, we talk adventures, but nothing real.

Iris is real—she is my *real*-fake girlfriend. It makes sense in my head. And fake or not, I'd choose her over Andrew any day.

———

IT'S seven and dark when I pack up my Jeep for home. Andrew tried one more time to get me to stay, tempting me with the morning powder of the mountain. But Iris might be waiting for me—I haven't been brave enough to message her and ask if she's still there or not.

I do pull out my phone to see if she's posted anything today. There's a new picture of Hazel—on *my* bed. Her Patty right beside her. I scroll down—once again searching for the mysterious post I'm sure Iris posted. She acted so strange about her phone that night and I could see Instagram was opened—she just wouldn't let me see anything else. But there isn't one. Maybe she got embarrassed and erased it. She was hiding something. It may not be my place—I get it—I'm not a real boyfriend. But I'd still like to know.

I drive seven miles above the speed limit. I'm ready to be home, I'm ready to see Iris. It's only ten after eight when I pull into my building's parking area. There's her little red Volvo. She is here. I made it in time.

I check my reflection in the rearview mirror… but my cheeks are red, my hair is a sweaty mess and I'm certain I smell as if I've been working out on a mountain all day. Not much I can do about any of that now. Iris won't care—I tell myself. Although, it might be better not to look haggard and smell like dirt and sweat when trying to woo a girl.

"Woo?" I say aloud. Did Carry Grant invade my body? I sound like I should be in a black and white film.

I leave all of my gear in the Jeep and head inside, anxious to see Iris. The door is locked—and I admit, I tested it, I might have scolded Iris if she'd kept it open. I unlock and inch the door ajar, ignoring my neighbor across the hall who's pretending she isn't watching me.

"There's been someone here all day," Mrs. Nampton says.

I turn. "I know. My, um, girlfriend has been here."

Her gaze goes dark—clearly Mrs. Nampton isn't following me on Instagram or she would have known about Iris. "You don't have a girlfriend."

"Yeah," I say, just wanting to get inside, "I know."

I step into my home, not looking back.

"Dennis!" I hear my neighbor call after me—she's never gotten my name right. She's called me Dennis for three years.

I shut the door behind me, but consider hurrying out. This isn't my place… but then, it is.

Except there's a green wall—just one—with a massive three piece picture of my trip to Bridal Veil Falls two years ago, my couch is facing the wrong direction and my TV is nowhere to be found. In fact, none of my furniture is where I left it. I walk around to face the couch—no throw pillows, but there is one Iris, cuddled up with a pillow from my bed, shoes off and sound asleep.

Not one fluffy, decorative, throw pillow, though.

It's hard to examine my living room with the woman sleeping on my couch.

Strings of her chestnut hair cover her face. She lays on her side, her face out, her pink lips half pressed into my pillow. My tan cushioned storage box has moved from one side of the room to the other. Inside is a blanket my mom gave me for Christmas last year. She said everyone needs a throw blanket in their living room. And until just this second I had no idea what she meant. I was like Andrew and decorative pillows—what's the purpose?

But Iris's legs curl up and her arms have chill bumps. I flip open the storage box and pull that unused throw blanket out. Making sure my steps are soft and quiet, I walk back to my couch —facing the wrong direction. Although, I do like having the window on my right and I'm guessing when I decide to pay attention to the green wall and the pictures, I'll like them too. But I'm not ready to care about those things just yet. I lay the blanket over Iris. It never would have fit me shoulder to toe, but she's covered.

Her fingers curl around her face. I can see green on the tips of each one, as well as the back of her hands. There's even a small streak on her forehead. I run my thumb across her soft skin, but the paint doesn't budge. It's dried and staying until she takes some soap to it.

She breathes out with my touch, adjusting herself so that she's more on her back and I can see all of her face now. "Dean," she hums.

I sit next to her, draping my arm over her middle and lean a little closer. "Yes?"

She doesn't answer. She's still sleeping.

Like I'm back in Chemistry and she's my experiment, I run my hand along her cheek, seeing if I can produce another word from her lips. "Iris?" I whisper, but she's out.

Her soft skin is fair with a touch of pink at her cheeks and her lips are rosy—always rosy. Always asking me to study them, to touch them, to kiss them. My eyes stay glued to Iris's kissable lips for far too long. I'd be tempted to kiss her now—if she hadn't told me a million times *not* to kiss her. Sometimes her words and her actions don't match—but then, maybe my head is making that up. Maybe, I'm seeing what I want to see.

Still, I bend and breath her in—like she just came from a garden. I probably smell like I just got back from working in a mine. I breathe and lean in until my lips just graze her forehead. "Sleep," I say in a hushed tone. "Stay."

After lingering too long and too near, I adjust the blanket around her shoulders and peer about my living room. I like the green—it's light and blends well with the photos and white walls next to it. I love the falls photograph—I have no idea how she split it into three, and hung it like that, but it looks like magic. It's like the other three walls are themed—kind of like her own living room. Only mine have the places I love the most in winter, spring, and summer. I'm in a few of the photos, but I'm small and active, skiing in one and climbing the side of a mountain wall in Boulder Canyon in another. I'm almost unnoticeable, just the way I like it.

The only thing missing is Iris and Hazel—but then, she has added Hazel. A small photo of just the two of us on a shelf. The only thing that would make it better would be Iris on my other side.

"Hazel?" I say aloud. I'm just remembering that she was supposed to come with Iris—no, she did come. I saw that photo of her on my bed. But—she hasn't come out to greet me. I haven't seen her at all.

I don't want to wake Iris and calling out for her dog—her baby, would most likely wake her right up. I stand from my perch next to Iris, the space around me becoming cold and empty, and go on a search for Hazel.

It doesn't take me long to find her. She's laying on my bed. Right in the middle. Her head perks up when she sees me, but she doesn't move. "Why are you in here and she's on the couch?" Not that I expected to see Iris in my bed… not that I'd complain if I did. My head can all too easily conjure laying down next to Iris, shifting my body so that it's flush to hers. She'd be cold and I'd wrap an arm around her middle, hold her close, and warm her. My vision is innocent—mostly.

I change from my ski pants and layers into a pair of flannel pants, no top, I sleep warm. Besides, I think I'm going to end up sharing this bed with Hazel tonight, it's going to be a sauna—but she doesn't look as if she has plans to leave and I'm not waking Iris after all the work she's done today. "What's wrong with the floor?" I ask her.

She tilts her head, her wiry fur curling around her mouth and eyes.

"I don't blame you," I say, sitting down next to her. "This is a Dreamcloud luxury hybrid mattress. I wouldn't want the floor either." I stretch out my legs and cross my ankles. Which Hazel takes as a sign to rest her head in my lap. I scroll through pictures from today, the ones I took and the ones Andrew shared with me.

There are a few that I'm anxious to show Iris. I like sharing this with her. I should have her teach me—I could be getting better quality shots.

"Iris," I say aloud. Her name is like a prayer. It's like oxygen. "Iris."

The cell in my hand lights with a message request: *@gram-gramgeorgia would like to send you a message.*

"Gramgram?"

I approve and open the message.

> @gramgramgeorgia: No Iris. She isn't responding
>   either.

I read through the lines and send Georgia a quick response.

> @deanlivingoutloud: She's still here. She fell asleep. I
>   didn't want to wake her.

Gramgram sends back a thumbs up and:

> @gramgramgeorgia: Did you feed her ice cream
>   again? I told you that would win her over.
> @deanlivingoutloud: No ice cream tonight. But I
>   definitely owe her a few pints.
> @gramgramgeorgia: Well don't waste time, Dean. We
>   like you!

I'm not sure what to say to that and I certainly don't understand what it means. *We* like you? Is she saying that Iris has feelings for me? Or… that she does? I show my phone to Hazel. "What do you think?"

She whines, but doesn't tell me anything. She is no help, though I'm certain she knows the answer.

TWENTY-SIX

Iris

I wake up to bacon... someone is cooking bacon. "Hazel?" No that's crazy. Hazel could never open the fridge. But then... who? I roll to the left—er, at least I try to roll to the left, but I can't... Flying upward, I remember. "I'm at Dean's!" I never made it home!

I peer around at Dean's newly decorated living room. The one I decided to remodel and then rest for a minute afterward. My minute of rest turned into sleeping... all night... at Dean's!

Whistling sings in from the kitchen—*Dean*. I pull in a breath and resist the urge to cry. I'm at Dean's... in my day old clothes, no makeup, and, ew, morning breath, and no toothbrush. Why don't I carry a toothbrush with me at all times? It should go wallet, cell, toothbrush!

"Hazel!" I whisper yell. She comes trotting in from the kitchen, no hurry, just living her best life. "Why didn't you wake me?" I gripe in hushed tones. "We weren't supposed to stay the night!"

"Hey, you're up!" Dean stands in the living room entrance—flannel pants and shirtless, a spatula in his hand.

My fingers grip the blanket that he must have laid over top of me. Oh cheese and crackers, I'm going to start drooling. I toss the blanket over my head, letting my bare feet hang out at the opposite end—you know, hiding like the mature twenty-six year old that I am.

"Iris?"

What do I do now, pretend I'm in a blanket fort and invite him inside? Nope. Maybe if I say nothing, he'll run back to his bacon and leave me be. I can sneak out. But he doesn't run back to his bacon. In fact, suddenly, my blanket fort moves slow and steady down my face, until my hair is a static science experiment and my eyes are planted right on him. Inches away, Dean leisurely pulls the remaining blanket off of my head. His bare chest with abs of steel towers right in front of my face. I can see his navel and the way his muscles contour around it. Why is his stomach staring at me like that?

Dean sits on the coffee table, meeting me eye level and I bring the blanket back up, just to cover my mouth with its offensive morning breath.

His forehead wrinkles. "You okay?"

"You don't have a shirt on and I don't have a toothbrush." I swallow. Shoot—*did I say that out loud?*

The corners of his lips turn up.

I totally did. I spoke my truth and now he's staring at me.

I work hard to concentrate on his eyes, where his lashes connect with his lids.

"That's right," he shakes a finger at me. "You have issues with nudity." The lines around his eyes wrinkle with the joke. When I don't laugh, he clears his throat and adds, "Sorry—just morning and I—I'll put a shirt on." He stands and takes two steps back. "I've got breakfast ready for you. As a thank you." His eyes circle the room we're in. "It's perfect, Iris. You outdid yourself."

I drop the blanket all together, distracted for a second with his praise. "You like it?"

His grin deepens. "I really do." He starts for the kitchen, but pauses. "There's a plate on the table for you." He turns to go, but doesn't even make it one step before turning back. "Um, where did you put my TV?"

My smile is forced and weak. "It's in your office—that spare bedroom."

"Of course it is," he says without a doubt remembering Gramgram's spare bedroom TV room.

"Oh crap! Gramgram! She'll be worried."

"Nah, she's good. She messaged me last night."

My brows cinch and for a brief moment, I forget the unbrushed teeth predicament I'm in. "Gramgram doesn't text."

"She does now." He winks… Dean winks at me. A shirtless Dean winks at me. What is this? Mornings with Magic Mike?

Ugh! My head is more than a little bit muddled. What is he trying to tell me? What did that wink say? Was it—*haha, Iris, you're so funny putting my television in my spare room.* Or maybe—*check me out, Iris, all this could be yours.*

I blink. Slow and long. It was definitely a—you're so funny—wink. I can't blame him. Of course he thinks I'm a goofball. I am!

With Dean out of the room, I jump to my feet. I am not staying for breakfast—me and my unbrushed teeth. No way! I hurry to the bathroom, pee, run my fingers through my bed head, and gargle a bit of warm water—which does nothing for my teeth growing ick by the second!

Time to go!

I charge out of the bathroom to see Hazel run into Dean's bedroom. "Hazel!" I whisper yell. But she's already on his bed. She loves his stupid mattress. I jog the three steps from the hall to Dean's room and smack both my hands on my thighs, calling to my pup. "Hazel! We have to go! Come on!"

"You're going?" Dean steps out of his master bath—still

shirtless, by the way—a few lathery toothpaste bubbles at his lips and a toothbrush in the hand at his side. "Breakfast—"

"I know! I'm sorry. I'm not packed and we're leaving for Tahoe this morning and—" my hands flail and all I can think is —*you're shirtless and I have grime growing on my teeth*. Thankfully, I keep those words inside of my head. They don't escape and it's a May Day miracle.

"Are you sure you don't want to stay and eat?"

"Hazel," I growl, while somehow keeping a forced smile on my face. "No. We can't. We need to go." To seal the deal, I hop over to the bed, grab my baby by the collar and tug her off the bed.

Dean walks the three steps over to us and runs a hand through his tousled hair, the boulders in his arm distracting me. "Okay. I wanted to thank you—better than just the words thank you, I mean."

I toss my hand in the air. "It's nothing." Then, trying to say goodbye, trying to leave, trying to get the message across that WE ARE GOING! I toss one arm around his neck for a friendly— we're friends—goodbye pat.

But Dean wraps both massive arms about my waist pulling me in for a hug. "Thanks," he says again. "The room is perfect."

"You bet." I pat his back like he's a baby to be burped. Pulling back, ready to escape, I try with my body as well as my words to say *goodbye*. And suddenly, I think I'm French, because I decide to do it with a closed lip, grimy teeth, kiss to the cheek. Only Hazel whimpers and Dean turns his head to look at her, just as I lay a kiss—with my super steroids morning breath—right on Dean's mouth.

His mouth.

Not his cheek, but his perfectly pouty, sweetly soft, freshly brushed mouth.

Yep, his mouth is on my mouth.

No, actually, my mouth is on his. I'm the one who pressed in.

I'm the one who instigated this, who connected minty fresh with unbrushed plaque.

It isn't romantic and it's isn't sexy. I hold my breath, thinking I can keep in the rank. But I know I can't. I can smell the mint from his toothpaste and soon enough I'm tasting it too. I don't know how because my lips are sealed shut, like a manila envelope closed up with super glue. He's not getting in. Maybe, I think, after a solid ten seconds, I should remove my lips from his.

I do. But I keep my mouth shut up tight. He is closer than he should be and his bare chest is making an impression over the entire front of my body as well as my mind. I will feel the softness of his skin and the hardness of his abs until the day I drop dead.

Here lies Iris. She was a lousy kisser and fantasized over Dean Cooper's abs.

Yep. That's what it will say, because I am going to die right here and now and there will be no time left for me to do anything else impressionable.

When Dean doesn't let go of me, I am forced to set my hands to his chest and push him away—only solidifying the memory of his shirtless body in my head—*oh forever*.

"I'll see you at ten!" I practically shout—all while staring at everything in this room—bed, floor, ceiling, everything, except for Dean.

"Iris, wait."

"See you!" I call and Hazel must know that I mean business, because she is on my heels. I snatch my shoes from the living room and dart outside, barefoot. Dean chases after me, but I shut his front door before he can make it outside with me.

I'm in my car and waving before he can make it down the steps of his eight story building.

For an hour and forty minutes—the entire ride home, I attempt to convince myself that I did not just awkwardly kiss Dean Cooper Hale. That did not happen. It was a nightmare and now I am awake. That's all.

As if sensing my discomfort, my phone rings and Ebony's face lights up the screen. I don't say hello. I don't ignore the call. I answer and blurt, "I kissed Dean."

There's a short pause before I can hear my sister applauding! "Woo! Woo!" she cries. "Aren't we feeling brave!"

"I am not brave!" I bark and Hazel jumps beside me. "It was an accident. I was fumbling and scattered! And my teeth are all grimy and my hair is a mess. I have morning breath, Ebony!"

"Ew. Geez. Then, why did you do it?"

"Cheese and crackers! Did you not hear me? It. Was. An. Accident!" I am bellowing in my car—yes, I'm on the verge of hysterics. "And now Dean is *never* going to want to kiss me because I kissed him and it was kind of like kissing a toothless grandparent—all tight lipped and smelly!"

"Calm down, crazy. How do you accidentally kiss someone?"

I pull in a breath, trying to calm my pounding heart. It's going to burst from my chest—which might not be too terrible. I wouldn't have to face Dean again. "I was trying to say goodbye. I went in to kiss his cheek—to like seal the deal, when he turned his head."

"Seal the deal?" I hear her mutter. "Who are you? When have you ever kissed anyone's cheek to say goodbye?"

"Today! Today is the day, okay! Now, stop talking." My car goes quiet and I sit there waiting—because I didn't actually expect Ebony to listen to me. But apparently she's going to. "How do I fix this?"

"Am I allowed to talk now?" she says and she sounds so big sisterly. Did she forget that we are literally the exact same age?

"What do I do, Ebony?" I tug on the ends of my long, unbrushed brown hair. "I should just forget it happened. I could pretend that I kiss everyone. In fact, the next time we're together I'll just start kissing everyone I see."

"Or not." She groans, disgusted by the thought. "You could talk about it."

"Nope! Hard pass. What else you got?"

"Well, don't start kissing every person you come across! That would be much much worse. If you don't want to talk about it, then just move forward. Go with pretending it didn't happen without the kissing everyone you come across part. You're about to attend a family wedding, Iris. You will contract some kind of disease if you kiss everyone there. Not to mention we have a couple of cousins who might creepily enjoy a kiss way too much."

I huff out a breath. "Pretend it didn't happen. Pretend it didn't happen." I whisper the chant. "I am about to be in a car with him for fourteen hours. What do I do if it comes up?"

"You… laugh?" she says, but it sounds like more of a question than an answer.

I have no idea what I'll do. I need to pack—so when I get home that will keep me busy. I'll pack up my best black high tops and my new navy blue dress for the wedding day—as well as clothes, shoes, and toiletries for the next few days. I also plan to start praying. I'll be praying all the way to Tahoe that Dean shows a little mercy and doesn't bring that awkward lip action up. Or maybe the Universe could give him amnesia—just of the last six hours. "What do you think, Universe? Amnesia?"

But I have a feeling the Universe is done making deals with me.

TWENTY-SEVEN

Dean

I've just parked when Iris comes barreling out of her house, bags in hand. Apparently we aren't messing around. I'm not going inside, no small talk, no attempting that awkward lip to lip action again. We are just getting up and going.

She has a suitcase handle in each hand and it's only because she has to pause to open the gate of the little fence surrounding her front yard that I'm able to make it over to help out at all.

"Hey," I say, making sure I smile when Iris looks at me with a scary grin that says—*I'm not awkward, you're awkward!* "Are we in a hurry?"

"Yep! Can't wait to get there! Let's go! Let's go!" She drops both bags to clap her hands and then tosses the medium bag my way.

Sure, let's hurry up so we can sit in a car and wait fourteen hours. It's not as if we'll be doing anything other than driving today. I'm hoping that the prickly thickness in the air will dissolve with a few car games and road trip tunes.

She charges toward the back of the Jeep with Hazel on her

heels. She opens the hatch and tosses the larger of the two bags inside. She tossed the smaller bag to me and I hoist it up as well.

"Two bags, huh?" I'm trying to talk—to say anything to get any kind of answer from this awkward Iris. But she's been on edge since she woke up at my house and sort of kissed me. I'm not really sure you could call it a kiss. Sure, our lips touched, but hers were pressed so tight, I doubt I could have pried them open with a crowbar. So, her mouth bumped into mine… is that a kiss? Usually, I know for sure if I've kissed a girl or not. But I don't this time. Part of me wants to ask her if it actually was a kiss. The rest of me would like to keep all of my body parts.

"One is for Hazel," she snaps, letting Hazel in the back.

"Oh. Right." I run my hand over the back of my neck. "Are we telling Gram goodbye?"

"Already done!" she shouts.

She's in the car and buckled up before I can lay a finger on my door handle. I type in the address to the resort and we are fourteen hours away from a blissfully bumpy few days.

The radio is playing, but there is no other sound in the car, even Hazel is avoiding us.

"So…" I say and I can't help but draw out the word. "This morning—"

"Nope!" At least she's looking at me. "Tell me every one of your favorites ever. *Ever.*"

"Uh. Okay." But I don't know what she wants.

"Favorite candy bar?"

"Uh," I grip the steering wheel. "I guess… a nut roll."

"What?" Her head whips my way, chestnut hair flying out like a Chinese fan. "That isn't a candy bar."

"Sure it is. They sell it in the candy aisle."

The rigidness in Iris's shoulders and back eases. She laughs— at me, but I don't care, as long as she's laughing. "How old are you? Seventy-five?"

"Have you had one? They're delicious. Sweet and savory all

at once." I glance over at her and a natural grin plays at her lips. She stares out the window and props her foot up on the dash.

"Yes. I've had one—only because Gramgram made me share one with her once."

"So, you know."

"I know that it's not a candy bar—that's what I know."

We go through a series of our favorites, things we didn't already know about one another. I even ask a few questions to bring in what I think I know about Iris—at least what I thought I knew about her a decade ago. I learn that her favorite band is now the Beatles—no longer One Direction. Both boy bands, though. I see a trend… Maybe she's ashamed of her love for One Direction and she's giving me her second favorite.

I ask her favorite color—still violet. She had this violet sweater that she'd wear every week when we were in high school. I couldn't remember her wearing anything as often as that sweater and once when a guy in our class called it purple, she corrected him. I don't know why I remember that—maybe because everything Iris did stood out to me. Still, it's just a hunch on my part. But when I ask her favorite color, she doesn't say purple, she doesn't say blue, she says *violet* and I feel triumphant.

Each favorite takes us down a tangent path and soon hours have passed and it's time to stop for food and gas.

We do swap seats so that Iris can take a turn driving, and then start back up again. The next time we stop, Iris yawns and her eyes squint with sleepiness.

"My turn to drive," I say.

She easily agrees, and when I suggest she lay back and rest, she doesn't argue. She reclines her chair and closes her eyes, leaving me with my thoughts and attraction and uncertainty on how to move forward.

I follow the GPS and Iris is still snoozing when I pull into the hotel that Shelia sent directions for—The Lake Resort. It's fancy —even in the dark. I'm already imagining a dozen places Iris will want to take photos of. It's right on the lake too—though it's hard to see this time of night. Her options are pretty limitless. Tahoe is one of those amazing places that holds what we normally think of as separate destinations. There are the snowcapped pine trees, majestic mountains, sandy beaches with a glassy blue lake. All together it really is something special.

"Iris," I say, running the back of my hand over her arm. When she doesn't move, I pull in, park, and reach for her cheek. I could tap her shoulder, but I want to touch her, really touch her. I run my thumb under the soft skin beneath her eye. "Iris," I say again, examining her pink pouting lips and long dark eyelashes. "Iris we're here."

TWENTY-EIGHT

Iris

———

Dean's hand cups my cheek and I pray I haven't been slobbering. Yesterday wore me out and driving today hasn't helped. I haven't slept like that in a car since I was two.

He peers down at me, his fingers still on my cheek. I blink and focus on his sapphire eyes. They're like lights, like beaming beautiful spotlights on this dark night, shining only for me. I press my cheek into his palm and then freeze. Okay—weird-o, that's not normal behavior.

I'm just trying to figure out how to get myself out of this when—*tap tap tap!*

A rap on my passenger side window has me up and if not for my seat belt—I'm pretty sure I would have ended up in Dean's lap. Dang that seat belt.

Shelia's nose presses against Dean's window and Travis stands outside frowning down on me. I'm still not exciting enough for him. Shelia waves and a claustrophobic energy fills me. We are surrounded. There's no getting out alive!

"Hey you!" Shelia sings to Dean through his windowpane.

"You made it! Travis said there was no way you'd end up coming."

My eyes swing from Shelia to Travis standing with his arms crossed glowering down at me. I'm not sure what I did to deserve such crusty looks.

Dean's brows raise and he attempts to turn his lips up in a smile, but I can tell it's difficult for him. He makes a small hand motion that says in a polite way—move, and we'll get out.

Travis doesn't budge from his spot, but Shelia nods and steps back so that Dean won't hit her with his door. I don't really care if I hit Travis. I open the door, pushing out harder than necessary and I hit him in his crossed arms. Ha! Take that stupid, Travis.

Dean and Shelia walk around to my side of the Jeep, Shelia has looped her arm through Dean's and that single action makes me really dislike my cousin.

"Yeah, Travis said you wouldn't show. It was all talk. I told him, I'm following him on Instagram now and the Dean I know wouldn't let me down." She says this as if Dean is here for her and not me. "But Travis said that Iris had made you up!" Shelia giggles while she clamps both her hands around Dean's forearm and shakes. "You feel like flesh and bone to me!"

"I'm real," Dean says with a false laugh. "Let me grab Hazel." He steps away from Shelia, but she holds tight to his arm.

"How long have you two been together?" Travis asks, his lip curled and his brows furrowed.

"Huh?" I'm staring at Shelia with her Hulk Hogan grip on Dean. I pat her hand and offer a down cast smile. "Shelia—you have to let go of him."

She giggles and shakes Dean's fingers. "Right." She gives him a wink and I dart a glance at Travis, his glare is still on me.

"How long? It isn't a difficult question."

"I don't know. What does it matter?"

He lifts one shoulder. "Shelia can tell you how long we've been together."

I scoff, and pretend I'm a preteen, giving Travis a full on eyeroll. "Yeah. *Shelia*, but not you. Well, good for her."

"I just find it—" His shoulders rise and fall and his poopy brown eyes bug. "What is that?" Travis hisses and turns his glower onto my Wirehaired Pointing Griffin.

"This is Hazel," Dean says, holding Hazel by the leash.

Travis's glare whips to me once more. "You brought a dog?"

Hazes snarls and bares her teeth at Travis. Hmm, she doesn't like him either.

"*We* brought Hazel. Yeah." Dean stands next to me and though he drapes his arm around my back I can hardly feel his touch. But aren't Shelia and Travis my excuse to play girlfriend? So, I loop my arm around Dean's waist—he is my "boyfriend" after all. Maybe it's Travis's unruliness, but it fires my bravery and even with the French goodbye looming in the back of my mind, I pull Dean's side close to mine. His arm around me tightens and I feel his warmth through my long sleeved, thermal shirt.

"I knew about the dog," Shelia says—and as much as she irritates me, I appreciate the backup. "She's Rizzo's support dog, so I made sure she had the pet friendly room."

I stiffen at the nickname—something Shelia and her sisters gifted me after we first watched Grease together. I strongly disliked Rizzo's character and somehow it became my pet name. But I don't mind Hazel being called my support animal. She does support me. I feel better whenever she's around.

"I'm allergic," Travis says.

Yes he is, just another reason I love my dog. She is the smartest, sweetest girl there is and if she happens to make Travis's nose swell up and turn bright red—even better.

"Well, then," Dean says, guiding Hazel so that she stands right in front of us, "you may want to back up, then. And," his brows lower, giving him a menacing look, "you will probably need to stay clear of Iris, she has this dog with her at all times."

"Whatever." But he waves a hand and Shelia trots to his side.

They start off toward the lights of the resort entrance, when Shelia turns back. "We're having appetizers and drinks tonight with a few of Travis's groomsman." Yikes. That's a late party. It's midnight. We're exhausted after traveling. But Shelia doesn't care. "Tomorrow you can get the feel of the place and—"

"Oh, Shelia," Dean says, "I made reservations for Iris and I tomorrow. We're going on a fishing charter for half the day. Would the evening work."

Her brow furrows.

"Wait, you did?" I probably shouldn't ask it in front of Travis, but I'm surprised. I knew Dean wanted to play—he needs to sail and ski and hike all in one day. I didn't know he'd be bringing me along.

"What about the dog?" Shelia says.

"I've got a playdate set up for Hazel."

I peer up at him, standing so close that the warmth from his body, like sunshine, soaks into me, his cedar and musk fragrance filling up my senses and making me loopy. "You do?"

"Yeah," he grins down at me and tremors run through my body—ones that will only stop once Dean decides to wrap his arms around me and hold me tight. So, I may be shaky for a while.

"Oh. Okay." Shelia's voice is faint in the back of my mind. Dean is too at the forefront to notice anything else.

His hand moves across my back and slips into mine. I peer at our fingers knotted together and then back to his face. He just smiles, faces forward, and looks as if fake dating is just another adventure.

"Oh, I almost forgot! I've got your key," Shelia says, taking a key card from her pocket. "I can show you to your room."

Travis leaves—not wanting to be around Hazel too long—and I am not sorry to see him go.

Pet rooms are on the bottom floor of the left wing of the resort—I'm also not sorry that the rest of Shelia's family, her parents and four sisters will be on the third floor, right wing.

We stand outside the door and Shelia hands Dean the key. She waits, like a bus boy seeing if we approve or not, and I just wish she'd go. When we step inside, Shelia follows. Ugh. I'm tired and worn from the drive and all I want is a little peace. *Run back to Travis, Shelia! Go!*

It is a nice room though—and Shelia's paying for it. "Look, Iris, a dog bed," she points to the far wall where, sure enough, a new plush dog bed waits for Hazel.

"Nice," I say, trying to be polite. There's a couch against the wall too, a door to the bathroom, and a bed—*one bed*. "One bed," I say and I feel as if every drop of blood drains from my cheeks. One bed!? I assumed we'd have two, Ebony and I would take one and Dean the other. Sure, it would be a little awkward, but awkward and I are becoming the best of friends. We've spent a lot of time together in the last three weeks. Just this morning, awkward and I made out.

Dean peers at me—what is he thinking? Does he think I've done this on purpose? That I'm trapping him into sleeping right next to me.

"One bed?" I mutter.

Shelia's brow furrows and I am about to give up the jig.

"One bed?" I'm a broken record.

"I think," Dean says, "she's wondering about Ebony. She is coming. So where—"

"Oh," Shelia's eyes bat up to the ceiling, "I'm not gonna make the two of you share a room with her. She's bunking with Shandon."

Dean's brows raise in question.

"My sister."

"Right." Dean takes Hazel off her leash—I see it in my peripheral, my eyes are glued to the one bed in our room, blood still drains from my head. Yep. I'm going to pass out. "We'll unpack and meet you down there." Dean sets a hand to Shelia's back and walks her out the door, closing it behind her.

"One bed," I whimper again.

"It's fine, Iris. I can take the couch."

But the dog bed looks more comfortable than that thin excuse for a sofa. I'm so embarrassed and I feel like a twelve year old girl who just got "the talk" from her mom. *That's* what happens in a bed? And my mother just gave me details. *Ew.* I slap both hands over my face, not wanting him to look at me— and still in my twelve year old mode. "I'm so sorry Dean. I'll see if they have another room for you. I didn't know. I wasn't trying—"

"Hey," he says, and his voice is so much closer than before. "I'm aware that you weren't trying to seduce me, Iris."

"Ughhhh," I groan into my fingers.

"Iris," he says through a laugh. My eyes are covered, but I feel his strong arms wrap around me, my face—still hidden in my hands—is pressed into his chest. I know because I can smell every inch of him. His cedar, musky, and manly scent is my own personal incense. "It's okay. You have nothing to be embarrassed about."

"But I do," I say through my hands—I'm not willing to bring them down yet. "I have so much to be embarrassed about. This whole escapade. I'm just sorry I involved you and made you feel uncomfortable."

His arms fall from around me and suddenly his hands are on my wrists. He tugs until he can see my eyes just peeking out. I peer at him for only a second before I cram them closed. Twelve year old Iris is making a comeback! Woo! Woo!

"I'm not sorry."

I open one eye.

"I'm happy to be here with you. I'm not sorry. Or angry. Or embarrassed, for that matter."

I open the other, my brows knitting. "You're not?"

One of Dean's warm hands cups my cheek, only an inch separating our bodies. "I'm not," he says. "Now, I'm going to shower—I need to wake up if we're going to that party tonight." His brows raise and his mouth cringes on the word party. I can't help it, my lips turn up with his playfulness. He lets go of me and I am instantly colder. He grabs his small rolling suitcase and heads into the bathroom.

The bathroom.

Where he will take off all of his clothes and get into the shower.

Naked Dean.

I yelp, clamp a hand over my mouth and Hazel trots over. "A walk?" I say to her. She sits and wags her tail, waiting for her leash. "I'm taking Hazel for a walk!" I bellow. A walk—far far away from naked Dean.

TWENTY-NINE

Iris

Two of Shelia's sisters have arrived already, as well as two of Travis's groomsmen. We make a big party, filling every seat at this large round table. We're just at the resort restaurant and bar, apparently it's open twenty-four hours. It's a nice night and we sit out on the deck—so I can bring Hazel. It ensures that I will sit on the very opposite side of the table as Travis—as far away as I can get.

Dean sits right next to me and slips Hazel pieces of his chicken paella. I don't see my cousins often—and this dinner has reminded me why. Sure, Shelia is a bit clueless, but not terrible—all of the time. Shandon likes to talk—whether she knows what she's talking about or not. She's got an opinion and she won't be done until she's made sure everyone knows it. Sherry complains—constantly. You could seat her at a golden table with a golden fork and have the best chef in America make her dinner, she'd still find something to moan about.

"Do your other sisters start with an SH?" Dean asks, halfway through our meal.

Oof—they don't like this topic. All three pairs of my cousins eyes find Dean.

Sherry rolls hers. "I hate my name."

"This again?" Shandon says. "Just because mom liked a few names doesn't mean that she had a naming theme. It just sort of happened. Our youngest sister doesn't have an "h" and that's proof that it just sort of happened."

"My name literally makes my skin crawl," Sherry says, as if Dean has just brought up the death of her favorite cat.

"It was just a question," I say. "He didn't mean anything by it."

"At least they answer questions." Travis's glare has turned into an Iris laser beam. It is on me at all times. Its entire goal in life is to open me up like a can of lying worms.

My heart thumps. Why can't I just give him an answer? Why can't I say a year ago? Or six months ago—that's when Dean and I met. Nothing sounds quite right in my head and then one of my stellar cousins is sure to bring up the fourth of July, when we all saw each other at Gramgrams. Why wasn't Dean there? Besides, I've already said I don't remember. I can't change my story now.

The table is quiet, the little bit of chatter amongst the groomsmen has quieted. I clear my throat. "I did give you an answer. You just didn't like it." I shrug. "I'm not sure why you care." It all comes out defensive—defensive and guilty. Ugh.

"What question?" asks one of Travis's groomsmen—I've already forgotten his name.

"I asked Iris when she and Dean met. Pretty simple question right? Something a woman usually remembers." Without bothering to look at her, he says, "When did we meet, Shelia?"

"Two years and one month ago. April something—"

"Right. April. Two years ago. She's got it." His brows raise, as if this proves something monumental.

"Good for you, Shelia. Sorry, Dean. Guess I've failed as a

girlfriend. I don't remember," my voice drips with sarcasm. I'd love nothing more than to see Hazel give this idiot a thousand doggy kisses. Maybe his face would swell up to the size of a watermelon. Maybe hives would cover his body and constrict his throat so that he couldn't talk until after the wedding.

"I'm not sure it makes a girlfriend at all," Travis snarls.

How does he know? And why does he care?

"Slow your roll, egg head," Dean says and his tone is anything but kind. Hazel's head lifts with Dean's tone and a low growl rumbles from her chest.

Shelia hisses a little and we all hear her say, "I told you that bowl cut was a bad idea."

Dean ignores her comment. "You haven't asked me. Iris may not know the exact day we met, but I sure do."

Travis smirks, brows raised. "By all means."

"September 24, 2012. Tenth grade English. She sat right in front of me and when she turned to ask my name, I knew I would never be the same again."

Travis's face goes red—but then I think mine does too. Tenth grade? English?

"Yeah, we've known each other a while. A *long* while. I've known Iris a whole lot longer than you—and a whole lot better. I have heard all about you and your pathetic excuse for a man. It's easy to believe every word."

Red has turned to purple—Travis looks as though his head may explode. "And why is that?"

"Because you're the idiot who let her go." Dean tosses another piece of chicken to Hazel, who sits at the ready—maybe to attack on Dean's command. "*That* tells me everything I need to know."

I hear it all.

But I am stuck on *tenth grade*. I am stuck on *English*. I am stuck on all the similarities my mind didn't piece together until this very second. I attempt to swallow, but the shock is too much.

There's no saliva to go down. I stare at Dean Cooper Hale. And a picture of my long lost friend blossoms. "Coop?" I say, my tone full of tremors.

I watch as Dean's Adam's apple bobs in this throat. "So," he says, less assured and all at once in a hurry. "Be nice to my girl-friend, or you'll find yourself in need of a new photographer." Hazel barks and bares her teeth toward Travis. Dean's chair scrapes along the stone floor. "Excuse us. It's been a long day." He holds a hand out to me and I can see in his face—he isn't sure I'll take it.

Truthfully, I'm not sure. But my hand has a mind of its own, it laces with Dean's and I stand. My legs are wobbly and I walk away with him—with Coop, my buddy from English who disap-peared at the end of our sophomore year, never to be seen again.

THIRTY

Dean

I ris sits on the bed, staring down at the floor and I worry that I've broken her. I shouldn't have said it, spilled my truth—at least not in front of all those people. I let her sit and I don't pressure her. Hazel lays across her feet and I sit on the couch, waiting for her to say something.

Finally she does. "I thought your name was Coop."

I swallow. "Yeah. Um, I remember when you asked for my name all those years ago. I said Dean Cooper. But I was pretty quiet."

"You were so sad." Her lashes flutter up and she looks at me, her voice quiet, her eyes pained.

I nod—I was, it isn't a fun topic. "You didn't hear me completely when I said my name, I guess. You repeated my name, as a question. You said, *Coop.* That must have been all you heard. It was easier for me to just agree."

"Huh." She nibbles on her bottom lip, her eyes sinking to the floor again. "How long have you known?"

I run a hand through my hair. "I—I remembered the night

your car broke down. That first night," I say, my tone timid—she must be angry. I wouldn't blame her.

Her eyes swing up to mine and her brow is wrinkled and furrowed. "That first night?" she says and there's more force in her tone than before.

"Yes. But I didn't think you would remember me, Iris. I wasn't in your life for very long. So, I just didn't mention it."

She shakes her head. "Why wouldn't I remember?"

I shrug and blow out a sigh. "I was a different person then. And I wasn't sure I was important enough to remember. *I* don't always like to remember that boy."

"Foster care?"

I nod.

"How did you end up there?"

I've told her some, but not everything. "My mom has a drinking problem. She's been clean for nine years. But she got herself into a lot of trouble the summer before my sophomore year." I don't go back to that dark time easily. Even before foster care, living with Mom hadn't been fun. I loved my mother, but she was like a selfish child for many years. "I was put into the system in the middle of September. Suddenly I had a new home, a new family, and a new school. That alone was enough, but then…" I swallow. I shake my head. I couldn't go there—not for anyone else. But this is Iris, that angel, who always had a smile for me.

"You said the people you lived with weren't kind." She watches me—waiting to hear about a past I want to forget.

"They were not."

"How?" That strain in her voice says she *needs* to know. But why?

I blink. "That's not a place I revisit, Iris." But she's quiet, waiting. I gulp down a swallow and plunge through. I am not that person anymore and I will never be again. "They didn't like me. They wouldn't speak to me. I was literally given the silent treatment for months. They'd talk around me and pretend I wasn't there. If they disliked something I did, I got pinched. I had welts the size of grapes on my stomach and arms. But at least the welts meant they were acknowledging me. Pretending I didn't exist sent me into a deep depression."

Tears pool in Iris's azure eyes, they spill over and slide down her cheeks. "I didn't know."

"No one knew." I muster my bravery—she has every reason to be mad at me, but I don't think she is. I stand and walk over to sit next to her on the bed. "I was forgettable and invisible. To everyone. Except you."

She slides her hand into mine, intertwining our fingers. "I'm sorry," she whispers.

"You have nothing to be sorry about. I've wanted to tell you thank you for years." For some reason my confession only makes more tears stream down Iris's cheeks.

Letting go of me, she gets to her feet and Hazel shuffles from Iris's toes to the dog bed in the corner. Iris stands in front of me, her long chestnut hair falling in waves over both of her shoulders. And for a moment, I think she's going to kiss me again. Iris leans in, arms around my neck, hugging me tight—not the fake boyfriend tentative touches I've gotten for the last three weeks— but a real embrace. Her body presses into mine, every inch of her touching me. I can feel her heart thundering, hear her breaths hitching, her tears leave tracks on my cheeks. Her lips, full and sweet, graze my jaw.

"I'm glad you're okay, Coop." She's still holding me, her cheek pressed to mine. Her words are a lullaby in my ear. And then, she's backing up. "I'm going to take a bath. I'll see you tomorrow."

"Tomorrow?" It's already tomorrow. Plus, we're sharing the same room. How long does she plan to stay in there? How long will I have to sit out here pretending she *isn't* in there?

———

JUST LIKE WE pretend that Iris didn't force her mouth into mine the day before, we also pretend that we've known all along that we were once teenage friends. I guess I did know. But now, Iris knows too. You'd never know that information was a new development, though. In fact, instead of her not remembering me or looking at me all pathetic because of who I once was, she studies me with what looks like adoration from time to time. When I catch her, she looks away. But I swear, it's not my ego—I've seen it.

I'm getting Hazel ready for the doggy playdate establishment I've found, as well as preparing for a few hours on the fishing boat. Iris has told me that tomorrow I should go skiing, hiking, and sailing—whatever it was I told her the day Shelia invited me to the wedding. She has plenty of work to do. And sure, that was the plan in the beginning. But I don't really want to leave her. Not with Travis the jerk leering and her cousins who are all—no offense to Iris—a little wacky.

Iris exits the bathroom in tight jeans, an army green tee tucked in, and an opened flannel shirt. She holds out her hands. "I've never gone fishing. Will this work?"

"You live in Colorado. How have you never been fishing?"

She lifts one shoulder.

"What am I saying? I'd never been fishing until Anson."

"He kind of changed your life then, huh?" She already knows this, but she's got more questions now. My answers are seen in a new light—I get that.

"Yeah." I shrug. "That's why I took his name."

"I'm glad you kept Cooper."

"Here," I pick up the fishing vest I bought her and hold it out toward her.

She takes it, unsure what it is and holds it up for examination.

A smile spreads across her face. "So many pockets. I can put all my lures and thingy-majiggy's in here!"

"Yes." I can't take my eyes off of her or the way her face lights up over a little fishing vest. "You have a place for all your majiggy's."

She slips it on over her red and black flannel shirt.

"You look official."

She tugs on the collar of her vest, grinning. "Sweet."

———

WE'VE BEEN on the charter boat an hour, we've learned about bait, how to attach our line, how to tie the hook, when to and when not to use a bobber, how to cast—all things Anson taught me years ago. It's finally time to actually fish.

I can see it isn't the most natural thing for Iris, but she's trying and I think we may end up waiting out here until a fish decides its life goal is to be caught by her.

I cast, and watch as her white teeth clamp down on her bottom lip. Strings of chestnut hair have escaped the elastic she's tied her hair back in and fly in front of her face. She ignores them as she removes the florescent green lure she attached five minutes ago—because she thought it was pretty. Now, she means business, she's going for the worm. The live worm.

"And this should get me a trout?" She points to the cup of worms in Mick's hand.

Our guide, Mick, raises one brow, studying the worm she points to. "Yeah. It should."

"Hand me the worm," she says as if it were a scalpel and she's about to perform brain surgery.

I'm being patient, I've had my Powerbait Trout Nuggets on my line and in the water for the last twelve minutes. I know—from fishing with Anson that fishing is about the right bait, time of day, and patience.

Iris might not be patient enough for this sport. I thought she might like it—and the truth is, she doesn't look bored, she has focused eyes and a determined expression. But she doesn't like waiting. This is her third bait change in twelve minutes.

Mick doesn't care. He's sixty-something and I paid for his services all day. He's amused by Iris's antics and I think would help her add a twinkie to her line if she asked him to.

Mick sets the worm in her hand, then rests his hands on his hips, watching my girlfriend—my *fake* girlfriend—with the biggest smile. I might be jealous if he weren't sixty and happily married.

One of Iris's brows raises over the other and she holds the worm out for me to see.

"Nice," I tell her, but I'm not sure if she'll be able to thread the live worm onto her hook. Iris kind of loves all things living—and I love that about her.

She holds the worm eye level, looking him right in the face and says, "Thank you for your sacrifice."

But before I offer to help, she screws her lips to the side, closes one eye and weaves the worm onto her hook. She holds it up, her face only inches from the thing and whispers something else.

I pinch my lips and hold in my chuckle. "What did you say?"

She blinks, her long dark lashes fluttering impishly. She clears her throat. "Never mind what I said." She points at me. "I will catch a fish and we will eat it tonight for supper, Dean Cooper."

She gives her line two extra feet, as Mick instructed, then sets her finger on the trigger and flips open her reel. Stepping back with one foot she tosses her line in one fluid motion—her best cast yet.

"Lovely," Mick says. "You've got this one, Iris."

She nods at him.

Walking with my line, I move a little closer, wanting to stand right by her.

"Dean," she says, a moan in her voice, "What are you doing? Our lines will get crossed."

"They won't," I say and I move my rod so that it faces away from us while I stand next to her. "Are you having fun?"

A breeze rustles her strings of fallen hair. "I am." Her lips peek just a little. "I didn't know I'd enjoy this so much."

"I'm glad." I trace a finger along her cheek, catch a few stray hairs and tuck them behind her ear—any excuse to touch her.

"I brought my camera too," she looks behind her. "After I catch my trout, I want to take some pho—" All of her attention returns to the line. It's tugging. All at once, Iris becomes a nine-month pregnant woman in labor. "Mick! Mick!" She calls. "It's coming! It's coming!"

I fasten my rod in Mick's boat buckle, keeping the line out—there's no time to reel it in—Iris's baby is coming!

I stand on one side and Mick on the other.

"Wait until he stops the drag!" Micks bellows.

We watch as Iris's line is dragged farther out to sea, clearly something on the other end. After only a few seconds it slows and then it stops all together.

"Now, woman! Reel it in!" Mick calls to her, his tone all business now. His smile is no longer light and playful, but determined. Iris is going to catch this fish—like a mother delivering her first child—and he is going to be her birthing coach.

Iris turns the reel again and again.

"Lift the rod," Mick reminds her of our training—our fishing Lamaze. "Point it to the sky as you reel!"

Iris does as she's told. She's doing it—she's pulling the fish inward—and then, it shoots out again, taking her line with him.

"No!" Iris stumbles forward a foot and then grabs hold of the line with her free bare hand. She's only clung to it for a second before she drops the rod all together, crying out in pain. Blood drips from her fingers and she holds her hand to her chest.

"Iris!" I crouch next to her.

But with her uninjured hand, she pushes against my chest. "My fish! Dean, get my fish!"

She's a strong little woman and the shove on my chest is more than insistent. Mick's already caught her rod, but he hands it over to me. I can feel Iris's eyes on me as I reel in her baby.

"Rod to the sky!" Iris spouts as if she's Mick and the one training me on how to catch a fish. She sits back in the fishing swivel chair behind me. "Reel him in, Dean!"

I do. I reel and reel. Finally, I have a speckled fish, as long as my forearm, wriggling against my hold. I hold up the rainbow trout—feeling somewhat like a proud papa—and show it to Iris. Tears brim in her eyes and she holds her injured hand to her heart. Blood soaks through her fishing vest and lines each of her fingers.

"Whoa, Iris." I hand the fish over to Mick who gets to work on digging out the hook. "Iris, your hand."

"It's fine." But she peers down and, for the first time, sees the blood. She's cut herself something fierce. "Oh." She groans and her face turns sickly white. "That is a lot of blood." She slides down in her seat a little, somehow turning even paler.

I kneel down next to her. "Let me see."

Her cut hand trembles as she sets it in mine. I run my free palm over her forehead. "You okay, mighty fisherwoman?"

"Mm-hmm." Iris shuts her eyes and it's like a pull that can't be helped—I lean in and brush my lips to her forehead. I breathe her in—roses with a faint smell of dirt and sea. Even on a fishing boat Iris smells good.

"Mick," I say, without looking at the old fisherman. "First aid kit?"

"Ho," he says and I turn my head just in time to see him toss the white box my way. For the next ten minutes, I play doctor… with Iris… which isn't nearly as fun as it sounds. I drown her cuts —two sharp lines across her two middle fingers—in clean water and dry them off with gauze. I find a tube of antiseptic cream that includes pain reliever and softly dab a generous amount across her cuts. Then I wrap both fingers in white bandaging tape.

Between the pain reliever and washing away the blood, pink slowly returns to Iris's cheeks.

I run my hand across her forehead, my heart beating faster than it should. "There. Are you okay?"

She nods and offers me a smile. "Thanks." Her lashes flutter and she still holds her hand protectively to her chest. "Can I see him?"

"Aw," I dart a glance at Mick, I know whom she means.

Mick's got Iris's rod back out in the sea, but he nods his head to the side where a large brown cooler sits. It's half filled with water and Iris's fish practically runs the entire length of the thing. It's alive and well, but it doesn't have any room to swim.

"He's here," I say, sitting on the seat on the other side of the cooler. I tip my head toward the thing and Iris slides her gaze from my face to her fish.

Her face brightens. "He's so big."

"Yeah," I laugh, glad she doesn't seem detoured by her fishing injury.

"And he's pretty. Look at his pink stripe." She chuckles. "I never knew fish could be pretty—I mean, other than Nemo and Dory."

"Rainbow Trout are known for their bright colors. They are a handsome breed." Mick's eyes stay on the water, a toothpick pinched between his lips.

"I need my camera," she says and reaches for the backpack at her feet. She pauses, shakes out her injured fingers, and then pulls Snappy the camera from her bag.

"You okay?"

"Yeah," she shakes out her hand again. "Just some stinging."

"That's gonna take a good week to heal," Micks says, taking the toothpick from his mouth and pointing it in Iris's direction.

"You're lucky you dropped the rod when you did. You never grab the line."

"Yeah, I've got that—now."

Iris urges me to pick up my rod again. I do and I cast out the same luckless bait I've been using, but I'm distracted. My mind is on her. She's photographing. She takes pictures of the view, of me, of Mick, and of her fish—a hundred of her fish. She talks to him. She tells him how pretty he is.

But it's when I hear her say, "You're so strong, aren't you, Puff Daddy? You almost beat him," that I know we will not be eating this fish. Not when Iris has given him a name and is cooing at it like he is her new born child.

Nope, we'll be throwing him back and Puff Daddy will live to see another day.

THIRTY-ONE

Dean

I am a gentleman—I promise. I have every intention of staying on this couch—this super comfy two inch cushion is lovely for my bed. But—then Iris starts whimpering in her sleep. At first I thought it was Hazel, pouting because we'd left her for most of the day. But she lay asleep on her dog bed—it's cushion about double the size of this couch.

"Iris?"

She doesn't wake. But I think her aspirin has worn off.

"Iris," I say again and yet I don't really want to wake her. I find an icepack in the mini fridge-freezer combo in our room and wrap her fingers around the bag. She's soft and gentle—even in sleep. I breathe her in as if sitting in a garden.

Her whimpering stops with the numbing of her fingers, but then chill bumps light up her arm and she shivers.

I have no idea what it would take to wake this woman up— she took two melatonin before bed and they are working. So, I lay on top of the comforter she's under and drape one arm around her—purely helpful, I'm a human heater, I have zero selfish motives. At least that's what I keep telling myself.

Iris rolls beneath her blankets, ice pack still in her grip—that must mean it's helping, right? She turns until her closed eyes and even breaths face me head on. In fact she breathes in deep, and nuzzles herself closer to me. I freeze in place, one arm bent and under my head, the other draped around her.

I've never watched anyone sleep before and I've always thought doing so was a little creepy. But I don't blink, I don't feel tired at all sensing the warmth of Iris's body so close and watching her lips and brows move in sleep. She is fascinating— and beautiful. Her lips are a siren calling to mine. I am in a famine and relief is just three inches away.

But—I starve. Because like I said, I'm a gentleman. And as much as I want to kiss Iris right now, she is totally unconscious. I'm not sure an earthquake could wake her.

No, instead, I set a silent timer on my watch to remind myself to go back to my crap couch by five a.m. No need to let Iris freeze, be in pain, or startle her in the morning. No, I am Jack Bauer—I can do it all.

THIRTY-TWO

Iris

Dean is gone when I wake in the morning, but there's a room temperature ice pack next to my injured fingers and two aspirin alongside a bottle of water on the end table. He is officially my hero. A scribbled note reads—*bringing breakfast, rest.*

You'd think I'd injured my entire body rather than cut up two fingers.

I'm warm—warmer than normal. I kick off my blankets and sit up in bed. It should be totally weird and awkward sharing this room with Dean and yet we act like there's plenty of space and we're just hanging out—like we have been for three weeks.

I pick up my phone and open Instagram. I might be getting the hang of this. I post a picture of Dean fishing, a selfie of the two of us he took with my phone before the action began, and of course Puff Daddy. Dean didn't even question when I asked if we could let him go before we reached shore. There's no way I could have eaten him… not after all we'd been through together. I am certain there is a Puff Mommy out there somewhere waiting for

231

him to bring home the bacon—or bait—or whatever fish bring home.

I lay my head back against the headboard and breath—and for some reason all I can smell is Dean. Dean. Dean. Dean.

The dream I had surfaces as I breath him in—he's everywhere! I don't remember it exactly. In fact, I can't envision anything, it's the feeling I remember—warm and wrapped in Dean's embrace. It was as if I breathed him in all night long. And apparently my head liked it so much, I am still breathing him in. I tap the back of my head against the headboard. "I am so stupidly smitten. How did this happen?" If I'm being honest, I started liking Dean from the minute he told me he knew what a wirehaired pointing griffon was. How is that even possible?

I message Ebony—feeling sneaky as I use Instagram messaging rather than our usual plain jane texts.

> @iris_me: When will you get here??
> @ebony_mccoy: Tomorrow morning. No falling in love
>   until I approve.
> @iris_me: You may be too late.

I sent that. I cannot believe I sent that! I am not in love with my high school friend turned hottie. I throw a pillow over my face and howl.

> @ebony_mccoy: Stop it, Iris! I mean it!
> @iris_me: I woke up smelling him—everything around
>   me smells like Dean. What does that mean, Eb?
> @ebony_mccoy: Have you been drinking coffee?
>   Coke? Dr. Pepper? You know you can't handle
>   caffeine.
> @iris_me: Water. That's it. I promise. He's amazing.
>   He's kind and fun. He's unpredictable and yet his

> goodness never surprises me. And he smells like
> heaven. Ebony, I am in trouble. What do I do?
> @ebony_mccoy: Try kissing him.
> @ebony_mccoy: For real this time.
> @ebony_mccoy: But wait until I give approval!

My phone is three inches from my face, my fingers at the ready to write her back when Dean walks in with two breakfast trays. I juggle my phone like a hot potato before slipping it into my night shirt.

Dean watches me with curiosity, one brow raised, and a quirky smile playing at his lips. "You and your phone have a funny relationship."

I clear my throat. "It's just Ebony. She's texting. About a guy. And... that's all." There. Truth. Not one lie in that sentence.

His brows cinch together a little and he gives a slight nod. "Oh-kay." He sets both trays on the table in our quaint room, it's right next to the sliding glass door that leads out to our minuscule deck and view of the lake.

"She'll be here tomorrow." I throw my legs over the side, ready to stand and stretch. "You'll like her. She's the best." I pause mid stand. "Oh." I peer over at him—very aware of my morning breath, but this time I know exactly where my toothbrush is. "Did you know her?"

"I knew who she was. But we didn't know each other. Mostly I knew what you told me."

I shut my eyes, trying to remember anything—but it was all so long ago. I just remembered that I liked Dean—aka Coop. And I always wanted to see him smile. I felt this strange need to protect that sad boy—at least in English. I never saw him outside our one common class. "What did I say?"

"It's been so long," he says, but I know his memory is better than mine. He recognized me, he remembers me asking his name and actual conversations we had. I know he remembers something. "You said she was brilliant and that one day she'd win a Pulitzer Prize. At the time, I didn't know what that was. I had to google it."

I laugh and scratch the back of my neck. "Yeah, well, she will."

"Do you remember when we were paired to do that report on Othello?"

"Yeah." I remember I asked our teacher to pair us—I didn't want anyone else with Coop. "You made me do all the writing."

Dean laughs. "And all the researching. I wasn't a lot of help."

I shrug one shoulder. "You had other things to worry about."

"I did." He blinks, his lids low, but his eyes slide up to meet my gaze. "And you're the only reason I passed English."

My head still spins with the knowledge. Dean is Coop. Coop is Dean!

I swallow and my eyes prick with moisture. I'm not sure why. It's a dumb thing to get emotional about. But after all these years, I get to know my friend again. "What did you bring?"

"Breakfast," he says. One corner of his mouth rises. "Rainbow trout omelets."

My eyes go wide and my mouth dries out like someone took a vacuum to it. "No." A Puff Daddy omelet. I can't.

He breathes out a laugh. "No. It's a cheese omelet and a fruit. salad." He turns his sights on Hazel, she's been patiently wagging her tail and waiting at his feet. "And," he says, "I brought you a little treat." He holds out a single slice of bacon.

"You are going to spoil her!"

"She's on vacation," he winks at Hazel. "Aren't you, girl. You're on vacation too."

My heart patters at the way Dean makes googly eyes at my dog. He caresses behind Hazel's ear and I can't stop staring. Hazel is the luckiest griff in all the world. And I am jealous... of my dog.

"So," Dean says and it ends my trance, "we have a few hours until the rehearsal dinner. Do you want to explore a bit?"

"I do. I mean, I would. But Shelia has my day booked. You should go. I know you had plans for Tahoe." I swallow, feeling the truth of these next words. "Don't let me hold you back."

"Nah," he says, shaking his head and pooching out his lips in a way that makes me think they're saying—*kiss me Iris, you know you want to.* "I'll hang out with you."

In the last three weeks, here's what I've learned about Dean, not only is he one of the kindest, sexiest men I know. He's also a protective sexy man. Yes, I added sexy twice. It's worth adding twice. Just look at Dean's biceps—any single, straight woman would add it twice.

So, I'm pretty sure he'll tag along to all the boring wedding appointments with me to be my sexy guard when it comes to my overbearing cousins and my pompous ex. But he doesn't need to do that. I'm a big girl. And I tell him just that. "You don't need to do that. I can handle myself."

"I know. But I'm here for the wedding. I'm here for you."

We stare at one another, neither of us speaking. A pin could drop and it may sound like a hydrogen bomb. A knock sounds on our hotel door—sounding like that hydrogen bomb and about making me pee my pants. I start my Kegel exercises right then and there.

Another tap. "Iris!" It's Shelia.

A round of giggles sounds on the other side of the door. And then a chorus of "Dean!" rings through. Ugh. Not just Shelia, but Shandon and Shayla too. *Joy.* The whole darn family. Okay, well not all of them, but close enough.

I pull in a breath—needing to gather a little sanity and strength. Then, I open the door—still in my pjs.

Shandon looks me up and down, her chin tracing the line of my body. "Nice shorts," she says.

Shayla pokes her head around her sister. "Is Dean still here?"

I swallow. "Yeah. We were just about to have breakfast."

"Mmm. Lovely."

"What adventure are you going on today, Dean?" Shelia reaches out a hand, running her fingers down Dean's arm.

"Aw, just wedding prep… right?"

Shelia laughs and Shandon and Shayla give each other a knowing glance. I'm just going to count myself lucky that Sherry and Serenity aren't here. "You can't come with us," Shelia says with a giggle.

"I can't?" He sets one hand to his hip, sweat pooling at his collar, he's already been for a morning run.

"Of course not. Girl day. You don't get to come for mani-pedi's." Shelia points a finger at him and I think for a second that she's going to bop Dean on the nose.

"Oh."

I shuffle my feet. "It's okay. Really. Go do something fun today. Hike and ski and anything else that calls to you."

Dean peers back at my cousins and I don't blame him one bit when after only a few seconds he says, "Sure. Okay. I'll meet you for dinner?"

"Rehearsal dinner, you mean." Shelia holds up a finger.

"That's exactly what I meant, Shelia."

I press my lips together and smile at my very fake boyfriend. He is adorable—for real.

THIRTY-THREE

Dean

I'm back from my hike an hour earlier than I planned to be. I can't stop my brain from running. This week is almost over. And then where will Iris and I be? What will she tell her family? Not to mention—my mom and Anson.

Shelia has Iris working, so I shower, clean up, and ponder a solution. But the only solution I want doesn't seem possible.

I'm getting ready to find Iris—I think seeing her might help me clear my head or maybe I'll just be all the more confused, when the buzz of a phone that isn't mine rings. Iris left her phone. I grab it—to take to her, in case she needs it. When the text that's come through lights up in a banner across her screen.

> Ebony: How's project kiss the boy going?

She's added a mermaid and a crab emoji—a reference I clearly don't get. But even more so, I don't understand what she's saying. She's asking Iris about kissing. Who would Iris be kissing? Besides… me?

I have to wonder—has my ego grown too big? Is my big head

the one asking this question or is it a legit question? But I can't think of anyone else Iris might kiss. I think I'd notice if she had another fake boyfriend in her pocket.

It has to be me.

Right?

I'm Iris's boyfriend—fake or not.

Is Ebony teasing her sister? Or serious? Why would Iris tell me half a dozen times that I'm not allowed to kiss her if she *wanted* me to kiss her? Then again—she kind of kissed me. I really don't know what else to call our faces smashed together.

I shove Iris's phone into my pocket and formulate a plan that could get me fake broken up with. I'll give Iris back her phone, but I'm going to spy while she reads that text from her sister. Iris isn't exactly adept at hiding things. In fact—is *this* why her phone keeps getting stuffed down her shirt?

My ego might be growing bigger by the second. But I'm out of here, Iris's phone burning a hole in my pocket.

When I get to the opened ballroom, where Shelia and Travis will have their rehearsal dinner and tomorrow their reception, I stand back by the kitchen. Iris is busy listening to Shelia spout instructions, holding up her camera every now and then, not to take a photo, but to check for spaces and lighting, I think. I've seen her do it enough these past three weeks.

"There's no passion there." Shelia's sisters have all walked in, next to the table right in front of where I lurk with the kitchen staff. I'm not sure which one spoke just now, but her tone of disgust is evident. I'm still amazed that Iris and these women are related.

"Absolutely not," says Shayla—I'm pretty sure when she dropped her napkin the night before and leaned down, giving me a full view of her cleavage, it was on purpose. "I don't know what Dean sees in her."

Iris? They're talking about Iris and me.

"He's hot," says Shandon.

"And Iris is at best a seven," that's Shayla again.

My head goes hot with their unkindness. Iris outdoes them by tenfold—in kindness, personality, and looks.

"You can tell he's not really into it. I mean, I'd be shocked if we aren't hearing a breakup story the minute this wedding is over," Sherry chimes into the conversation. And it's like she's reading into my fears. These women are so cruel. What will they say when Iris and I aren't together directly after this event?

"You can't blame him, though," says Shayla. "You should hear some of Trav's stories about her."

"Iris isn't exactly *desirable*... walking around in her tennis shoes, her dog with her wherever she goes," says Shandon.

The others laugh. It's all I can do to keep my mouth shut. They're a bunch of bullies. And they're bullying the one person who'd never deserve it. My head burns with annoyance. My eyes slide to Iris in the middle of the room. *Sweet Iris.* She doesn't deserve such censure. She swings her camera so the strap is about her middle and Snappy lies at her back. She's looking at wherever it is that Shelia is pointing—so focused, so diligent—all while her cousins talk behind her back and Travis gives her the stink eye.

And that's when I break. *Enough.* I can't take it anymore.

I move forward, pushing through the sea of cousins. They part for me with songs of,

"Dean!"

"Oh!"

"Hey, there."

I ignore them and charge to the center of the room. I plant myself in front of Iris, who blinks up at me. The room spins as I cup one hand about the back of her neck, my other finding her waist and dragging her flush to me. There's vulnerability behind her robin's egg eyes and her breath catches. I lean down and she doesn't push me away or yell that I'm not allowed. I press my mouth to hers, soft, sweet, and waiting. She kisses me back—nothing awkward about it.

Iris rises on tip toes and tangles her arms around my neck. My teeth graze on that bottom lip she's always tempting me with and I deepen the kiss. I don't care that we both need to breathe. I need Iris. I need her kiss. I need her like I need sunshine and water.

I hold her as close as I can, as close as is physically possible, my mouth moving with hers. She tastes like strawberry and her breath is warm and inviting mixed with my own.

Iris.

She is my favorite adventure.

In so many ways, I've loved Iris for a decade.

Someone clears their throat—loud and disturbing. But I am happy to ignore them. I don't loosen my hold on Iris and her arms stay tight around my neck—as if she has been wanting and waiting for this kiss as long as I have been.

"Iris!" Shelia whines.

Another clearing of the throat—Travis—and Iris freezes in place. Her lips turn to stone with our scandal.

Iris drops back onto the heels of her feet, her fluttering lashes kissing my cheeks along the way.

"What's going on?" Travis snarls.

"Sorry," I say—not sorry at all. "It's hard to be separated from Iris for too long."

Travis rolls his eyes with my response. Shelia's grin turns lopsided. I'm not sure what she sees in Travis. Out of all of her sisters, I think Shelia might be the nicest, so how did she get stuck with a bum like him. Then again, he tricked Iris into dating him too.

"We've got a bit more to do and then I promise to give her back." Shelia chuckles.

She speaks to me and I politely make eye contact with her,

but Iris's gaze sears me. I'm almost afraid to look. What if she's repressing slapping me in front of her family?

But then—that isn't what her kiss said.

No, that kiss said so many things that Iris hasn't yet voiced, things I'm not creative enough to make up.

I shift my head, locking gazes with Iris. "I'll be waiting," I tell her and leaning down I peck her swollen lips once more. She doesn't say anything. And I'm a little afraid that everyone in this room will know that that was our first real kiss. I'm not counting when our faces collided back at my place.

I sit at a table—purposely near the cousins. I want them to see me and keep their goosy traps shut.

For the next hour I watch Shelia boss and instruct Iris and a dozen other people—all so that tomorrow will go off without a hitch. I don't know what Iris is charging her cousin, but I do know it's not enough.

The room starts to disperse and I can see the exhaustion in Iris's face—it's been a long, taxing day.

She trudges over to me and I stand, my legs achy from sitting too long in this folding chair. I hold out a hand for her bags and she gives them up, no argument.

"Are you ready to go?" I ask her.

"Are you ready to talk?" she replies.

I am ready. I might be ready to spill my guts and face rejection—if that be the case. If there's even the smallest chance for me and Iris, it's worth facing.

"Where's Hazel?" I ask—feeling like a jerk for not realizing sooner that she isn't with Iris.

Iris's shoulder brushes mine, my fingers itch—ready to take hers. She rolls her head back like her neck aches and flutters her lashes in annoyance. "Travis kept having allergy attacks. I ended up taking her to the doggie daycare place again. They were nice and it was better than Travis yelling at her."

"Shoot. I'm sorry. I would have taken her with me, but I thought you'd want her nearby."

"I know. I did." She shrugs and peers up at me. "It's not your fault. Let's just go get her, okay?"

I nod, pricks of pain in my fingers move up to my wrist and into my forearm. I slide my hand into Iris's, intertwining our fingers—it's the only thing that will cure this constant ache. When she twists her neck to peer at me again. I use my free hand to wave to the cousins. "See you, ladies."

"Listen," I say when we're halfway to our room, "you're exhausted. Go take a bath. Relax. I'll grab Hazel and get us something to eat, then meet you back at the room."

"You're sure?" she asks and in that moment she looks so vulnerable. It makes me wonder when was the last time someone took care of Iris? She's young and strong and gifted. But not invincible.

"I'm sure," I say, knowing I'd like to take care of her for as long as she'll allow me. "I'll be back in thirty minutes. Relax." I lean down—almost on instinct and press a soft kiss to her pink, full lips. They are ripe and I'd like to devour them. I won't—not yet. But I won't hide anymore either.

"Thirty minutes," she says, holding her pointer finger to her lips, "and then we'll talk."

THIRTY-FOUR

Iris

"Surprise!"

I jolt, my back hitting our resort room door and knocking it closed, my hand presses to my thundering heart. I squint my eyes to see my attacker better. "Ebony?" My sister wasn't supposed to be here until tomorrow.

Her eyes lock with mine and her brows narrow—assessing me. "Iris," she says, her tone low. Her coffee brown hair is pulled back in a high ponytail that makes her glare feel even fiercer. "What did you do? You were supposed to wait to fall in love until I approved!"

"Shh!" I hush her. Moving away from the door I set both hands on her right forearm, pleading. Besides, can she really see *that* just by looking at me?

"Who's going to hear me?" She flaps her arms at her sides like a dead fish. "What happened? Where is this Dean?"

"He went to get Hazel." I drop her arm and pace once, then twice right in front of her. "And... he kissed me."

"Iris," she says, snatching hold of my wrist and stopping my jaunt. She questions me with just her eyes—she calls it our twin ESP.

"Yes," I say, answering her unasked question. "Like a Jack and Rose level kiss."

Her deep brown eyes widen. We've always been suckers for Titanic and we've rated Jack and Rose's kisses a million times. "Iris," she moans and pulls me in for a hug.

I cling to her, now that she's got me here, in her arms. It's been months since I've seen or hugged my sister and life isn't the same without her close by. I miss her. Desperately. The thought brings tears to the surface.

I don't make it to the tub—as Dean suggested. I lie on the one bed in this room with my sister and for thirty solid minutes Eb and I talk, non-stop.

We're sitting with our backs against the headboard, our feet —exactly the same length—stretched out overtop the comforter, when the lock mechanism sounds with Dean's key card. Ebony pauses mid sentence and we freeze—like we're kids about to get caught doing something naughty.

"I picked up some Ben and Jer—" Dean halts when he sees me and my twin sister atop this bed.

It's a strange thing—I know that Ebony and I look a lot alike, but we aren't identical. Her hair is a darker shade of brown than my own, but the biggest difference is our eyes. Mine are a clear blue, while Eb's are a deep brown. They stand out when we sit side by side.

"Ebony," Dean finally says. He just has the word out when Hazel rips her leash from Dean's fingertips and hops up onto the bed—right onto my sister. We've both missed her. "I should have grabbed more food."

"It's fine." Ebony waves her hand. "I ate."

"Are you sure, I can—" Dean shoots a thumb over his shoulder. He's nervous and adorable... and possibly looking for an escape.

"Nope. Stay. Let's chat." Ebony scoots to the edge of the bed, stands and holds out a hand for Dean to shake. She's all sisterly business.

Ebony takes her job as my one minute older sister very seriously. For the next two hours she asks Dean a dozen questions. We'll fall into a natural discussion and just when we all think we're enjoying ourselves, Ebony throws out a, "What's your opinion on the Las Vegas Raiders?" or a "How did you feel about the season finale of Friends?" My personal favorite, "Are you team Edward or team Jacob?" When Dean has no idea what my sister is talking about and asks, "Is that political? Edward Martinez—the senator?" she loosens up and lets the questions go.

Finally, Ebony lifts her wrists to study her watch. "Blech." Her pretty face sours. "I have to go sleep in Shandon's room."

"You can stay here," Dean says, pointing to the bed. "I'm on the couch." His eyes dart from my sister back to me. "Or I can sleep in the Jeep tonight."

"Nah. I'll survive." Though she makes a horrid face, making me giggle.

I nibble on my lip—nervous and anxious to be alone with him.

"Goodnight, sister." Ebony wraps her strong arms around me and I hold my sister close.

"See you in the morning."

Ebony's squeeze on me tightens though. "No shaving your legs," she whisper yells into my ear. "But I do like him." Her lips press to my cheek and then she's broken away, scratching Hazel's beard, before waving to Dean and escaping out the door.

And Dean and I are left alone.

"How are your fingers?" he says, lifting my hand with his, his touch is soft and kind, and fills my stomach with flutterings.

"Okay." They're sore and pink and my dressing needs changed. "Shelia had a panic attack when she saw me. She asked if I could still click the camera clicker." I smirk.

245

"Nice," he says, his tone flat.

I tug on the tape around my fingers, but I don't get far.

"Let me." He pulls out his own first aid kit.

I sit on the bed, one leg pulled up, my black Converse shoes still on my feet.

Dean sits next to me and I watch his fingers, expert and gentle as he strips the tape covering my wound, his face inches from mine. "Hey, they don't look too bad."

I swallow at his nearness, at the quiet, at the vulnerability that fills the space between us. He washes my cuts with a wet wipe and applies new antiseptic.

"Dean, why did you kiss me today?" The words stick in my throat, but I get them all out. I want to know.

He shrugs one shoulder, his eyes still on my hand. "You kissed me—I figured your rule about our lips not touching had been broken. So—"

"So I had already broken the rule... and that's it?" I study him, heart pounding and insides tremoring. Maybe I shouldn't have said anything. But how could I not?

His eyes sweep up to lock with mine. "And—"

"And?"

"And. I wanted to."

"Okay." I gulp. He *wanted* to. Dean wanted to kiss me. Does that also translate to—*I like you*, because it doesn't have to. I'm old enough to know that fact. Sometimes a man will charm a woman, kiss a woman, sleep with a woman—simply because he can.

And yet... I don't think Dean is that kind of man. The past three weeks tell me he isn't. But more than that—the Dean I knew a decade ago wouldn't have done that.

"Is that okay?" he asks like we're both teetering on a ledge.

Is it? I mean, I've only been trying to figure out how to make that kiss happen for the past week. So, despite the thunder in my ears and pounding chest, I'm gonna have to go with, "Sure."

He pulls out a strip of white bandaging tape, his eyes on his work, and wraps the bandage around the middle of my ring and middle fingers. "Okay, then." His eyes flutter up until they lock with mine. "You're all set.

"I'm exhausted," I whisper—and I don't even have to lie. I don't know what that kiss is going to change, but I can't think about it now. The fear of it changing *nothing* might induce an anxiety attack—so it's best not to think. Our *talk* will have to come later.

"Sure," he nods and stands, ready to make his bed on the couch. "Do you need some aspirin?"

"Um, yeah," I say, content to let him take care of me.

Dean rifles through his personal first aid kit until he finds what he wants, a little bottle of white pain meds. He hands me a bottle of water, then drops two pills into my outstretched palm, covering my hand with his.

"Thanks." I swallow, the warmth of his hand spreads over my skin like pancake batter on a griddle.

Dean leans toward me and my breath hitches. His soap and cedar scent devours me and I close my eyes. His lips brush my forehead. "Goodnight, Iris."

I mumble out a goodnight that I'm not sure is audible and lay my head against the pillow. Dean turns out the lights, but my eyes can still make out his form lying on the couch. I'm not sure my head or my heart will let me fall asleep tonight. Not with Dean so close, and so far away, all at the same time.

———

WEDDING DAY. I'm up early—Shelia has me taking pictures from pre dressing drinks with the bridesmaids to the last minute of the reception tonight. I slip into my new blue cocktail dress—it's comfortable and Shelia approved. I didn't mention my shoes to her—and I was grateful she didn't ask. I'm afraid I would have lied. I sport my black Converse high tops, in all their glory, and I'm happy with the look. I can move in this dress and maybe my feet won't be completely dead by the end of the night. At least I'm not in heels. I've pulled my hair back—all business, but I know I'll let it down before the night is over. I can't handle the ponytail headache.

Dean is ready to go—ready to be Hazel's plus one for the day. I'm grateful she'll have him and they'll both be close if I need them.

He's too cute in his long-sleeved button up. That top button undone, tempting the world. Does he have any idea how sexy he is? It's no wonder my cousins haven't stopped drooling since they met him.

Dean smiles when he sees me and I try not to fidget with my dress. "You ready?" he says, interrupting my roller coaster day dreams.

"Oh. Yes." I blow out a huff, letting my thoughts roll off my back. There's work to do! "Let's do this."

"Iris," he says, grinning, and pausing my exit. "You look beautiful."

My cheeks burn and I nibble on my lip. "Thanks." I swallow. "You too."

I swear his smile says more than he's letting on. But what? I don't know. I may never be able to figure it out. Why? Because I'm Iris and I don't understand what men like Dean want. I realize now, I'm not what Travis wanted... but that doesn't bother me anymore. He isn't what I want either.

But Dean... I want Dean Cooper Hale. More than I've ever wanted anything. More than I'm willing to admit.

———

THE REST of the day is long and a bit of a blur—I won't remember a lot of this until I scroll through the thousands of pictures I've taken. Even in my favorite shoes, my feet ache from this all day event that's just now winding down.

Hazel has hung out with Dean all day—far from Travis. She sits with him now, while the bride and groom and a few stragglers are left on the dance floor. I am ready to put my feet up. I trudge to the table where Dean, Hazel, and Ebony sit. Dean has spent way too much time with my sister today. I have no idea what she's asked him or prodded from him, but Gramgram has nothing on Ebony. So... I can only guess. Not to mention, Dean has surely figured out by now who is the more exciting twin. And it isn't me.

"Hey guys," I say, putting on a smile for my family and friend. I lay Snappy back into my camera bag, knowing I've got some gems—including a fabulous picture of Shelia pushing cake up Travis's nose.

I might enlarge it.

And frame it.

And stream twinkling Christmas lights around it.

"Hey baby girl," I give Hazel a much needed snuggle and plop into a chair next to Dean.

"You okay?" Ebony asks, sipping on her drink, her brows cinched in worry over me.

"Yeah. It's over. So, I'm great."

"You need a foot rub."

I scoff, my lips twitching at Dean's suggestion. "You are not giving me a foot rub in the middle of this reception hall."

"You need one."

"I don't!"

"You don't?" he says, and his tone says he doesn't believe me.

"I don't." I pull in a breath. I have worked all day. And maybe I deserve a minute of fun. It wouldn't be crazy for a romantic couple to... *dance*. Right? My feet have a little life left in them. And my longing for closeness with Dean makes me brave. I stand, nervous tremors in each of my limbs. "Do you want to dance?"

249

Ebony hikes one brow at my forwardness. We both know this is out of character for me.

"What?" I say with a shrug. "A boyfriend would probably dance with his date. No?"

"He definitely would," Dean agrees. He tosses Hazel's leash to Ebony and reaches out for my hand, entwining our fingers. Dean leads me onto the dance floor, only half a dozen couples remain and I ignore them all.

I set my hand in his. My opposite arm drapes over his shoulder where my fingers fidget about his neck. His muscles are like a boulders beneath me. His arm slides around my waist and he pulls me close. I can feel the grooves of his toned abs through my cotton dress. He is everything a man should be, and my insides erupt in fireworks upon touching him.

Dean nestles his head next to mine, his cheek and lips at my temple. "You're beautiful, Iris."

"The dress is new."

"It's not the dress," he clears his throat, "I like the dress, but it's *you*—in the dress."

"Thanks," I say, my voice a whisper, my heart thundering. I shift an inch, which only has me facing his neck and breathing him in—I repress the urge to kiss his Adam's apple.

"I mean," he says and his voice has playful confidence, "if we're talking clothes, my favorite would be your shoes."

I tilt my head, peering up at him on instinct. "My shoes?" I'm in my new royal blue cocktail dress and… my black Converse high tops.

"Yes. I am crazy about your shoes, Iris."

I smirk a little—he's such a goof. Then, somehow on this dance floor, glued together, in this fake relationship… I become *courageous*. I am brave—like Dean's dad told him he could be. I reach up on tip toes, slide both arms around Dean's neck, and peer into his sapphire eyes. They seem to give me permission and I connect my lips to his. Dean's arm around me locks in place and he returns the kiss—not a show for everyone around us, but as if no one else were watching.

We are a spectacle.

But I don't care.

I pretend that it's just the two of us on this dance floor and we aren't tangled up in fake titles and real feelings.

THIRTY-FIVE

Dean

I ris has left me breathless a dozen times tonight, but I hadn't expected her to kiss me on the dance floor—in front of so many members of her extended family. At least it's not her mom and dad. I haven't met Iris's parents—they've been in Nepal for a month. Gramgram stayed home. So of her immediate family, the only one with a view is Ebony. But if Iris doesn't care, I'm not going to worry about it.

The song ends—and I'm not being cocky, really I'm not, I just think Travis is a big egotistical imbecile, because Iris and I end the party. The minute the song goes quiet, Travis claps his hands, loud and commanding. "Show's over, folks. Thanks for coming." He sets a glare on Iris and my protective nature kicks in. She got one dance. One kiss. And then he ended the night. He didn't even let Shelia get her grand bride and groom exit.

I've met guys like him. He doesn't want her. But he's pretty annoyed she isn't at home pining for him. He's a creep.

"I'll get your things," I say in Iris's ear. The wedding crowd wakes up with Travis's announcement and they aren't quiet. "You grab Hazel?" I brush my lips to her cheek.

I'm gathering the equipment Iris stashed in the kitchens when Ebony walks in. "Well," she says, hand on one hip, her hair a shade darker than Iris's is pulled back and straight, while Iris's waves down her back, "that just got *real*."

I straighten up. "Excuse me?"

"For a fake boyfriend—that was a very real kiss."

I run my hand over the back of my neck. I'm not sure what to say to her—Iris and I haven't discussed our feelings. I told her I wanted to kiss her—she said okay. It's not exactly clear where we're at. I lean back down, packing Iris's lenses and tripods into her equipment bag.

"Don't break her heart, Dean Cooper."

I stand and peer at her again.

"Yes, I know who you are." She lifts one shoulder. "I mean, I don't really, because I have no memory of you. But Iris does."

"I won't break her heart."

"You want to know the problem with being fake for too long?"

I breathe in and out, waiting. This is Iris's person—not only her sister but her best friend. Anything Ebony says could make or break me.

"You start to forget what's real and what isn't."

I shove my hands into my pockets, leaving Iris's things on the ground. "I've never been good at pretending."

One brow quirks above the other. "Good. I approve."

"Of?" I ask, not following her train of thought.

"*You*," she says. "Now, prove it to my sister, she's not going to believe you."

Ebony starts for the door and I feel a surge of panic with her declaration. "Wait." I shake my head, still trying to make sense. "Why wouldn't she believe me?"

"Iris has no idea how good she is or what she deserves."

My gaze darts from side to side, adrenalin pumping. "Ebony —are you saying that Iris has feelings for me?"

She mutters under her breath, something that sounds a lot like, "Holy cow, they're both clueless." She sets one hand to her hip and speaks more clearly. "You'll have to ask her that." She steps from the kitchen, only to peek back inside. She looks like a floating head—and it makes me wonder what might have been in that punch I drank. "And, I was never here!" she barks, only to jet out of view once more.

———

I CONTEMPLATE on Ebony's words for the rest of the night. She's right—Iris has no idea what she deserves. She's better than she knows. And maybe she deserves more than me. But at least I know I'll die trying to be worthy of her. I have to prove to Iris that I'm here for real and I'm here for the long haul.

This is going to be fun.

If Iris wants to get rid of me, she's going to have to have a *real* fake breakup. Because, I'm all in.

Iris exits the bathroom at six in the morning, no makeup, hair pulled back, in black leggings and a long taupe shirt that's way too baggy for her slender figure—and of course, her black Converse high tops. She looks good enough to eat.

She rolls her personal suitcase out and I meet her halfway.

"Morning," I say, reaching up to cup her jaw and cheek. "I'll take this."

Pink floods her cheeks and it might be my second favorite color—right after robin's egg blue. "Oh." She presses her lips together, her long dark lashes fluttering up to see me better. "Thanks."

Leaning down, I take the bag, and the opportunity—while I'm here I kiss her cheek and more color floods into her face.

The Jeep is almost packed, with only Hazel's bag left. Iris and I both head back inside for it and on the way I pick up her hand, lacing my fingers with hers.

"Hey! Hey!" Shelia calls from across the parking lot. "Rizzo! Rizzo!"

I squeeze Iris's fingers, knowing how she despises the nickname.

"Thanks for everything, cuz." Shelia's feet jog in place like she's a four year old who needs to pee and she weaves her arms around Iris's middle. "Have a safe trip!" She turns to me. "Oh Dean!" She plants a kiss on the corner of my lips and only giggles when I jerk away startled.

The back of Iris's hand covers her smiling lips. She's laughing at me. But I don't mind. I love that smile. "See you, Shelia. Congratulations."

Shelia hurries off and we're left alone. Iris's azure eyes glisten when she smiles at me. "I'm sorry. She's a bit much." She goes to open the door to our room once more, but I hold tight to her hand. I don't let her go.

She peers back around, one brow lifted in question.

I pull her close in answer.

"Dean," she says. "No one is around." Her head tilts to look at me. "You don't have to do this."

"I refuse to have the last lips that touch mine be Shelia's."

Her pretty brows cinch and she looks at me in wonder—she still doesn't understand. So, I close the gap between us, brushing my lips, soft and gentle against hers.

"You don't have to do this," she whispers against my mouth —her body rigid rather than melting into my own.

"What if I like doing this?"

"Do you?" Her lashes flutter, tickling my cheek.

I dip my head and brush my lips from her shoulder to her jaw. She hums, going limp in my arms and tilting her head so that I have easy access to her neck.

"Ohhh, this is confusing."

"It doesn't have to be," I tell her, lifting my head to meet her eyes.

Her brow furrows. "Dean, I know who *you* are and I know who *I* am and—"

"And I know that I'll never deserve you," I say, interrupting her sad monologue.

"You, not deserve me?" She bobbles her head in a shake. "Dean, I'm not exciting."

"You are."

"I'm not fun."

"You are," I tell her.

She breathes in, her chest rising and falling, but she isn't smiling yet. "You are everything I've always known I can't have," her eyes skirt the ground, she can't even look at me.

"And you are everything I've ever wanted. "Iris," I whisper in her ear, "you… are… *everything*." I press one more kiss to her throat.

"Everything?"

"Everything," I tell her.

"How is that possible?" She tilts her head to peer up at me.

"How is it possible that I've fallen for the best person I've ever met? It's pretty simple really." My heart thunders in my chest. "And Iris, I'm exhausted."

Her brows knit, her eyes search my face with worry.

"I'm tired of resisting you. I can't do it anymore."

I can see she wants to give in to me. Give in, Iris! Give in!

"If you want to get rid of me, you're going to have to stage a fake breakup," I tell her.

She blinks, her gaze locking on mine. "And cause a scene?"

"You wouldn't want that. Would you?"

Her teeth clamp down on that bottom lip I love so much. I'm still not certain she knows my intentions. "I wouldn't," she says.

I lift the corner of my mouth in a grin and lean down to claim her lips once more. I'll never get enough. I'm already figuring out how to rent out my apartment and move to Ft.

Collins. I'll need to claim those lips and feel Iris's heart beat thump next to mine daily. She is like oxygen and unless she tells me to leave, I don't plan on going another day without her.

Epilogue

IRIS

Two Months Later

I hold up my phone, camped out on the couch and too tired to get up. "But I'm logged in as me, so I don't see how—"

"Are you in settings?"

"Yes, but maybe they limit you to two accounts," I hold my phone out to Dean so that he can just do this for me. My brain is fried after three engagement shoots and two weddings this week.

He plops onto my couch, Hazel at his heels. "Gimme," he says snatching the phone from my hand. He leans in and steals a kiss before looking at my phone. "Come on, you know the drill. Shoes off." He pats his lap with his empty hand.

Dean has rubbed my feet after every full day photoshoot I've had in the last month. I don't even argue anymore. I can't—not when he's the only reason I don't wake up limping and achy.

I kick off my Converse—new yellow high tops that Dean bought me when my business account reached one thousand followers.

"Okay, I'm in!" he says, as if we're secret spies on a case. We kind of are secret spies... "What did you want to name it?"

I stare up at my white ceiling, throw a pillow beneath my head, one of my feet in Dean's left hand. "I was thinking @HelloHazel."

"Perfect." He types one handed, then says, "She's requesting her first friend—"

"You?" I ask, Hazel loves Dean almost more than me these days. I can't blame her. In the past ninety-one days—since I first saw Dean on the side of the road, we've only spent six days without him. I think we both agree that we like life much more with him in it.

"No. Gramgram."

I rest my arm overtop my forehead and keep my eyes on the still silent clouds of my ceiling and giggle.

"Do you have her first post planned?" he asks, eyes still on my screen.

I lift up on one elbow. "Yes. You know that picture I took of the two of you last week."

"Iris—" His tone is low and menacing and I feel his laserish eyes on my face. "The one where she's licking frosting from my face?"

"You mean, the one where you asked her for a kiss and she gave it to you? Yes. That one."

He sighs. "Got it." His fingers click across my phone. Then he hands me the device and I lay back, holding it above my head with both hands. Hazel's first post—via Dean—the picture of me and Hazel, from two months ago, when I fell into the bathtub. The caption reads:

@HelloHazel: Just sprucing up for a night out with my man.

"Dean!" I suck in a gasp, but my false horror is short lived. I can't help the laugh that escapes. Instead of anger, I choose revenge.

I make my own Hazel post. It's a picture of Dean—he smiles as Hazel lays a big kiss right over his chin and frosted lips—and I write:

> @HelloHazel: I know exactly why she loves him. He is an excellent kisser.

My eyes are magnets to his face as I hand the phone over to him. This isn't exactly how I'd planned to tell Dean that I love him for the first time—but I do, and it feels kind of perfect.

He reads the post. His eyes on the screen for five seconds and then ten. I swallow and involuntarily hold my breath.

Dean sets the phone on the coffee table. "You love me?"

"I love you," I say, clamping down on my lip.

Like a professional wrestler, in one swooping motion, Dean is up, his legs straddling mine, a hand on either side of my head. "And this is how you tell me?" he says hovering over top of me.

I lift one shoulder where I lay.

He tickles my sides while nuzzling my neck, his five o'clock shadow making my skin prickle from head to toe.

"Dean!" I bellow through a laugh.

His hands go still and his kisses turn gentle as they make their way from my jaw to my lips. His warm body wraps me up, enfolding me in strength and tenderness. "I love you too, Iris McCoy." His lips brush mine with each word.

It's sweet and it's sensual—that is until Hazel joins in on the kissing.

Bonus Epilogue

Iris

"DEAN HAS A LOT OF NICE FRIENDS." I run my fingers through Hazel's hair. Her head lazily lounges in my lap—pretty little lazy girl.

"Irisss—" Ebony says into the phone, dragging out my name. There's clicking in the background. She's typing. I'm talking.

"You could come visit before summer ends and meet one of them."

"Iris!" The clicking stops. "Do *not* try to set me up!"

"But Ebony, I just want you to—"

"You know that I am married to my job right now. I'm trying to get Clark to take me more seriously. If I could be his lead sports writer, I'd get to travel. I could write what I wanted rather than take whatever spin Clark thinks I should."

"You can still do that." I stop petting Hazel and lean my head back against Dean's couch. Dean and I are going to the falls today, Bridal Veil Falls—the picture stares at me from my green wall across the room. Just looking at it makes my stomach bubble with excitement. I get to meet those falls today, in person!

And yet I can't stop thinking about my sister in Seattle— alone. No sweet pup, no adorable adventuring boyfriend, and no waterfall.

"We both know, I can't chase my career if I'm chasing some man." I picture her glasses down on her nose, concealing a little of the glare from her chocolate brown eyes.

"Why not? I am." It's true and she knows it. My career has boomed since I met Dean. "What does Beth say?"

Ebony groans and her clicking starts up again—how that woman can talk on the phone and type is beyond me. "Beth, who has a different date every other week? Well, of course she thinks I should—how did she put it? *Get some.*"

"Ew."

"Beth isn't exactly a one woman man—not anymore anyway. So, sure she's mentioned me doubling with her before—"

"Ooo, do that!"

"I don't want to do that, Iris. Really, it's not like I haven't been asked out. I'm just not interested right now. Stop worrying, okay? I'm happy."

"I hope so."

"I am! Geez, meddling sister." She grunts, but a laugh comes out instead. I know she loves me and she knows I love her. Ebony—well, she's always been my other half. But my life has changed and grown for the better, and I just want the same for her.

"I love you, Ebony." I say, just as Dean walks into the room. He's holding up a pair of hiking boots with a giddy smile on his face. *Ew*—boots, but I do love that smile. Besides, Dean *and* the falls—I think I'd wear high heels if he told me they were the only proper attire.

"I love you, too, Iris. Now, stop worrying about finding me a date."

"Fine. I'll stop worrying," I say as Dean leans down to place a soft kiss to my lips. It's quick and chaste and makes me need one of those personal handheld fans. He leaves the boots on the floor next to the couch and slips out of the room to finish preparing for our outing. A small hum escapes me.

"Iris?"

I blink myself back to the present. "Right. Fine Ebony, I'll stop worrying because I know when Mr. Right comes along, you'll lose yourself. For the better. And you'll finally see that you can love and write."

THE END

———

Keep reading, for a peek at the next book in the {INSTA} Series…

{INSTA} Connection
Chapter One

Ebony

I AM NOT in love with Instagram—as my sister, Iris at times likes to accuse me of. I just like the mindless break from time to time. Besides, had it not been for Instagram, it's possible I never would have found out that my sister had the hots for her very fake boyfriend. I helped them! Instagram helped them! She shouldn't judge either of us.

No… not in love, not addicted, but I do enjoy the break. I duck down in my office chair, and prop my feet onto my desk, taking a five minute break before I haul my story down to my editor. I know he'll have *comments* on my Samurais piece—more comments than I want to hear.

I scroll through Instagram, laughing at a post from my old college roomie, Coco. It's a meme of Sean Lake, Seattle Samurai's goalie, with a soccer ball smashed against his distorted face. The caption reads: *I don't always cry when I get hit in the face... First I make sure someone is watching.*

> @ebony_mccoy: Well, Sean's doing an excellent job of
> making sure he's seen this year.

I add a crying emoji to my comment for good measure. If I could, I'd add this meme to my article, but Clark would cut it before he even glanced over my clever caption. Living in Washington has made my *honest*—not prejudiced—articles about the Seattle Samurais professional soccer team a bit of a touchy subject. Clark, my editor, wants me to give the people what they want—a piece about their beloved team and the comeback they'll be making… *any minute now.* But heck, I can't change their losing record or the fact that their current goalie has lost his touch.

Before I can scroll past the meme, a comment pops up on my smartphone screen. A reply to my comment on Coco's post.

@jetjacobson10: You don't think that hit would bring
tears to your eyes?

I press my lips together. I don't mind I good debate. I also don't mind stating my opinion. Loudly.

@ebony_mccoy: I think I would have used my hands
to catch the ball.
@jetjacobson10: This isn't little league.
@ebony_mccoy: Are you sure? Because Sean is great
at acting like he's six years old.
@jetjacobson10: Sean Lake is a professional athlete.
Maybe show a little respect.
@ebony_mccoy: I'd have more respect if he cried
less.
@jetjacobson10: Let me guess, you played fullback on
your high school team? You were fast, which
meant you rarely got hit?
@ebony_mccoy: Wrong. I've never played.
@jetjacobson10: Sure… now I get why your opinion is
valid.

I giggle and slump down in my office chair, not offended and entertained by his comment. It's something I would have said.

@ebony_mccoy: And your opinion is valid?
@jetjacobson10: Anyone who has been hit in the face
with a soccer ball as many times as I have has a
valid opinion.

Laughing, I type in three chortling emojis. Jet Jacobson follows my crying-laughing faces with a soccer ball and a little frightened emoji face, hands covering his eyes. I set my fingers to my phone, ready to respond, my mouth pursing to hold in my chuckle.

"Ebony—it's four."

Heart thrumming, I drop my phone, pound my feet to the ground, and fly upward in my office chair. "Clark! Hey. I didn't see you there."

"I noticed." My boss's bushy brows rise and his eyes pointedly look to the phone now on my desk.

"Research," I say.

"You have a laptop right there."

"I do," is my only defense.

When I don't say more, Clark points a finger my direction. "I want the Samurais piece on my desk in five minutes."

"Yes. Of course," I say. He walks away, and I add, yelling through my opened office door, "It's ready to go!"

I clamp down on my thumb nail with my teeth, wheel my chair near the opened door—making sure Clark is out of sight. Once his backside disappears down the hall, I push off with my feet and slide my wheeled office chair back in place at my desk. I snatched up my phone and blink, letting my facial recognition open the screen back up to Instagram. Is jetjacobson10 still there, waiting for my reply? Or has he gone back to work—or whatever he does at 4:00p.m. on a Thursday.

@jetjacobson10: Really? No questions? No guesses?

He asked the question two minutes ago. Two minutes… it feels like a long time in the cyber world, where any and all information pops up on our handheld devises in an instant. Maybe he's moved on, he probably didn't have time to wait around for my response.

@ebony_mccoy: Questions? I don't need to ask any.

I text with one hand, while typing on my laptop with the other. I google his name: Jet Jacobson. For good measure, I add the number ten, hoping I can find something in the thirty seconds it will take for him to respond—if he's still around that is. I could search through his Instagram if it's public—but I don't want to leave Coco's post... just in case.

Maybe Iris is right about me and Instagram.

My google search produces results right away, though. While his Instagram profile picture is a child's drawing and tells me nothing, Wikipedia brings up a picture of a dark haired man, M-shaped hairline, twenties, tanned skin, white teeth, sweet smile.

My heart skips—with a photo.

Whoa—Ebony... bickering with a stranger, while a good time, should not cause any hearts to skip.

I swallow down my instant attraction and read the first line Wikipedia has to offer me: Jet Jacobson is an American soccer player who after playing for four years for the European team, SSC Madrid, Jacobson is back in the states, playing for MLS Next Pro, the Atlanta Rhinos.

Huh? Next Pro, that's minor league. Before that he played in Europe. No wonder I haven't heard of him. I would have remembered that face had I seen it before.

I tell my eyes to return to my phone screen, it's ridiculously difficult taking my gaze from Jet's smile, though. Butterflies come to life in my gut, just looking at him.

@jetjacobson10: Is that right?
@ebony_mccoy: That's right, Jet Jacobson, #10 of the Rhino Football Club.
@jetjacobson10: Ha. Ha. All you've proved is that you can google. Isn't that right Ebony McCoy, sports journalist for the Seattle Times?

He adds,

@jetjacobson10: I thought you'd have more respect
for you boy Sean, Ms. Seattle Times.

I smother a laugh that for some reason feels like bursting from inside of me... or possibly bursting from my ovaries.

@ebony_mccoy: I'm not the only one who can google.
And I respect the deserving, it's not dependent on
geography.

I hit post and glance up at my wall clock. I have one minute until Clark is going to lose his mind. I snatch up the three pages that make up my Samurai piece and hurry out the door. I speed walk down the hall, then tap on my bosses office door.

"Enter."

"Hey," I say, holding up my pages. "Samurai piece. Right on time."

He doesn't say a word, but holds out his hand, his eyes still glued to his computer screen. "I'm going to assume that you took my notes to heart." His eyes drag up to me. "We live in Washington, Ebony. The people here want to hear positive antics and hope when it comes to the home team."

My teeth pinch at my inner cheek. "Yes. I did. I talk about their new assistant coach and what his expertise will bring to the team. But I can't make up a new ending to that last game, Clark." I clear my throat, then mumble to myself, "Or beginning, or middle."

His glassy blue eyes—that I swear see straight through me—dart from my pages to my face like a whip. "Try." He holds my work back out to me.

"Clark," I moan. "How am I supposed to add hope into *that* game? They are literally hopeless."

"When you report for ESPN you can take that route. But you work for me, for the Seattle Times. Let's make Seattle happy."

"It's not as if I have the power to get Seattle a new goalie. Because that's what they need." I snatch up my papers—my story —it's honest and witty and spot on. The Samurais need a goalie with a backbone.

"Ebony—"

"Got it," I groan. "*Hope...* I'll find some." Even if it's fictional.

"You have until five."

I know exactly which lines to delete and which to add to please Clark—even if it goes against my inner journalist conscience. I can complete it in ten minutes. So... it can wait a second.

My chat with Clark took an entire six minutes. Will my new friend be waiting to banter with me? Or will he have gone by now?

I shut the door to my office, toss my pages on my desk, and snatch up my phone. I slunk into my plush office chair and swivel away from the closed door. There isn't a new reply from @jetja-cobson10, but there is a new comment.

Coco.

@coco.crisp.99: Dudes. Have you heard of a DM? Try it.

I blink, slide my gaze to the message button of my Instagram feed. My heart skips and I'm pretty sure my ovaries leap with the little number one lit up in the corner.

———

Pre order {INSTA} Connection HERE!! Coming soon! Or find it on Amazon!

Let's Stay Connected

Thank you for reading {Insta} Boyfriend. I hope your heart fluttered and you laughed out loud.

Sign up for my weekly newsletter for giveaways, deals and more sweet reads! As well as information on the rest of the {INSTA} series! Sign up *HERE!*

Sign up comes with a FREE book!

Love,

Jen

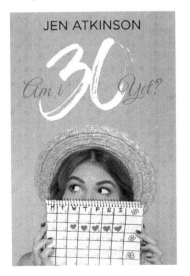

**If reading a physical copy of this book type in:

https://dashboard.mailerlite.com/forms/264735/75215388316533951/share

Acknowledgments

THANK YOU!

I have so much thanks and love in my heart. God is good. He loves me and He's helped provide a way for me to write and to find my people. I am so grateful to know that with all that goes on in the world, my ambitions and desires mean something to Him.

I am so grateful for a fantastic team of beta readers and editors! First, thank you to my Sam. You are one of the few people on the planet who will tell it to me like it is—with love and without judgment. I appreciate that more than you know and it makes me love you—amazing, beautiful, strong woman—all the more! Also, thank you for always being my go-to person with graphics and covers and such. I know you'll be thoughtful about the project and honest. And you know if I don't hear back from you within the hour, I'll have my mind made up already. Haha!

Marisa, this was your first beta read for me and I'm hooked! You are talented and so helpful! Thank you for your time and skills and thoughts. I'm so glad that Instagram makes Portugal feel closer to Wyoming than it actually is!

LeeAnn, you are a dear beautiful friend and I appreciate your support and help so much! You always find my misspellings—why are there so many?? Haha! And I appreciate it so very much. Thank you for always taking time for your little writer friend.

Kristol, thank you, sweet friend, for your time and effort! I am truly grateful for your thoughts and suggestions. They are unique to everyone else's and I need that! I appreciate you so much.

To my honey—I love you. Thank you for making my writing a priority. Thank you for being proud of me. Thank you for answering questions like—how would a man say this? Or—what's a good name for a minor league soccer team based in Atlanta, Georgia? I appreciate your support more than you know. You're my favorite. I love your smile. I love your laugh. And I especially love when you make dinner.

I'm grateful to my kiddos for their love and support. They are the best four humans I know. They are inspiration. They represent everything good in the world. They are truly amazing—and hey, I totally made them!

I am so thankful for the past six months of Bookstagram! I love and appreciate my Bookstagram friends so much. I'm grateful for other authors who have helped me learn this platform and for the many readers I've met. You have blessed my life! Thank you!

Thank YOU for reading {insta} Boyfriend. Cheers to Iris and Dean and the rest of the {insta} series! Please consider taking two minutes to leave a review on Amazon. It will help this girl out immensely!

Xoxo,

Jen

———

P.S.

An extra special thanks to Sam, who always helps me with research.

About the Author

Photo by Halle Garrett Photography

Jen Atkinson is a born and raised Wyoming girl, who believes there is no better place on earth. She lives next to one of Wyoming's many mountains where the wind regularly whips through her hair and bites at her cheeks.

Jen has been dreaming up love stories and writing them down since she learned her ABC's. While Jen writes a variety of genres, they're all going to contain a love story and a HEA. Jen is currently working on her RomCom stand-alone series, The {INSTA} Series.

You can get more information on Jen's novels, as well as other clean romances by subscribing to her weekly newsletter. You'll even receive a free RomCom ebook for SIGNING UP!

Made in the USA
Columbia, SC
04 October 2023

23857857R00157